A note from Tracie

Dear Reader,

I cannot believe that just over a year since Captivated By You released, here we are with Devoured By You, the sixth book in the series. Time sure flies.

I had enormous fun writing this book. Blaize and Jill are electric on the page from their very first meeting and it just gets hotter from there.

If you've been around a while, though, you'll know things are never that easy for my characters. I like to put them through it quite a bit, make them earn their HEA. This book is no different, I can assure you ;-)

Enjoy reading Devoured By You. I'd love to hear what you thought once you've finished reading. Why not join my

A note from Tracie

Facebook reader group Tracie's Racy Aces, and take part in the discussion over there.

In the meantime, turn the page and dive in to the sixth installment of the Kingcaid Billionaires. Enjoy every page.

Happy reading.

Love,
Tracie

Chapter 1

Jill

**Handsome *and* astute.
What are the chances?**

Success was a strange phenomenon.

Ambitious people, like me, strived to reach the mountain summit, slipping and sliding and falling on the way to the top. Sometimes we ended up with a bloody nose, or a bruised ego, but we picked ourselves up and carried on, not because we wanted to, but because we *had* to.

For so long, I'd lived with this rabid need to make it to the pinnacle of my career, certain that when I achieved a goal I'd had since I was six years old, happiness would be there, waiting for me, arms outstretched. The proverbial pot of gold at the end of the rainbow.

Instead, imposter syndrome became my new best friend. And until I discovered a way to beat that fucker, I had this awful feeling that I'd remain stuck with the worst writer's block *ever*. Hitting number one on the *New York Times* and the *Sunday Times* bestseller lists was simultaneously a dream come true and my worst nightmare. I'd set a bar, yet a singular thought whirred inside my mind.

What if I'm a one-hit wonder and everything that comes afterward sucks?

I pushed the depressing notion to the back of my mind and boarded the plane for a much-needed holiday with three of the best friends a girl could wish for. I refused to let this crippling doubt stop me from enjoying this break. I needed it. Badly.

Before I hit burnout.

An author friend of mine had slammed into that wall a few months ago. She still hadn't recovered. I didn't want to end up like her, exhausted and unable to type a single word. It was for this reason I'd agreed to the trip. My best friends had gotten together, like the three witches of Eastwick, and staged an intervention.

And here I was, turning left on the plane for the very first time. I'd earned a treat, and a first-class ticket from London to Miami where I was due to meet my girlfriends before starting our two week adventure, was my chosen gift.

My jaw hung open as I copped a first look at the exclusive cabin. Wow. Talk about luxurious. A steward, smartly dressed in a navy uniform and a blue-and-gold tie, showed me to my seat. *I mean, I could have found it.* There were only fifteen in total. *All part of the service, I guess.* But when he asked me what time I'd like to book the first-class bathroom—equipped with a proper shower, no less—I gaped.

"Um, I'm not sure. Just..." I motioned with my hand. "Whenever."

"As you wish, Miss Rowe."

I made myself comfortable in the middle seat—I'd rather not be beside the window—and accepted a glass of crisp champagne from a different member of the cabin crew. A woman took the seat to my right. I smiled at her. She responded with the coldest stare. Okay, people in first class weren't the talkative kind. Got it.

Maybe this wouldn't be as much fun as I'd thought. That shower, though. I'd have to do that, if only for bragging rights with my friends.

I dipped into my carry-on bag for my latest novel. I read the first line and sighed. Dreadful. *You can do better than this, Jill.* Could I, though? If I was capable of better, then why hadn't I *done* better? For six months, I'd worked on this manuscript, and it was still a big steaming pile of crap.

"No good?"

The silky smooth American accent came from seat 1A on my left. I turned to answer, a cordial smile in place. Ohhh. A swarm of butterflies took flight in my stomach. *He's gorgeous.* I hadn't a clue why, but I'd expected to come face-to-face with a middle-aged man and have to craft a polite way of signaling that I wasn't in the mood for chitchat. Instead, sitting across the aisle from me was a guy in his late twenties or early thirties. Medium-brown hair curled over his white shirt, and his eyes were the color of the finest jade. He had a perfect aquiline nose, model-worthy cheekbones, and a jawline that I'd give up this seat to run my teeth along just once.

"Sorry?"

He pointed his chin at my book.

"Ah. No. It's terrible." I wasn't lying. If my editor saw this, she'd drop me faster than I could type "Goodbye, career."

"Then why read it? Life's too short to force ourselves to do things we don't enjoy."

I attempted a wry smile. "If only it were that simple."

He flashed a set of perfect white teeth and removed a brushed-gold laptop embedded with a logo I couldn't make out from his bag. Seconds later, he began typing, long, slim fingers moving effortlessly over the keyboard, his eyebrows dipped in concentration.

All righty, then.

Maybe he thought I'd given him the brush-off with my answer. Or perhaps he found me boring.

Ouch. *Stop with the self-flagellation, Rowe.* My confidence was already teetering on the precipice. It didn't need a helpful shove over the edge of the cliff.

I returned to reading. Every word burned my eyes. The sentences were staccato and unvaried, there was far too much telling instead of showing, my descriptions were cloggy and lacking any kind of color, and my characters were two-dimensional arseholes.

What had happened to me? I used to find writing a joy, yet the more readership I gained, the worse I felt. Once upon a time, I could knock out ten thousand words in a day, and those words needed hardly any editing. The best I could do with this book would be to set fire to it and start over. But what if I couldn't? What if this offense to literature was the last thing I ever wrote?

"Isn't this you?"

I let the book fall into my lap and once more turned my attention to the handsome stranger. He'd spun his laptop so the screen faced in my direction. Staring out at me was... me.

I groaned. Stupid author bio. I hated that picture, too. I looked like such a prat. The photographer had insisted on that silly pose. Said I looked "author-y" in it—whatever that meant. My publisher had gushed over it, and the next thing I knew, it was everywhere.

Worse, though, was that my beautiful stranger had caught me reading my own book. From his point of view, I must look like an egotistical jerk.

"Um, yeah."

"Wow, an author. That's impressive."

"It really isn't."

"Don't talk yourself down. Millions of people would love the talent and discipline it takes to write a book, and you've written fifteen."

He'd... counted.

Also... sixteen, if we included the... the... *thing* I held in my hands.

"Thanks," I muttered.

The plane slowly reversed onto the taxiway. I hated the takeoff part. Once we were airborne, I'd be fine, but this first bit—

"Sometimes it helps to talk about it."

I frowned, refocusing on the man to my left once more. "What? My dislike of taking off?"

His lips twitched. "No. Although, we can talk about that if you like. I was referring to your exasperation with your latest book."

"Exasperation? Who says I'm exasperated?"

"I do. You've sighed thirteen times in less than two minutes. I could be wrong, but that sounds like exasperation to me."

Ugh. Handsome *and* astute. What were the chances?

"I'm sure you don't want to listen to my woes, Mister...?"

"Better than musing on my own." He flashed that perfect smile again. Good God, he really was beautiful. "Call me Blay." He offered his hand.

I reached across the aisle and shook it. His palm was warm, his skin soft, and he held on to my hand a little longer than I'd consider normal for two strangers. A delicious shiver trickled up my spine. "Jill."

"Yeah, I know." His smile widened.

Oh, yeah. Stalker extraordinaire.

"What does the *T* stand for?"

"Huh?"

"'English author Jillian Rowe writes as J. T. Rowe,'" he parroted from my bio. "What does the *T* stand for?"

"Ah. I'm not telling. A girl's got to have some secrets."

"I bet it's Tilly."

I chuckled. "Jillian Tilly Rowe. Not even my parents would be that cruel." I winced. The last time I'd spoken to my parents had been the day they'd discovered I was a romance author. Porn, my God-fearing mother had called it. She'd given me an ultimatum: give up writing "that disgusting smut" or forgo a relationship with them.

I'd chosen my characters. They rarely let me down. Unlike my mum and dad. Nor did they sit in judgment on every decision I made.

Either Blay didn't see me flinch, or he chose not to probe. Instead, he said, "Jilly Tilly Rowe," laughing heartily at his joke.

"Tease me all you like. I'll never tell."

"Then you leave me no choice. To me, you'll always be Tilly."

I raised one eyebrow. "Always? You mean for the next nine hours until we land in Miami and we never see each other again?"

"Did you notice we're in the air?"

I hadn't. For the first time in my life, I'd gone through takeoff without clutching the armrests once.

"You're a miracle worker."

He held a hand across his stomach and performed a seated bow. "One of my many talents."

"What do you do for a living?"

One shoulder lifted. "Oh, this and that."

"Ah, a man of mystery."

"As we're on a flight from London to Miami, I think that should be *international* man of mystery, don't you?"

I wrinkled my nose. "Like Austin Powers."

"I don't have the teeth to pull off Austin Powers."

"Nor the velvet suit."

He smoothed a hand over the arm of his jacket. "Were they velvet or suede?"

I shrugged. "Potayto, potahto."

"That's a very American saying from a very English girl."

"I write mainly American characters."

"Why's that?"

"America is such a diverse country. It gives me a wealth of opportunity. I could write cowboys, or Wall Street types, or Hollywood playboys, or Texas oil barons."

"And do you?"

I laughed. "No. I write pretty dark romantic suspense that could be set in any location. I love a good kidnapping."

His eyes heated, and he ran his gaze over me, a slow appraisal that made my fingers and toes tingle and my stomach do several somersaults.

"Is that an invitation?" he murmured.

I stroked my bottom lip, drawing his eyes to my mouth. I wouldn't say I was an expert flirter, but I didn't completely suck at it, either. A little frivolity on an otherwise boring flight would make the time go faster. We were both adults. And single.

Right?

I risked a glance at his left hand. No ring.

"Are you spoken for?"

He smirked. "Is that the kind of language you use in your novels?"

"Sometimes. It depends on the character."

"No. I'm not spoken for." He looked me over for the second time. "Was that the right answer?"

My stomach flipped again. If my flirting skills were passable, Blay's were off-the-freaking-charts outstanding.

Clearing my throat, I picked an invisible thread of cotton off my sleeve. "It wasn't the *wrong* one."

His pupils flared, and his stare probed, searching for an answer to an unasked question. The answer, by the way, was a big fat yes.

"I'm rather glad I took this flight, Tilly."

I might adore that nickname. "Me, too."

Chapter 2

Blaize

I'm waiting for the punch line.

WHAT A PLEASANT SURPRISE THIS TRIP WAS TURNING out to be.

I'd expected a long, dull commercial flight to Miami—foisted on me because my father needed the company jet—with nothing to occupy my thoughts other than dread that grew like a weed.

Instead, Cupid had tossed me a lifeline, a distraction I'd badly needed to take my mind off the cruise ship launch.

Jill "Tilly" Rowe was a delight.

A hazel-eyed beauty with mocha hair that kissed her shoulders, high, proud cheekbones, perfect lips, and a body created to torment heterosexual men into selling the family silver for just one touch.

And she was sitting in the seat right across the aisle.

Lucky me.

"So, come on, then. Tell me what the problem is with this book. Talking it through with a stranger who doesn't know the first thing about romance novels might help."

Her nose wrinkled as if she'd smelled something bad.

Ah. Not convinced I'd be at all helpful.

I chuckled. "I promise I'm not one of those assholes who think romance books are bits of fluff, or mommy porn, or countless other misogynistic put-downs women get for loving the idea of love and happy endings." I motioned to her. "What harm can it do?"

She massaged her temples. "It's complicated. I'm not sure where to begin."

"I usually find starting at the beginning helps." I accepted a glass of champagne from the steward.

Jill helped herself to an orange juice. "You're a funny guy."

"I try."

She sipped her juice. "I've always loved reading. I started dabbling in storytelling in high school, but it was only after I left college that I dared to dream that I could make it my full-time job." She flicked a bit of lint off her sleeve. "I self-published my first novel a year after I graduated, and I went on to publish another fourteen novels. I was doing okay, more than making a living, and I was happy. Then a TikTok that a reader made about my last book went viral, and everything changed."

"In what way?"

"One of the biggest publishers in the world contacted

me. They wanted to re-cover and rebrand that book and get it into every bookstore in the world. The idea of seeing my precious baby on bookshelves turned my head, and I signed a five-book deal."

She pulled a deep sigh up from the pit of her stomach.

"They kept their promises. My relaunched book hit number one on the *New York Times* and *Sunday Times* bestseller lists a week after the new copy went live, and it's stayed on those lists in the six months since."

"Isn't that a good thing?"

She waggled her hand from side to side. "Yes and no. I mean, it's a dream come true to know how many people have read and continue to enjoy my books. That's what I do this job for, really. The readers. They're the ones who matter. They're the ultimate judges of whether something is good or bad, and I have some of the best readers in the world."

It all sounded pretty damn perfect so far. "I'm waiting for the punch line."

She gave me a tight, brief smile. "My publisher wanted me to write a follow-up in the same world, with the same couple, and that's where the problems began."

Taking another sip of OJ, she stared off into the distance. I didn't interrupt, choosing instead to use the gap in conversation to study her profile.

Jillian Rowe was my type of woman. Attractive, intelligent, financially self-sufficient, a delightful conversationalist.

A body made for fucking.

My groin heated. The upcoming maiden voyage of

Kingcaid's newest cruise ship—the largest in the world—had absorbed all my time recently, and sex had taken a back seat. Like most guys my age, I thought about sex at least a hundred times a day, probably more. And sitting across from a gorgeous woman who ticked all my "yes, please" boxes had kicked my libido into high gear.

"—editor wants the first three chapters, and they're awful. Just awful."

Fuck. I'd missed half of what she'd said.

Focus, dickhead. You offered to listen. Now fucking listen.

"Why do you think they're awful?"

She shook her head. "The characters are flat, the sentence structure is hideous, there's no real hook to grab the reader, and there's far too much telling rather than showing. The whole thing feels forced. And the worst of all is that I don't know how to fix it."

She picked up the book and flicked through it, then tossed it back into her carry-on bag.

"I thought publishers only printed the paperbacks once the book was finished."

"Oh, they do. But I always get a copy printed for myself. I've had the same process since I first started publishing. It helps me to see issues far easier than reading on my computer or on an e-reader. And this way, I can make notes in the margins."

She heaved another heavy sigh. Her third. Or maybe fourth.

"I can't send her this crap."

"She might be able to offer advice. Isn't that what editors do? What's the worst that could happen?"

She laughed bitterly. "Well, let's see. My publishers could drop me as a client. Although, maybe that wouldn't be a bad thing. Ever since I signed that damned contract, I haven't been able to write for shit." She ran a hand around the back of her neck. "Strike that. Getting dropped would be the very *worst* thing that could happen."

"Why? You were successful before. You can be again."

The minute the words spilled from my tongue, I knew I'd said the wrong thing. She pursed her lips, and her foot jiggled.

"It doesn't work like that. If I get dropped by my publisher after one book, it'll ruin my reputation. No one will ever take me seriously again." She tugged on her earlobe. "I can't expect you to understand. I bet everything you touch is successful." She motioned to me. "I mean, when was the last time you suffered from a loss of confidence, or a bout of imposter syndrome? If you ever have."

"This morning."

Her eyebrows kissed her forehead. "Really? You strike me as the kind of man who oozes self-assurance."

"We all play the game, Tilly. Some of us play it better than others, but most people suffer from the odd hit to their confidence from time to time. It's how you react that counts."

"How did you react?"

"I told myself that it would pass and my day would pick up." I ran my gaze over her, my intentions in plain sight. "And it did. Spectacularly."

Her cheeks reddened, and she tucked her chin into her chest.

Adorable.

"I wish my doubts would pass."

"They will."

"When?"

"Finding a pleasant distraction helps." I waggled my eyebrows.

She laughed. "I suppose you're applying for the job."

"Applying? Oh, Tilly, I've already landed it."

"I'm guessing your moment of self-doubt wasn't female related."

"Correct."

The steward crouched beside Jill's seat. "What can I get you for lunch, Miss Rowe?"

"Oh, I haven't even looked." She glanced around haplessly. "What choices do I have?"

Ah. Not a seasoned first-class traveler.

"I can recommend the filet," I said. "That's what I'm having, and it's usually good. Or salmon if you don't like red meat. I can't offer an opinion on the vegetarian option, but if you don't like any of those, they'll make you something else. If they have the ingredients on board, that is."

She opened her mouth, then shut it. A second attempt at speaking was more successful. "The salmon, please."

"Good choice," I said.

The steward noted down her selection and mine, and shortly afterward, he returned with our food.

"Would you like to join me?" I pointed at the guest seat opposite mine.

"Or you could join me."

I laughed, rising to my feet. This woman, I liked. A great deal. "What the lady wants."

The steward set up the table for two, and I sat down, shaking out my napkin. Jill lowered her head and sniffed.

"That smells *amazing*."

"It's not gourmet, but it's passable."

"Passable?" She screwed up her nose. "I'm guessing you've never traveled in the economy cabin?"

Chuckling, I shook my head. "Guilty as charged." I cut into my steak. Rare, just how I'd requested before I'd boarded.

"I've never traveled first class before," she confessed. "A treat to myself for hitting number one bestseller."

"It's important to celebrate our successes."

"I'm still working on that one."

I grinned. "Me, too."

Lunch took a while to get through because we talked so much. Jill Rowe was not only gorgeous, intelligent, and great company, but she also had that sarcasm-laden humor that the British had mastered.

My eyes lingered on her face as she sat back in her chair and let out a contented sigh, simultaneously rubbing her stomach. She caught me studying her. The air between us crackled, a definite shift in atmosphere now that we'd eaten.

"So, what now?" she asked huskily.

I reached for her hand, drawing it to my side of the table. Turning it over, I traced the lines on her palm. "My grandmother reads palms."

"Is that so?" Her voice dropped another octave.

"It is. I learned one or two things from her."

I drew a figure eight on her palm. Her hands were

dainty, the nails painted in a delicate pink. They'd look great wrapped around my dick.

"Such as?" She cast a furtive glance at me, then returned her attention to her palm. Her tongue darted out to dampen her lips.

Flirting. So fucking good for the soul.

"Well, see this line here?" I traced a path in a downward trajectory, starting from the tip of her middle finger. "This is the fate line. Not everyone has this."

"So I'm special?"

My lips twitched. "That you are, Tilly."

"What else does it mean?"

"Well, it's quite deep, so this means you're strongly controlled by fate. You're likely to plunge headfirst into fatalistic events." I looked up at her. I could get lost in those eyes. "Such as meeting a handsome stranger on a plane."

She licked her lips again. Heat filled my groin. That tongue would also look good on my dick.

"Are you—"

"Miss Rowe?"

I glowered at the steward hovering next to her seat. *Read the fucking room, man.*

She pulled her gaze from me to give her attention to him. I might have him fired.

"Yes?"

"The bathroom is available for you now, ma'am."

"Oh." She smiled at him. "Thank you."

Slipping her hand from mine, she smiled at me, too. Except it differed from the smile she'd given him. He'd gotten the polite version. I received the sultry, lust-hazed version.

"I won't be long."

As she stood, I grabbed her wrist.

"Hey, Jill?"

"Yeah?"

"Leave the door unlocked."

Chapter 3

Jill

Sex in the first-class bathroom?
There's an experience I never thought I'd have.

"LEAVE THE DOOR UNLOCKED."

My knees shook during the short walk to the bathroom at the rear of the first-class cabin. I slipped inside, resting my forehead against the door. I had a choice to make, and I could stand here all day and pretend I was considering both options, but it would be a big fat lie.

There was only one option. A distraction of the best kind. If I left the door open, then I'd get off this plane in Miami as a fully paid-up member of the mile-high club.

Not that it was a club.

Or I didn't think it was.

Maybe there *was* a club, with regular meetups where

we all sat around quaffing expensive champagne and regaling the other members about the day we gained entry.

You're losing it.

My heart thudded too fast, skipping the odd beat, which made me light-headed. I stared at the door handle. How long would it be before it turned? What was the appropriate amount of time to wait in these situations?

Good God, Jill.

I'd promised myself that I'd let my hair down on this trip, do things I'd never done before. But I'd thought those would be things like zip-lining through a rainforest, or driving a buggy through sand dunes, or riding a jet ski.

Having sex with a beautiful stranger who read palms, had listening skills that bypassed most men, and would win Olympic gold in the flirting category hadn't crossed my mind.

Why would it have?

I could lock the door, have my shower, and return to my seat, politely thanking him for his offer but explaining that I wasn't that kind of girl.

Except I wanted to be that girl. To be reckless, and to bank a story I could use in a book one day. The one-night stand was a hot trope, and the consensus was to write what you knew. Although, I'd always thought that was a ridiculous notion. If we only wrote what we knew, then how would paranormal romance books exist? Or sci-fi? Or historicals?

I made my way over to the sink and stared at my reflection in the lighted mirror. If I was going to have sex on this plane, at least I wasn't in economy.

Imagine trying to get it on in those tiny spaces? One of

us would have to sit on the loo. Probably him. That way, I could—

The door opened. Blay slipped inside, locking it behind him.

Fuck.

Fuck, fuck, fuck.

My stomach vaulted. His molten eyes met mine in the mirror.

"I wasn't sure if I'd find it locked."

I licked my lips and swallowed past a narrowed throat that resembled a compressed straw. Maybe I had a nut allergy, and any second, I'd collapse onto the floor. The cabin crew would find us both in here and know what I'd been about to do.

You don't have a nut allergy. Calm down.

He prowled toward me. Literally prowled. I shifted my position.

"Don't. Stay where you are."

I gripped the sink. Only way to stay upright. My thighs trembled. His large hands gripped my hips. I breathed in through my nose, catching the scent of expensive cologne and a musky maleness. My clit pulsed, and a heaviness settled between my legs. He moved my hair out of the way and ran his nose along my neck.

"You smell like sin." He breathed in deeply. "My kind of girl."

"Have you done this before?" My voice came out breathy, like an actress in a 1930s black-and-white movie.

"Not on a commercial jet, no."

"You've flown on a private jet?"

A low chuckle rumbled through his chest. "I *own* a private jet."

"Then why aren't you on it?"

He nuzzled my ear. "My father needed it." His hands cupped my breasts, homing in on my nipples as if he could see right through my shirt and bra. "Lucky for me that he did."

Spinning me on the spot, his mouth took mine. I gasped, surprised and unprepared. My hands clasped his shoulders for support. He was everywhere at once. Hands, body, mouth, tongue. It was all so good.

So fucking good.

My worries vanished, quashed by a single kiss from a man who'd studied the art of kissing. He must have. It was *perfection*.

He burrowed his hands beneath my shirt, and my bra loosened. Both items of clothing ended up around my neck, and he suckled on my nipple with a combination of urgency and languor. That made little sense, but my brain had stopped producing logical thought from the moment he'd kissed me.

"How long do we have?" I moaned as he bit my nipple and then soothed it with his tongue.

"Not nearly fucking long enough," he growled. "But it'll be worth it. I promise."

My skirt dropped to the floor. He hooked his thumbs into my knickers and yanked them off me. I pulled my shirt over my head and threw it off to the side. My bra, too.

"Let's fix this power imbalance." I tugged off his tie while he shrugged out of his jacket. My fingers fumbled to unfasten his shirt buttons, so much so that he took over,

24

revealing bronzed skin over a taut chest, defined shoulders and arms, and a positively lickable six-pack that was every hetero girl's wet dream.

His trousers and boxers joined my clothes in a pile on the floor. I paused for a second, memorizing how he looked with his stunning face, perfectly toned body, and thick cock jutting out from his hips.

What a romance hero he'd make.

I wished I'd brought my phone so I could take a picture, but a mental one would have to do.

"Is this going in a book?" He smirked.

"Do you read minds as well as palms?"

"As a matter of fact, I do." He ran his hand over my hip, settling it on my arse. His eyes zeroed in on my boobs. "I'll expect a signed copy."

He kissed me again, cutting off my reply. Walking backward, he took me with him. I squealed as icy water gushed over me, soaking us both.

"That's cold."

"I'll keep you warm."

My back hit the wall. Fisting my hair, he tugged it to the side, exposing my neck to his lips, his tongue, his teeth.

God, he was *feral,* and I couldn't get enough.

I pulled his hair, matching his savagery. He bit me harder, as if the pain of tugging out his hair from the roots spurred him on. Spinning me, he pressed my cheek to the tile.

"Don't. Fucking. Move."

The warmth of his body left me. I risked a glance over my shoulder. He picked up his jacket and reached into the inside pocket, producing a condom.

I laughed. "Did you plan to seduce a stranger on this flight?"

"No. But it's better to be prepared."

He set the condom on top of the shower gel, and his body covered mine again. His hands were *everywhere*, touching, squeezing, pinching. I reached behind me. Time to cop a feel of my own. In less than a second, he had my hands pinned above my head.

"I'm in charge, Tilly. You'll touch when I say you can."

Every single muscle south of my belly button squeezed at the same time. My sexual encounters were usually a more even affair. I'd never had a man assume control, not to the extent Blay was.

I *loved* it.

Yep. Going in a fucking book. I might have to switch genres and write erotica under a new pen name.

His thumb circled my butthole. I tensed. That was one hole I hadn't let a man breach.

"Ass virgin?"

I nodded.

His thumb disappeared. I wasn't sure whether the emotion sweeping through me was relief or disappointment. Maybe a little of both.

"Open your legs."

I shuffled them apart.

"Wider."

"Much wider and I'll be doing the splits. That way lies disaster. Trust me."

A gruff chuckle rumbled through his chest. "Thank fuck my father needed the company jet."

My chest swelled. When I'd given my credit card to

the travel agent who'd booked this flight, I'd thought it an exorbitant extravagance.

Now, I was thinking it might be the best ten grand I'd ever spent. A memory to last a lifetime.

He slid his hand between the wall and me and pushed two fingers inside me, gently massaging me from the inside. He didn't shove them up me as if he were stuffing a chicken. I groaned. The man should give lessons on how to work a woman's body into a frenzy.

"Feel good?"

"God, yes."

His thumb strummed my clit. I gasped. "I bet you play guitar."

He laughed. "As I child, I did."

"I knew it."

He nibbled along my shoulder. "You're incredible. How are you single?"

"I'm married to my job."

"Same, Tilly. Same."

His cock nudged between my ass cheeks. I stiffened. If I wasn't all that keen on the idea of a thumb up there, then a massive cock was an absolute no-no.

"Relax. I'm not going to take your ass virginity." He removed his fingers and turned me to face him. "Better?"

"I'm not a prude."

He flashed a toothy smile. "I'd say that ship has sailed."

"Good point, well made."

He picked up the condom. "As much as I could spend hours playing with your body, we're on a clock. And I'm salty about it." Tearing through the packet, he took it out and handed it to me. "Put this on."

I glanced down. "I don't have the right appendage."

He laughed again. "Yep. Incredible."

Grinning, I pinched the tip and rolled it onto his dick. "Look, it fits."

He grabbed a fistful of my hair and tipped my head back. "I'll never fucking forget you."

Before I could answer, he speared me. I hissed through my teeth at the unexpectedness of it. Then he moved, and I was lost. Our teeth clashed, our tongues battled, and our bodies moved in a frictionless dance. He lifted me, hooking my legs over his hips. The sound of running water drowned out my gasps of pleasure as my perfect stranger pummeled me. A wild thrill coursed through my body. This was dirty, raw, forbidden. His lips bruised mine as he drove himself into me faster and faster. I moaned, the pleasure almost too much to bear.

"Come, Tilly. Fuck, come."

He shifted his angle, and his pelvis rubbed my clit.

"That's it," I breathed. "Right there."

He did it again, and I came apart, cresting, falling, except instead of smashing into the ground, I floated away on a cloud of pure carnality. Blay grunted, thrust twice more, stilled, and then emitted a gratified sigh. Seconds later, he lowered me to the floor. He pulled out, took off the condom, and stuffed it in tissue before putting it in the bin. I reached for a towel and wrapped it around my body.

"They'll know, won't they?" I pointed my chin at the door.

He nodded. "Does that bother you?"

"No. It probably should, but no."

Devoured BY YOU

Life's full of surprises.
Some I could live without.

Things I'd hoped for/anticipated
on this vacation:

- Have a wonderful, relaxing time with some of the best friends a girl could wish for.
- Overcome the crippling doubt that had taken hold since I achieved Number One *New York Times* Bestseller status.
- Send my editor *something* to stop her from messaging me seventeen times per day.
- Get a tan.

Things I didn't expect to happen:

- Joining the mile-high club.
- Engaging in an altercation with a Hugh Hefner wannabe.
- Finding myself in a life-and-death situation.
- Falling in love.

Blurb

Nor did I expect to have my happily ever after torn from my grasp by a cruel twist of fate.

But one thing that clawing myself to the top has taught me; I'm a fighter.

And this is one battle I will win.

"Good." He pulled me to him and kissed me, hard. "You'll never see them again, so why worry?"

I wouldn't see Blay again, either. And the devastation tearing through my insides was the most worrying thing of all.

Chapter 4

Blaize

Lucky for me, nature had blessed me with an overactive imagination.

Miami International Airport was crammed with tourists, most of whom stumbled around trying to figure out where the fuck they were going. Kids screeched in that earsplitting way they'd mastered, and that caused every childless traveler to grimace and glare at the parents who were, for the most part, impotent to stop the little darlings making the goddamn sound.

I shouldn't imagine they enjoyed it all that much, either. At least I had an escape route.

"What does your luggage look like?" I asked Jill as I plucked my brown leather carryall off the carousel.

"Um, pink, large, and heavy." She stared at my bag. "Is that it? That's all you've got?"

"I travel light."

"No shit." She pointed to two enormous bright pink suitcases slowly making their way toward us. "They're mine."

"You like to travel incognito, then?" I grinned.

"I'll have you know they're the height of fashion."

"I'll take your word for it." I put out an arm as she surged forward to get them. "Allow me."

"Are you this chivalrous with all your mile-high conquests?"

I heaved the first one off the belt. "Jesus Christ Almighty. What have you got in here?"

She shrugged. "Shoes, clothes, emergency chocolate."

The second suitcase was heavier than the first. "And in here?" I huffed, setting it beside the first one.

"My vibrators."

Suppressing a bark of laughter, I ran my tongue along my lower lip. "What a shame they weren't in your carry-on."

"It is. A terrible tragedy." Her eyes traveled over me, and she nibbled the corner of her mouth. "What would you have done if they had been?"

My dick stirred to life. This woman could make me break my cardinal rule of never returning for seconds. I didn't do seconds, but fuck if Tilly wasn't tempting me.

"I'll leave that to your imagination."

Was that a look of disappointment sweeping across her face? I checked my watch. Damn. Even if I was tempted, I didn't have time.

"Can I offer you a ride anywhere?" Maybe we could do it in the back of my car.

"I'm meeting my friends. But thank you."

"Oh." Now *I* was the disappointed one. "Let me walk these out for you, at least." I put my bag over my shoulder and extended the handles on her cases.

"Are you sure?"

"Of course. I'll send you the medical bills if I get a hernia."

"You're all heart," she replied drolly.

A smile pulled at my lips. I would miss this woman more than I should for someone I'd only met nine hours ago.

I wheeled her gargantuan luggage to the arrivals hall, and for the first time in my life, I couldn't think of anything memorable to say. I'd have to let the sex do the talking for me.

I stuck out my hand. "It was nice to meet you, Jilly Tilly Rowe."

As her palm touched mine, I had the urge to ask her to meet me for dinner tonight. Then I recalled that I already had plans with a business associate. Not to mention that would smash the "no second bites of the cherry" rule.

"And you, Blay No-Last-Name."

"Ah. International man of mystery, remember?"

Her eyes softened, and she stood on tiptoes and kissed my cheek. "I'll never forget."

The warmth from her lips stayed with me during the entire ride out to the Port of Miami. Kingcaid's newest addition to our cruise ship empire towered majestically above every other ship at the docks.

My stomach flipped, the familiar worries crawling back now that my female companion wasn't around to quash them.

One point five billion dollars of my family's money rested on the success of this venture.

One. Point. Five. Billion.

Every time I thought about it, my stomach knotted and my palms began to sweat. I could not allow this venture to fail. The problem was, the cruising business was cutthroat and unforgiving, and the next wannabe constantly strategized ways of overtaking you and becoming number one. It wasn't a business for the faint of heart, that was for sure.

There were *tons* of VIPs booked on this sailing, most notably Scarlett Rose, a Hollywood A-lister who'd recently divorced her longtime manager in a blaze of publicity. Scarlett alone had seventy million followers on social media, with an influence that spread far and wide. If she wasn't happy with a single element of the service offering, she could sink this venture with one scathing tweet before it'd gotten off the ground.

To add to my stress, it was widely known that Scarlett was a royal pain in the ass, although her many fans were oblivious to the true woman beneath the public persona.

Every contract I'd signed from the moment I'd envisaged this project had given me sleepless nights and chest pains. It *had* to go well. If it didn't... I couldn't bear to let the thought fester. I'd rather throw myself overboard than disappoint my father.

Sometimes I wished I'd never pitched this idea to the board. I'd gotten a lot of pushback at the time, and even Dad had cautioned me against taking the plunge. But I'd battled on, and when it had come down to a split decision and I'd had the casting vote, I'd pushed the motion through. The exuberance of youth and my father's faith in me to run a business he'd built from the ground up had driven me forward.

Looking back now, with the benefit of hindsight, I'd been an idiot.

Most projects of this size had problems. Nothing this large ever went smoothly, but as we'd edged closer to the maiden voyage, the problems had kept mounting up, and my previously unshakable belief in my abilities had begun to waver.

There was a concept in business called the Peter Principle, which stated that, in a hierarchy, people rose to a level of respective incompetence. Translated: if you pushed hard enough, high enough, eventually you'd over-reach, and fail spectacularly.

What if this project was beyond my capabilities?

What if I, or someone on the wider team, had missed a crucial element?

Given that I was the CEO, the buck stopped with me, so even if one of my team fucked up, I was ultimately responsible. I'd be the one to bring bad press to the family name if anything went wrong or if the customer satisfaction surveys weren't at the target level of ninety-five percent or above.

My greatest fear was disappointing Dad and having him think he'd made a mistake putting me in charge of such a large business, a cornerstone to the Kingcaid Vacations brand.

So far, I'd met his high expectations, but all I'd done

was take over an already successful business with an established board in place. This cruise ship was my brainchild, though, my baby, and my reputation, and that of my family, rested on its success.

Despite the air-conditioned car, sweat dampened the back of my shirt, and tingles plagued my chest.

Breathe.

Everything would work out.

It had to.

I exited the car outside the welcome area for our VIP sailors. John Simmonds, the ship's captain, strode toward me as I entered through a set of sliding double doors.

His beaming smile should have calmed me down.

It had the opposite effect.

John had probably thought he'd won the fucking lottery when he'd landed this gig. A brand-new ship with all the bells and whistles of modern technology was probably a seafarer's wet dream.

Easy for him. He didn't have a one-point-five-billion-dollar target on his back.

I was the unlucky sucker with that label.

"John." I shook his outstretched hand, exuding the confidence expected of the CEO of the company. "Forty-eight hours until we sail. How's she looking?"

"One or two issues I'd like to discuss with you."

And the hits just keep on coming.

"Like what?"

John cocked his head. "Come on, let me show you around."

I'd toured the ship many times, watching with fascination as she transformed through the various stages to the opulent finished product I'd envisaged. The executive committee had poured over every minute detail, tweaking and changing things until we, as a collective, had agreed we'd created a magnificent ship.

An adult-only ship, Serenity stood twenty decks tall and had the capacity for eight thousand passengers and four thousand crew members. On board were thirty gourmet restaurants and eleven themed bars. Each night, three Broadway-standard shows would play to packed theaters.

As far as rooms went, there were twelve sumptuous penthouses, and three decks of VIP accommodations that I'd named the Kingcaid Royalty suites. There were two swimming pools, an enormous gym and spa, and a VIP-only sundeck with personal cabanas, an open bar, and Michelin-starred food on demand.

Four and a half years of hard work had brought me to this place, and I'd never felt sicker in my entire life.

What made matters worse was my elder brother, Nolen, choosing the maiden voyage for his long-awaited honeymoon. Nine months ago, he'd married the love of his life, Marlowe, when their little girl was two months old. Neither had wanted to leave her at that age, hence their delayed honeymoon.

I could have done without the added pressure, though.

At least my parents hadn't descended on me. Now *that* would have been pressure.

John led me into the Crown restaurant, the jewel in our gastronomy offerings. The restaurant was aft, with huge picture windows that would give diners a magnificent view of the wake as the boat cut through the water. The place was a hive of activity, all fixated on an enormous hole in the ceiling.

"What the fuck is this?" I hissed.

"We had a leak. A burst pipe. They're working on it now."

"Extensive damage?"

"Not too bad. Just poor timing." He put a hand on my shoulder. "It'll be fine."

As a singular event, this wasn't a big deal. But it was the way the problems kept piling up that was getting to me.

Only last week, I'd received an email that informed me the entire badge-scanning system had gone down, meaning our passengers wouldn't be able to access anything on board, including their cabins. The outage had only taken a few hours to fix, but if that happened while at sea, our customer satisfaction scores would plummet.

The entire future of this highly expensive venture rested on a spectacular first outing. I needed all passengers, but especially those with a large reach, to get off this ship and gush to their followers about how fabulous it was. Word of mouth based on personal experience was far more powerful than the slickest marketing campaign.

We left the team fixing the leak and continued our tour. We ended on the top deck, where the VIP area was located. Passengers who booked one of our suites received a different wristband from everyone else, giving them exclusive access to this part of the ship.

As we approached, the door was open. I pulled it shut, but the locking mechanism failed to activate.

Great.

One more fucking problem I could do without.

"Get maintenance on this, will you?"

"Will do."

John made a call, and a few minutes later, a maintenance crew arrived. We continued our tour, but the mushrooming issues were a constant thorn, spearing my liver.

The logical side of my brain knew that complications were unavoidable, but that didn't stop me from striving for perfection. I couldn't help taking everything personally, despite having a large team who were all there to support me. It was in my nature to own every obstacle and to berate myself when those obstacles proved troublesome.

We didn't come across any more concerns, and after speaking to as many of the crew members as I could, I said goodbye to John and left the ship, making my way back to my car.

"Home, please," I instructed my driver.

Home was a twenty-million-dollar estate on Indian Creek Island, also known as "Billionaire Bunker." A three-hundred-acre oasis with each of the forty homes enjoying unrivaled waterfront access. I liked the privacy of it, away from the frenzy of Miami Beach.

After my driver dropped me off, I walked straight into the bedroom and let my bag fall to the floor beside the bed. I flopped onto the mattress and knitted my hands behind my head, staring up at the pristine white ceiling for a few seconds before closing my eyes.

The moment I did, Jill's luminous, intelligent hazel eyes looked back at me. Eyes I could stare into for hours, a full, plush mouth I could kiss for days, the knockout body I'd never tire of.

God, what a woman.

If she were here now, I'd christen this bed, the huge walk-in shower, the hot tub, the fucking dining room table, the kitchen countertop. I'd bang that incredible woman on every single hard and soft surface in this house until my dick ached and she was wrung out from all the orgasms I gave her.

What the hell am I thinking?

She was a onetime deal.

A dalliance.

A way to quash the boredom and extinguish the voices in my head that made me want to puke out of sheer panic over this damn ship. I was thirty-one, and I'd never been on a second date. I was married to my career. There weren't spare hours in the day to nurture a relationship, especially now, with everything riding on this launch.

Maybe the attraction was the fact that she'd admitted she was married to her career, too. Kindred souls who recognized they weren't cut out for monogamy.

Wonder where she's staying.

I reached for my phone. Picked it up. Put it down.

This was crazy.

I'd met an exceptional woman, enjoyed amazing sex, and said goodbye.

That was how it should be.

If I weren't so on edge about this cruise, then I'd never consider a second hookup. Orgasms gave me momentary peace, but I could have one of those without the added complication of sending mixed signals to a woman only meant to be transitory in my life.

I unbuttoned my pants and gripped my dick.

All I needed was my imagination.

Lucky for me, nature had blessed me with an overactive one of those.

Chapter 5

Jill

Time to forget Blay "No-Last-Name" and party!

DON'T LOOK BACK. DO NOT LOOK BACK. DON'T YOU *dare look—*

I glanced over my shoulder. My stomach vaulted at the sight of Blay's tall, imposing figure cutting through the throng of passengers all gathered to meet up with loved ones. He narrowly avoided getting hit in the face with a bunch of roses brandished by an overenthusiastic boyfriend who thrust them at his girlfriend before crushing the delicate flowers between his chest and hers. Blay didn't even appear to notice. He disappeared through the sliding doors and out of my sight.

I sighed, deep and regretful. *What did you expect, Jill?*

Sex with a guy I'd met on a plane hardly lent itself to something more. I didn't even want more. I couldn't afford entanglements of any kind until I'd fixed this disaster of a book.

Putting Blay "No-Last-Name" out of my mind, I rolled my two suitcases across the tiled floor, stopping every three seconds to reaffix the damn bag that kept slipping off my shoulders. An excited squeal drew me to a stop. I'd know that high-pitched screech anywhere. I turned on the spot.

"Jilly!" One of my best friends, Addison, enveloped me in a bear hug that almost broke at least two of my ribs, and my mouth ended up full of her out-of-control red curls. "Oh my God! I thought your plane would never get here."

We'd landed on time. But that was Addison. She loved a bit of overexaggeration.

"Where are Raya and Kelsey?" I asked, referring to my other two besties who'd helped to support Addison in her "friendivention" when they'd realized I needed a break away before I broke.

"Kelsey's parking the car, and Raya went to get coffees." She linked her arm through mine. "Miami Airport is a disaster."

"All airports are a disaster."

"True story."

Grabbing one of my suitcases, she tugged it, and me, away from the arrivals hall. I pulled the other one along, giving up on the stupid bag that refused to stay on my shoulder. It hung off my wrist, banging into the suitcase with every step.

"There's Raya. Hey, babe!" Addison yelled across the line of people waiting to order their drinks, and an even longer line of customers hovering by the pickup point. A few people looked behind them in irritation. Addison couldn't care less. She didn't have the embarrassment gene. "Look who I found."

Raya waved her arm in the air, then picked up a cardboard cup and pointed at it. I hadn't a clue what that meant. Could be "I got you a coffee," or it could be "Do you want a coffee?" I nodded, the gesture working under both scenarios.

Someone grabbed me from behind. "Boo!"

I jumped, whacking Kelsey on the arm. "You scared me, you daft cow."

"Charming. What a way to greet your best friend."

"Ahem. *One* of her best friends." Addison stuck out her tongue at Kelsey, who returned the gesture.

My heart bloomed with love. These women were my ride-or-dies. I didn't know what I'd do without them.

Kelsey was an editor who'd once worked for a large traditional publishing house and now freelanced. Not for me, I might add. We'd agreed long ago that it was better for me to work with an editor I wasn't so close with to avoid any conflict.

Addison was an author I'd met after I'd written a short story for a charity anthology. She'd been one of the curators making sure the stories aligned with the anthology requirements. She'd slid into my DMs and pronounced us best friends forever. Most authors were introverts. Not Addison. She put the "E" in extrovert and forced my introvert out of my shell and into the real world. I adored her.

Raya was my graphic designer extraordinaire, without whom my book covers wouldn't shine and my social media posts would look like a five-year-old had worked on them. Keeping Raya on after I'd signed with my publisher was one of the demands I'd had written into the contract.

"No need to fight over me. There's plenty to go around." I patted my distended stomach. "Especially after all that delicious food on the plane."

"How was first class?" Addison nudged me. "Any celebrities on board?"

"Not that I saw."

I'd only had eyes for one passenger. A beautiful man with vibrant green eyes, soft brown hair, and a magical cock. The memory of the orgasm he'd given me had me pressing my thighs together.

Heat raced to my cheeks. Kelsey's keen brown gaze homed in on me.

"Why are you blushing?" She planted both hands on her hips. "Oh my God. Did you meet someone on the plane?"

My friends could read me far too well. It scared me sometimes. I took my coffee from Raya and sipped. "Let's get to the hotel and I'll tell you everything."

The journey out of the Miami Airport reminded me why I never hired a car when I visited America. There were too many lanes and not enough rules. Kelsey had lived in the area her entire life, so for her, this was a breeze. If I'd been behind the wheel, I'd have had an accident by now. My fingers brushed the rough edges of the paperback as I dug around in my bag for my sunglasses. A ball of dread circled my stomach. What the hell was I going to do about this pile of crap? My editor wouldn't contact me during this trip, but she'd be on the case the day after I landed, demanding to see something. Anything.

Maybe I should rip out the pages and send her the cover. That was the only thing about this book I loved. The rest of it made me want to stab myself in the eye with a needle. I never used to be like this. Writing was my happy place, yet now, every word felt forced, the weight of expectation killing my creativity.

Did every author who'd achieved sudden success feel like this, or was it just me? Maybe I should reach out to someone like Colleen Hoover and ask her advice?

As if. I didn't have the guts to write to Queen Colleen. Besides, she probably received a gazillion emails a day. No one had the time to reply to even a fraction of those, even with help.

Ugh.

Check-in at the hotel went smoothly, and an hour after I'd landed at the airport, we entered our two-bedroom suite. I sank onto the couch.

"Jet lag sucks." I closed my eyes.

"Oh, no, you don't." Kelsey dropped beside me, and Addison took up space on the other side. Raya perched on the edge of the coffee table. "Deets, missy. Then you can take a nap before dinner."

I groaned. "Fine. But someone get me more coffee."

Addison got up to make me a cup, pressing it into my hand. All three of them leaned in, agape. I blew on my nails. The second I spilled, this room would erupt. We'd probably get chucked out of the hotel for causing a disturbance.

"Are any of you members of the mile-high club?" I

paused for effect as three jaws dropped simultaneously. "No? Just me, then."

As predicted, all three of them screamed, questions firing at me from all angles. I waited for them to get it out of their systems.

"How did it happen?" Addison demanded when the excitement quieted. "Who came on to whom?"

"Um... a bit of both. Although, he was the one who made the ultimate move."

"Which was?" Raya urged.

"I went to use the shower room. Did you know first class has, like, a proper bathroom with a shower and everything? I didn't."

"Focus," Kelsey said.

I grinned. "Anyway, I got up from my seat, and he grabbed my wrist and told me to leave the door unlocked."

Kelsey pretended to faint, covering her forehead with the back of her hand. "Oh my God. What a dreamboat."

"What about the sex?" Addison asked. "I mean, sure, he might be great at the seduction part, but what about the delivery part?"

"His 'delivery' "—I air-quoted—"was exemplary."

"Ugh. Why don't these things ever happen to me?" Addison pouted. "If I treated myself to a first-class ticket, I'd end up sitting beside some old bald guy who'd regale me with boring stories of the war or something. You, lucky bitch that you are, ended up sitting next to Mr. Hotness." She arched a perfectly shaped eyebrow. "He was hot, right?"

I fanned myself. "I have third-degree burns to prove just how hot."

"I need to hook up with a hot guy." Addison pointed between her legs. "Before my pussy seals up."

"You and me both," Kelsey chimed in. "I'm hoping for some action on the cruise."

"Me, too." Raya's dark blue eyes sparkled. "So, are you planning on seeing him again?"

"No. I didn't even get his last name, although he knows mine. So I guess the ball is in his court." I rubbed the back of my neck. I should have pressed for his surname. However, if I had, what would I have done with it? He'd clearly kept his identity a secret *because* he wasn't interested in seeing me again. Rejection sucked.

"Ooh, a mysterious man. Intriguing."

"Or well practiced in this kind of thing." The thought popped out unintentionally. I shrugged to hide my disappointment. "Anyway, I had fun. But I'm far more excited about spending the next sixteen days with you bitches."

All three girls piled on for a group hug. "Us, too."

My friends headed down to the hotel swimming pool, leaving me in peace to take a nap, but I struggled to fall asleep. I tried to tell myself it was because of excitement about the trip, but the truth was I couldn't stop thinking about Blay. Those piercing eyes of his that had bored right through me, the intelligent conversation we'd had, how a single touch had sent a burst of electricity through my veins. The way my body had accepted him as if he'd been created just for me. The sex. God, the sex.

If I ended up comparing every sexual experience to that one, I was completely screwed—no pun intended—on the sex stakes. It wasn't only the illicit nature of it that thrilled me. It was the complete package. Gorgeous guy who could string a sentence or two together, who listened to my woes about my book, and who gave me an earth-shattering orgasm into the bargain.

In the end, I gave up trying to sleep. I took a shower, then sat on the balcony and listened to the sound of the waves. Music from the pool deck drifted up to me. I rose to my feet and peered down at the swimming pool eleven floors below. Several people were in the pool doing aqua aerobics with a rather enthusiastic woman in a leopard-print swimsuit miming the actions on dry land. And right at the front, unsurprisingly, was Addison, giving it her all. I smiled. Sometimes I wished I could be like that, so outgoing and ebullient. I was fine in small groups, but in large crowds, I faded into the background, preferring to watch rather than take part.

Kelsey waved, nudging Raya sprawled beside her on a sun lounger. I waved, too, trying to send a message not to rush back on my account. Being alone for a little while longer wasn't a problem for me. Kelsey either didn't get the message or ignored it. She packed up her things while Raya went to get Addison out of the pool.

We dressed for an early dinner, all of us voting to eat at the hotel restaurant tonight. We had another night in Miami to enjoy before boarding the ship on Saturday, ready for our two-week cruise around the Caribbean. This way, if I crashed, I could go to bed and leave the girls to enjoy the rest of their evening without them having to escort me back to the hotel.

"So," Kelsey said as soon as we'd ordered cocktails. "How's the book coming?"

I might have known she'd be the first to ask. "Awful."

"You always say that," Addison said. "And then you turn out amazing work that readers devour."

"Not this time." I looked over at Raya. "The best thing about this book, by far, is this lady's talented cover design. But the inside is a gigantic pile of steaming horseshit."

"I'm sure that's not true," Raya said.

"Babe, it is. I know authors are always the harshest critics of their work, but I'm looking at this dispassionately and it's just dreadful." I ran a hand through my hair. "And the worst part is I don't think it's fixable. Which is a big problem. I've bought myself some time with my editor by telling her I really need this break, but she's going to want to see something when I get home. If I send her what I've got, that's it." I drew a finger across my neck. "Bye-bye, career."

"Stop being so dramatic," Kelsey, in her inimitable direct style, said. "You're not that person."

She was right. Dramatics annoyed the hell out of me. My sister, Karen, whom I hadn't seen in years after she'd sided with my parents over my "disgusting porn," could turn the slightest drama into a major crisis. These days, I avoided anyone with those specific personality traits.

"I know." I sighed. "It's the pressure of the previous book getting to me. If this one isn't as well received, then I'll have failed, won't I?"

"Oh, Jesus." Kelsey rolled her eyes. "Don't make me slap you."

"Ooh, if we're lining up for slaps, can I get in on that?" Addison grinned, her green eyes twinkling with humor.

"If you say something so ridiculous again, even *I* might

51

have to get in line," Raya weighed in. And she was the pacifist amongst us.

"But what do I do?"

"Want me to read it?" Kelsey asked.

I shook my head. "It's a nice offer, but—"

"Your ego is a little delicate right now, and the last thing you need is me coming in with my red pen and reaffirming your concerns."

I loved how she knew me so well. "Exactly. Maybe if I leave it for a couple of days, then go back to it, the answers will magically appear." I doubted it, but voicing that would probably earn me those slaps.

"That's a good idea," Addison said. "Let your brain work on it subconsciously, and I bet when you open it again, you'll know exactly what needs to be done. Work on the first few chapters so you can give your editor something to keep her occupied while you review the rest."

Just talking to my girls made me feel brighter.

"Course..." Addison winked at Kelsey. "They say to write what you know, so maybe you should write a story about a hookup between a sex-mad author and a rich, hot guy getting it on at thirty-five thousand feet."

"If I wrote contemporary instead of romantic suspense, I might just do that. But I need a disaster to make my books work, like a plane blowing up, or a villain out for revenge against the heroine, or..." I paused for effect. "A kidnapping."

"All together now," Kelsey said, waving her hands in the air.

"Because we do love a good kidnapping!" all three girls yelled at once.

I laughed. That was my signature phrase. And it was true. I *did* love a good kidnapping. In my books only, of course.

"Well, if you're not planning to write *Hot Guy Meet-Cute at Thirty-Five Thousand Feet*"—Addison winked again—"then it's my duty to. Course, I'll need all the intimate details about hot guy and his hot rod."

I removed the umbrella from my tequila sunrise and set it on the table. "In your dreams."

Chapter 6

Blaize

Googling is a dangerous pastime.

Nolen let go of Marlowe's hand and pulled me into a bear hug. "It's great to see you. Thanks for picking us up from the airport, although we could've easily organized a town car. I'm sure you're maxed, what with the launch tomorrow."

My stomach tensed, a muscle twanging low in my abdomen, but I faked a smile. "It's not a problem." I hugged Marlowe. "You look great. How's my gorgeous niece?"

"Growing up too fast. She took her first step last week."

"She did? Wow, that's amazing." I looked at Nolen accusingly. "You should have messaged me."

"I messaged the family WhatsApp group," he replied.

I grimaced. "Ah. Sorry. I'm a little preoccupied."

55

"It's fine." He clapped me on the back. "Is there anything I can do?"

"Yeah." I grinned. "Pay for dinner."

I grabbed two of their suitcases and wheeled them out to my car. My driver navigated the busy airport traffic with ease, and a few minutes later, we were on the freeway headed to my house. Marlowe scrolled through her phone, showing me pictures and videos of Makenna.

Regret weighed heavy in my chest. The last time I'd seen my niece was at Nolen and Marlowe's wedding last September, when she was only two months old. After this launch was over, and life steadied a little, I'd make more time for the family. I felt as if I was missing everything, and while work *was* my life, so were the people who meant the most to me. At least I'd get to spend some time with my brother on this trip. I was only sorry that Kadon couldn't make it, but summer was his busiest time, and I couldn't expect him to up and leave his business to help support mine.

I showed Marlowe and Nolen to the guest bedroom and left them to freshen up. Taking a seat out by the pool with a freshly made pitcher of iced tea, I scanned my emails, answering one or two while I waited. Distracted, I found myself opening Google and typing in "J. T. Rowe, Author."

Pictures of Jill filled my screen, and below, a selection of her published novels. I traced my fingertip over her face, my mind throwing up images of her smooth, pale skin and rosy nipples. My palms prickled. Logic told me I'd never see her again, but if I did, for her, I'd break my principal rule for a second taste. Maybe even a third. Or a fourth.

Jesus Christ. Who even was I?

"Who's that?"

Like a kid caught looking at dirty pictures, I dropped my phone screen down. "No one."

Nolen flopped into the chair next to mine. "You're blushing. You never blush. Come on. What gives?"

I sent a scowl in his direction. "Nothing gives."

"What are you two cooking up?" Marlowe took the seat next to Nolen.

"Blaize was drooling over a woman on his phone, but he won't tell me who she is."

"He's entitled to a private life, Nolen. Leave him alone."

"Ha." I jabbed a finger at my brother. "Listen to your wife. She knows best."

"Although..." Marlowe released a slow smile that built. "I'd like to know who's piqued your interest, Mr. One-Night Stand." She held out her pinkie to Nolen, who hooked his around hers and laughed.

I groaned. "Will you two quit it?"

"Sure. No problem."

Nolen leaned his elbows on the table. The glint in his eye should have warned me of his intentions, but the lack of sleep and the stress over tomorrow made me a second too slow. He grabbed my phone before I could and leapt to his feet.

"Ooh, J. T. Rowe. An author, no less."

"Give me the phone." I tried to snatch it back. He whipped it out of my reach.

"How do you know the lovely Miss Rowe?"

A lifetime of living with Nolen told me he wouldn't

stop bugging me until he'd gotten answers. I returned to my seat. "I met her on the flight from London. That's all."

Nolen sat down, too. He gave my phone to Marlowe. "And was that 'met' in the biblical sense?"

"There is no 'met' in the biblical sense."

"You know what I mean. Did you...?" He waggled his eyebrows.

"For fuck's sake. I thought marriage and fatherhood would have forced you to grow up a bit. Makenna's more of an adult than you are."

"Stop teasing him." Marlowe passed me my phone. "She's lovely. You should call her."

"I don't have her number."

"But you have her bra size, I bet," Nolen drawled.

A laugh burst out of Marlowe. Great. I'd hoped my sister-in-law would side with me.

"What makes you think I behaved in any way inappropriately?"

"Because I know *you*."

The truth in that statement coaxed a chuckle from me. "Fine. We hooked up. It was pretty spectacular, and yeah, I admit, if I'd gotten her number, I'd probably call it. But I didn't. So can we just stop now, please?"

"Check her website," Marlowe said. "Most authors have a website with a contact form."

I gestured dismissively. "I've got enough on my plate with the launch."

"Any insurmountable problems?" Nolen asked.

Apart from my rapidly waning self-belief? "The usual snagging, that's all."

"Well, we're really looking forward to it, aren't we, Nolen? A much-needed break."

Wish it was a break for me. Still, in fifteen days, I'd be sitting back here with the maiden voyage behind me, and celebrating a job well fucking done.

I hoped.

Chapter 7

Jill

Not today, Satan.

"Wow! Would you look at that?" I craned my neck and shielded my eyes from the sun. "She's huge." I linked arms with Addison, a ball of excitement leaping around in my stomach. "I'll get lost."

"As long as we get lost in a bar, I'm good." Addison squeezed me tighter. "We're going to have the *best* time."

We lined up for check-in. Booths surrounded the reception area, each one manned by a member of staff, the Kingcaid logo stitched into their black-and-gold uniforms. I'd never been on a cruise before, and what a way to pop my cherry, so to speak. Serenity was the largest cruise ship in the world and had more activities on board than any of her competitors. There wasn't a chance we'd have time to get around to them all, not with the on-land excursions we'd already booked and paid for.

Plus, you have to find some time to look at that damned book.

I pushed the unwelcome thought to the back of my mind. *Not today, Satan.*

A handsome guy in his thirties beckoned to us. Addison nudged me and giggled. "We're off to a great start." Bouncing forward, hips swinging, she handed over her passport. "Are all the guys on board as gorgeous as you?" She fluttered her false eyelashes.

"Ignore her." I elbowed her out of the way and gave him my passport, too.

He smiled in that friendly yet distant manner of someone who'd heard it all before. "Miss Rowe." He looked at my passport and then at me, then swiped it through a scanner. "Welcome to Kingcaid Cruises. Is this your first time with us?"

"It's my first time, period."

"Yeah, she's a cruising virgin," Addison said.

She had a mischievous look in her eye, which, experience told me, meant she was about to say something outrageous. I stood on her foot before she made an inappropriate comment about sex.

"Ow. That hurt."

"Consider it a warning."

She wrinkled her nose and made a face. "I'd have thought sex on the plane with a stranger would have loosened you up, but it appears not."

Somewhere behind me, Kelsey laughed, and the poor guy booking us in turned beet red. I did, too. I should have broken her bloody foot rather than just standing on it.

"You're brave, considering we're sharing a room, and I'm vindictive enough to shave off your eyebrows while you sleep."

"You wouldn't."

"Oh, I would. Now behave."

I smiled at the mortified man on the other side of the podium. He handed me my passport along with a black wristband that also had the Kingcaid logo imprinted on it. He raced through the other three check-ins—I didn't blame him—and sent us on our way, his expression awash with relief.

"You are so bad."

Addison grinned. "It's all part of the fun." She narrowed her eyes at me. "You're not really going to shave my eyebrows, are you?"

I tapped a finger against my lips. "Maybe just the one."

Another member of staff escorted us to a VIP reception area where nibbles and drinks awaited us. Two Kingcaid Royalty suites had cost an absolute fortune, but if this was a taste of the service we could look forward to, it'd be worth every penny.

Contrary to popular rumor, I wasn't rich. Far from it. Self-publishing was expensive by the time you added up editing, cover design, formatting, and marketing costs. Not to mention website hosting, graphics, email programs, and a myriad of other expenses. And even when I'd been picked up by a publisher and hit number one on the *New York Times* and *Sunday Times* bestseller lists, my publisher had taken a whacking great slice of that pie. But I'd promised myself that I had to *try* to celebrate the success I'd had, even if the idea of losing it kept me awake at night. To me, this cruise was the physical embodiment of celebrating success.

We barely had time to enjoy the hospitality before a crew member invited us to board. Excitement curled in my belly as we crossed the gangplank. A member of the entertainment staff greeted us, holding up his hand for a high five. Addison, in her inimitable style, wrapped him in a huge hug and kissed his cheek. Unlike the guy who'd checked us in, this one looked thrilled with the attention.

"See you later, sweetie." She held her hand above her head and waved as she skipped on board.

"Bank on it," he called after her.

"Jesus," Raya muttered. "Five seconds and she's scored."

"That's Addison." I linked arms with Raya, who, if anything, was more introverted than I was. "Just go with the flow. It's easier that way."

Raya grinned. "This is going to be epic."

"You got that right."

We entered the ship and stepped into a large atrium. All four of us stopped dead, jaws dropping. The designers of this ship had spared no expense. Everywhere we looked screamed opulence. As VIP suite passengers, we could board before everyone else, giving us time and space to really look around.

"Whoa." Kelsey craned back her head, gazing up at the glass ceiling twenty floors above us, beyond which the bluest sky shone through, casting the entire area in dazzling light. "I saw this on their website, but the real thing is a whole other experience."

"Come on," Addison said. "Let's check out the suites."

The four of us rode the elevator up to the eighteenth deck, which housed the Kingcaid Royalty suites. One deck up were the penthouse suites for the real moneybags on this cruise, and above that, a VIP area separated from the rest of the ship where suite and penthouse residents could enjoy additional services not available to regular cabin passengers. I guessed they had to justify the exorbitant price tag somehow.

"Forward or aft?" Addison queried, peering at the chrome plate on the wall that showed the cabin numbers. "My glasses are in my bag. I can't see a damn thing."

"Forward." I led the way toward the front of the ship, stopping a few suites from the end. Our suitcases were already waiting for us.

"This is us." I held my black wristband to a plate on the wall, and the lock clicked. Kelsey did the same with the adjacent suite. "Ready?"

Simultaneously, we opened the doors.

"Oh my God!" Addison squealed as she ran inside. "Look at this place!"

I grinned at Raya and Kelsey. "See you in ten for drinks on the balcony." Following Addison into the suite, I closed the door and gazed around.

Luxury. That was the first word that sprang to mind. The space was vast with an enormous king-size bed, a fully stocked bar, and a marble bathroom with a walk-in shower and a jacuzzi tub, as well as two monogrammed plush robes.

There was even a living area with a corner couch in soft suede and a small dining table. But the real wow was the huge balcony. I opened the sliding doors and stepped outside. Two thick, padded loungers were placed in the sun, and there was a three-seater couch and a bistro table with two comfy chairs.

I raced to the railings, gazing down at the streams of people crossing the gangplank. To my left was the bridge, protruding out over the ship far above the sea, so close I could almost touch it. I waved at the crew members. One waved back. Whipping around, I grinned so wide my cheeks ached.

"This is *unbelievable.*"

"I know!" Addison hugged me. "I can't believe we're here. Finally." Returning inside, she flopped onto the bed. "Which side do you want?"

"Either."

"I'll take this side, then. Closer to the bar. Speaking of." She sprang from the bed and inspected the rows of top-shelf liquor. "How about a cosmo to kick off the festivities?"

"Sounds good to me." A knock came at the door. "Better make that cosmos for four." I wrenched it open. "Okay, bitches, let's get pi—"

It wasn't Kelsey and Raya.

"Oh, sorry about that."

The young woman standing outside our suite smiled. "Not a problem. It's an exciting day. I'm Soraya, your Royalty suite assistant. Can I come in for a minute?"

The suite next door opened, and Kelsey and Raya appeared.

"You might as well do us all together." I jerked my chin

at my friends standing behind Soraya. "Save you from making the speech twice."

Soraya glanced behind her. "Oh, of course." Standing out of the way, she motioned to Kelsey and Raya. "Please, ladies, after you."

Soraya gave us the rundown of the kinds of services afforded to those in the Kingcaid Royalty suites. It was clearly a rehearsed speech, one she'd probably practiced over and over to get it right, but I instantly took to her. After this, going back to my normal life wouldn't be easy. I could get used to this kind of pampering.

"Oh, and finally," Soraya said, "we're delighted that our CEO, Mr. Kingcaid, will join us on the cruise, and as you're Royalty suite guests, he'd like to extend a personal invite to an intimate gathering tonight on the VIP deck." She handed over two cards that had our names printed on them. "Just bring these with you. The reception starts at seven o'clock, an hour after we set sail."

I scanned the invite. "Thanks. We'll be there."

"Wonderful. Well, if there is anything you need at all, you can contact me via the ship's app, or dial 626 on your telephone. I'm here to make sure your trip exceeds all your expectations, so please don't hesitate to reach out to me."

"Thanks so much." I showed her out and closed the door. Wafting the cards in front of my face, I grinned. "Girls, get ready to party."

Chapter 8

Blaize

Well, I'll be damned.

ONE OF THE PROUDEST MOMENTS OF MY LIFE WAS standing on the balcony of the owner's suite and looking down to deck six, where scores of excited passengers streamed onto my cruise liner.

There had been many times over the last year in particular where I'd wondered if this day would ever come. And while my stress levels would remain high until the cruise was over and the last happy customer left the ship, I took momentary comfort because, so far, things appeared to be going okay.

The damn leak was fixed, the badge system hadn't had any more outages, and my team seemed to be handling any other snags without involving me, which meant they were minor inconveniences rather than anything that a customer might have cause to complain about.

Opening my phone to the welcome speech I'd written for tonight's VIP reception, I read it over one last time. Making speeches came naturally to me, but somehow, this one felt different.

Was different.

This cruise ship was my baby, my vision, my fucking neck on the line. I'd never shied away from responsibility in my life, and I didn't intend to start now. But Christ, I wished I could fast-forward the next two weeks and know everything had gone according to plan.

Someone knocked on my door. Probably Nolen. I put my phone down on the glass coffee table and crossed the suite to answer it.

"Ta-da!"

My cousin Aspen planted a kiss on my cheek and waltzed inside, her dyed purple ponytail swinging as she hauled two suitcases behind her.

My jaw dropped. "What the hell are you doing here?"

As far as I knew, Aspen was not on the ship's roster. One of my team would have told me if she was. Which meant that somehow she'd slipped through security with no one noticing, and also meant that I had a big fucking problem less than four hours before we were due to set sail. If security was this lax, I'd have to scrub the whole cruise, unless I could find the source of the problem. Fast.

"Charmed, I'm sure."

"It's not funny, Aspen. You don't have a ticket, which means you don't have a wristband." Everyone had to have a ticket and a wristband. Including me.

70

"Yes, I do." She shook her hand in the air. Sure enough, there it was, a black wristband.

"How... what... who?"

"Where, when, why." She giggled. "Chillax, Blaize. It's totes legitimate."

"If that's true, how come I don't know about it?"

"Because we wanted it to be a surprise."

She wrapped her arms around my waist, and I automatically drew her to me. As the only female child out of nine in the family, Aspen was special.

"Who's *we*?"

"Nolen."

I ground my teeth. Might have known. He hadn't said a goddamn word at dinner last night. Aspen disentangled herself from my hold and shook her finger at me.

"I know that face. Don't be mad at him. It was my idea. I haven't seen you in ages. That's all. And I wanted to tell you how proud I am of you."

Adoration blossomed in my chest. Aspen might be Roman and London's sister rather than mine, but I loved her just as much as they did. We all loved her, as annoying as she could be sometimes.

"You nearly gave me a fucking heart attack. I thought you'd bypassed security."

"Are you joking? Your security guys almost strip-searched me before they let me on board."

I arched an eyebrow. "I see you're still prone to overexaggeration. Don't you think twenty-eight is too old for that?"

"Oh, shush. Give me another hug." She tucked her arms underneath mine and squeezed. "I've missed you."

I kissed the top of her head. "Missed you, too."

"Good. Because I'm bunking with you."

A laugh rumbled through my chest. "And what if I'd planned to invite a woman along?"

"First, so what? There are two bedrooms, and I have earplugs to drown out the noise of the headboard rattling the wall. And second, that would mean you're dating, and we all know you don't date."

"I might have changed."

She snorted. "Yeah. Sure."

Sashaying past me, she beelined toward the larger of the two bedrooms like she had a built-in homing beacon. Or, more likely, if I knew Aspen—which I did—she'd studied the layout before arriving.

"Oh, no, you don't." I gripped her elbow, steering her toward the other bedroom. "That one is yours."

"No fair. I'm a lady. I have things."

I eyed her suitcases, busting at the seams. "Too many things," I grumbled.

"Typical man." She scanned around. "It's nice, although I think you should do the gentlemanly thing and switch."

"I never said I was a gentleman." Gentlemen didn't fuck strangers on planes.

I loosened my tie and unfastened my top button. Every time I thought about Jillian Rowe, a strange sensation gripped me. A kind of longing to see her again, if only to satisfy myself that I still didn't believe in seconds.

A test of sorts.

One I'd undoubtedly pass.

Aspen knelt on the floor and opened her first suitcase. She rifled through it, brandishing a two-piece swimsuit in the air. "Order of events. Swim. Eat. Then stalk Joz Raynor and turn on the charm."

"Who is Joz Raynor?" The name was vaguely familiar, but not enough for me to zero in.

She gaped at me, then shook her head with the kind of disappointment a mother might show to a child she'd discovered playing hooky.

"All work and no play makes Blaize a heathen in the music world." She plucked out a pair of glittery sandals. "Joz Raynor is a rock god. I've been trying to sign him to my label for ages, but he's so damn difficult to reach. His manager is an asshole. But here..." A glint lit up her eyes. "He's allll mine."

Aspen ran the Kingcaid Music label out of New York. Over the last four years since she'd assumed full control from my uncle Jacob, her father, she'd signed some amazing, talented artists—according to the music press, that was. As for me, I was too busy with my overflowing plate to keep up with the latest "big thing."

Looked as if this Joz Raynor was the latest big thing.

She disappeared into the adjoining bathroom, reappearing a few minutes later, dressed for the pool. "What are your plans for the rest of the day?"

I rolled my eyes. "Let me see. Launching a one-point-five-billion-dollar cruise ship, maybe?"

"You're not actually driving it, though, right?"

Taking a deep breath, I closed my eyes for a second. *God, give me strength.* "You don't 'drive' a ship."

"Sail. Whatever." She flailed her hands in the air. "You know what I mean."

"No, I don't 'sail' or 'drive' it. I have a captain and an entire crew responsible for that. But there are other things I have to do."

"Such as?"

"Let's put it this way. If one of your major signings was headlining at Madison Square Garden, what would you be doing?"

She wrinkled her nose. "I hate it when you bring logic to the party."

"You go and enjoy yourself. Don't get into any trouble, and *do not* annoy my guests. Any of them. If Joz Raynor puts in a complaint about you, I swear to God, I am selling you out at the next Kingcaid Group board meeting."

"He won't. Promise. I'll take the softly, softly approach."

I didn't even want to know what that meant. "Just watch yourself. This is an important two weeks for me, and if you want to stay aboard, you'll bear in mind my stress levels."

"I'll be the epitome of supportive." She drew her phone from the back pocket of her jeans. "Siri, email Carly and ask her to book Mr. Stresshead a full-body massage at Serenity's spa."

"If you've sent that, I'll murder you with my bare hands."

Laughing, she sprinted for the door. "Gotta catch me first."

My lips formed a smile that wouldn't quit. As flighty as

Aspen sometimes came across, she was as hard-nosed in business as the rest of the family. She was only trying to loosen me up a little. She had, too. The tension tightening every muscle in my neck had lessened, and that all-too-familiar knot in my stomach wasn't there either.

For now.

Picking up my phone, I went over my speech one last time.

K

At seven o'clock, flanked by Nolen and Marlowe, with Aspen leading the way, I entered the VIP area on deck twenty. A few guests were already assembled, with more arriving every minute, and by the time seven thirty came around, the deck was packed. I circled the gathering, chatting with a few celebrities who, in my experience, needed their egos stroked far more than the average person.

Aspen scanned around, her shoulders dropping after she'd checked out the entire space.

"No sign?"

Joz Raynor was proving to be rather elusive thus far. Aspen had spent most of the afternoon touring the ship, looking in bars, restaurants, and everywhere in between.

"No. But I will not be beaten." She beseeched me with her hazel eyes. "Of course, it'd be easier if I knew which penthouse he was staying in."

"Not a chance." I pointed two fingers at my eyes, then swiveled them to point at her. "I'm watching you. If I get the slightest inkling that you've been hanging around on deck nineteen for any other reason than coming or going from the owner's suite, I will have the helicopter take you to the nearest deserted island and leave you there."

"You're so touchy. You never used to be this touchy."

"That's because I didn't have a one-point-five-billion-dollar price tag on my head before. My priority is my customers, not you. And Joz Raynor, like every single other passenger aboard this ship, deserves to enjoy his vacation in peace." I motioned to Nolen. "Help me out here."

He raised his hands to the sides of his head. "I'm staying out of it. This is my honeymoon. *My* priority is my gorgeous wife." He pressed his lips to Marlowe's temple and slid an arm around her waist.

"Fine, but do me one favor."

"What?"

"Monitor Miss Determined here while I give this speech. Then you're off the hook for the next two weeks."

"Deal."

I moved through the crowd, getting stopped once or twice by various people. Eventually, I made it to the small podium the crew had set up for me.

I tapped the microphone. "Good evening, everyone. My name is Blaize Kingcaid, CEO and joint owner of Kingcaid Cruises. I'd like to take this opportunity to welcome you personally to Kingcaid Serenity. If you'll bear with me for a few minutes, I'd—"

My gaze fell on a woman standing a few feet from Nolen. She stared right back at me, her lips parted, her eyes wide.

I froze, my well-rehearsed speech spirited away on the salty breeze, leaving me thrown—and speechless.

Jillian "Tilly" Rowe.

Well, I'll be damned.

I'd wished for a chance to test my beliefs that second helpings weren't my style, and I'd gotten it.

And instantly, I knew... I'd failed.

Chapter 9

Jill

This wasn't supposed to happen.

I STUMBLED BACK A COUPLE OF STEPS, MY THIGHS quivering under the heated stare of my perfect stranger. Blay, *my Blay*, wasn't an international man of mystery at all. He was Blaize Kingcaid, the fucking owner of this multibillion-dollar ship. For a second, I blamed myself for being so stupid and not realizing earlier, but I brushed it off. Who looked up the CEO of the company when booking a trip? Not me.

Murmurings radiated through the crowd, all eyes on Blay, who'd frozen right in the middle of his speech. And still he stared at me, and I stared right back at him.

"Has he had a stroke?" Addison said in a too-loud voice. "Should we call the coast guard? Nine-one-one doesn't work out here, right?"

Words stuck in my throat. I attempted to swallow, my heart hammering like a caged bird bidding for freedom.

"Oh my God," Kelsey whispered from my left-hand side. "Don't tell me he's... he's..."

"He's what?" Addison demanded. Less than a second later, she gasped.

Raya, God bless that woman, clamped a hand over Addison's mouth before she could blurt out what all my friends now knew.

Blay cleared his throat. "My apologies, ladies and gentlemen. I lost my train of thought for a second." He palmed the back of his head and finally released me from the intensity of his gaze. I let a breath go and reached for Kelsey's hand.

"As I was saying, I'd like to take a few moments of your time to welcome you on board Kingcaid Cruises' brand-new ship. The team here is at your disposal. Our job is to ensure that you create memories to last a lifetime. Therefore, please, if there is anything we can do to make your stay more comfortable, reach out to me or any member of my crew."

He jumped off the raised platform and cannonballed toward me. Gathering my wits, I sucked in a lungful of salty air and braced myself.

"Come with me," he said, gripping my elbow.

He steered me away from the crowd, but not before Addison's proclamation, "Oh, he's gone all alpha on her. How swoony," reached us both.

I peeked up at him. A muscle drummed in his cheek as if he was grinding his teeth. Maybe he was, and who could blame him? He wouldn't have expected a woman he'd banged on an airplane to turn up on a cruise ship he owned, knowing there wasn't anywhere to run to. Other than leaping overboard, which, to me, looked more appealing by the second. Swimming back to Miami wouldn't take that long, right? How far could a cruise ship travel in ninety minutes? Five miles? Ten? I could make it. Probably.

We descended a flight of stairs and arrived in a corridor. He opened a door and motioned for me to enter.

I ran my gaze over the suite. Wealth oozed from every square inch. And here I was thinking my accommodations were top-notch. This... this was on another level. There was so much space that I could move in here and live happily for the rest of my life. Great view for writing, too. Although, I doubted even a killer view could save my current manuscript.

"I didn't know—"

Blay spun me around. His lips crushed mine, his tongue attacking me with the ferocity of a wild animal. He tasted of expensive whiskey and the lingering smokiness of rich coffee, coupled with the smell of his cologne that made me want to do very bad things. Large hands gripped my bottom, fusing me to his massive erection. I dropped my handbag on the floor and held on to his shoulders for support.

A groan rolled through his chest, vibrating against mine. "Jesus, Tilly." He kissed my jaw, my throat, my bare shoulder. "This wasn't supposed to happen."

"What wasn't?" I gasped as he tugged down my dress, and my boobs spilled out.

"This. Us. You being here."

81

He captured one of my nipples between his teeth. My stomach twisted. I should stop this, but I couldn't. I was a slave to my body, a slave to him and everything he made me feel. Kissing Blay was like standing on the shore as a wave was sucked out to sea, and you knew when it came back in, it'd demolish you, yet you remained in place, ready to embrace your destruction.

He kissed me again, devouring me with the skill of a man proficient in seduction. The rest of my dress slipped off, gathering in a bunch around my feet and leaving me in a skimpy pair of knickers and kitten heels. I yanked off his tie, and he did the rest. Lifting me effortlessly, he carried me through to the bedroom.

I landed on the firm mattress, Blay caging me with his body. He rocked back on his heels and traced a fingertip down my throat, between my breasts, over my stomach. His gaze didn't leave me for a second. I was on fire, my veins charred, my lungs filled with ash, the unexpectedness of the last five minutes leaving me breathless and impatient.

"I don't do seconds, yet I haven't been able to stop thinking about you." He lowered his head and grazed his teeth over my nipples. Groaning, I writhed beneath him.

"Have you thought about me?"

I nodded.

"Good. Because I'm going to fuck you on this bed, on the couch, on the floor, on every surface in this suite. I'm going to burrow so far inside your body that it'll take a crowbar to pry me out."

A shot of blistering heat ignited between my legs.

Filthy words spoken in his husky voice were my catnip. He planned to wreck me, and I'd let him, too.

He fingered the hem of my lace underwear. "Are these expensive?"

"Yes." God, I sounded breathless and ridiculous. Like a novice porn star trying out OnlyFans for the first time.

Riiiiip. The material came apart in his hands.

"I'll buy you a new pair. Ten pairs. A hundred." Scooching down the bed, he sucked my clit between his teeth.

"Fuck," I moaned, greedily lifting my hips and thrusting my vagina into his face.

"We had to rush on the plane. This time, we've got all night."

His tongue surged inside me. I reached behind my head and gripped the headboard, using it for leverage.

"That's it, Tilly. Ride my fucking face."

I groaned, coiling and twisting my body, grinding against him as if I hadn't had a mind-altering orgasm just two days ago.

"Jesus, you taste like all my fantasies rolled into one. So good, Tilly. So fucking good."

Pressure built in my abdomen. *Not yet.* I wasn't ready for this to end.

Blay's large hands clamped onto my thighs, splaying me wide open for him. "Christ, you're wet. Come on my face. Come hard, baby."

None of my previous boyfriends had been dirty talkers, and I'd never have thought I was the kind of girl who'd get turned on by it.

News flash: I *was* that kind of girl.

I exploded, the rush of endorphins and Blay's talented tongue and filthy mouth tipping me over the edge into the sort of electric climax I wrote about in my novels but never expected to have. Twice now, this man had made me come so hard I'd almost lost consciousness for a moment or two.

The bed tilted, or maybe it was the ship on the ocean waves. Blay flipped me over, gripping my hips to pull me into a kneeling position. The rip of a condom packet gave me a few seconds to prepare myself.

The shrill ring of a phone interrupted us. Blay cursed loudly. He let it ring out. The head of his cock nudged my entrance, but as I pushed back and he thrust forward, the phone rang again.

"Motherfucker," he muttered.

"It might be important."

He leaned over me, pressing his lips to my shoulder blade. "As important as this? As important as you? Not to me, it isn't."

A thrill surged through me. "What if the ship's on fire?"

"Let it burn."

He didn't mean a word of it, but the sentiment made me feel like a queen.

The phone rang a third time. I groaned, burying my face in a soft feather pillow. "Answer it. The damn thing's ruining my buzz."

A rough chuckle echoed through his chest. He leaned on me, pressing me into the mattress and rolling us onto our right-hand sides in a move far too skilled to be his first attempt. A sour taste flooded my mouth, and a fiery ball of jealousy lodged in my stomach. I almost laughed at the stupidity of it. Everyone had a past, although I had a hunch that Blay's past was much raunchier than mine. Probably raunchier than most people's, if his smooth move on the plane was a peek into his sex life.

"Don't move. Don't make a sound." He thrust into me, balls deep, then stilled.

"What is it?" At first I thought he was talking to me, until he followed up with, "This had better be life or death."

Oh. My. God. He'd answered the call while his cock was buried inside me. I clamped a hand over my mouth to stop the burgeoning laugh that threatened to blow my cover. The man had no shame. His fingers played with my nipples, his erection pulsing inside me. I swallowed a moan.

"Oh, hell. Can't you calm her down?"

I glanced over my shoulder. Blay blew me a kiss, then rolled his eyes. Whoever needed calming wasn't worrying him, so it couldn't be a catastrophe. His palm traveled over my abdomen and covered my mound, his middle finger flicking my clit. I anchored my second hand over my mouth and let my groan break free.

So good. So fucking good. Blay still hadn't moved. The man had enviable self-control.

"Fuck's sake. Fine. Tell her I'm on my way."

He pulled out of me. Gripping my chin, he turned my head toward him and kissed my lips, hard. "Don't go anywhere. I'll be back as soon as I can."

I rolled over, biting down on my disappointment. "I'll go. I can see you're busy."

"You're going nowhere." He arched a brow. "Do I have to handcuff you to the bed? Because I can and I will."

A giggle tickled my throat. "You shouldn't make promises you can't keep."

Pulling off the condom, he tied a knot in it and disappeared into what I presumed was the bathroom. I lowered my head. *Oh. He was only joking.* I sat up and swung my legs over the side of the bed to stand.

"I told you, Tilly, you're going nowhere."

I glanced behind me. Blay, cock still half-mast, was running the belt from a bathrobe through his fingers. He picked me up and threw me onto the bed, his muscular thighs straddling my hips and rendering me unable to move.

"If I'd known you'd be here, I'd have brought supplies. But as my handcuffs are at home, along with an array of vibrators, butt plugs, cock rings, and anal beads, this will have to suffice."

His eyes sparkled. I wasn't sure whether he was kidding around or if he really had the contents of Christian Grey's red room at his house. My clit tingled.

"Shame."

"Isn't it?" He grabbed my wrist and wrapped the soft belt around it.

"You're not really going to tie me up, are you?"

He grabbed my other wrist and did the same, then anchored me to the headboard. Running his nose between my breasts, he bit one nipple first and then the other.

"One thing you should know about me, Tilly. I always keep my promises." Climbing off the bed, he dressed in record time. "When I get back, we're going to fuck, then talk about why you're on my ship, then fuck again. And again. And again."

He straightened his tie and turned around.

"Blay, come on."

Glancing back at me, he tongued his canine, his gaze lazily roving over me. "Don't go anywhere." Laughing, he walked out of the bedroom.

"What if I have to pee?" I yelled.

"Hold it. The orgasms are better with a full bladder."

The next thing I heard was the unmistakable sound of a door closing. I waited a few seconds for him to come back and tell me it was all one big joke.

He didn't.

Chapter 10

Blaize

Act your ass off, Kingcaid.

Stomping down the narrow corridor, I muttered a multitude of curse words under my breath.

Fucking movie stars.

Correction, fucking *diva* movie stars. Most A-listers I'd met over the years were pretty solid, if less than ordinary, people.

Scarlett Rose was about as opposite from solid and ordinary as one could get. She believed her own hype and only ever surrounded herself with sycophants who told her exactly what she wanted to hear.

Argh. Why did she have to choose my cruise to celebrate her much-publicized divorce from her husband and former manager? Couldn't she have taken a Celebrity cruise? More fitting, no?

And who named their child after one of the most famous divas who'd ever graced the literary world? Maybe she came shooting out of her mom's vagina a raving bitch, and her parents decided payback was due.

Less than two fucking hours into the voyage and she'd already found something to complain about. Worse, apparently, *I* was the only sucker on board that she'd talk to. Or rather, rant at.

I'd understand if her complaint was an actual issue, but having to wait an hour for a masseuse to fit her into their schedule when she hadn't booked in advance was the epitome of a first-world problem.

Fix a smile, be nice, nod in all the right places.

If I made a stand, it'd only take me longer to return to Jill. A shiver raced down my spine. I couldn't fucking believe she was here, on my ship, my captive for the next two weeks. The forced proximity should have given me itchy feet, a desire to escape, yet the complete opposite occurred. She made me want to shirk my responsibilities and spend the next two weeks drinking from her pussy and fucking her until my cock fell off.

Metaphorically speaking.

Just to be thorough, I called the spa to confirm Scarlett's eight-thirty slot as I made my way to her penthouse. If this woman thought I'd spend the entire cruise at her beck and call, she was in for a rude awakening. There was being professional and putting my customers' needs first, and then there was being a complete pussy-whipped idiot.

There was only one woman pussy-whipping me, and it wasn't Scarlett fucking Rose.

I'd already agreed to provide security to accompany her around the ship and keep away autograph hunters after she'd declined to have her own bodyguards join her aboard. Her reasoning? She'd wanted to enjoy the cruise like a normal woman.

Scarlett Rose and *normal* did not belong together in the same sentence.

I knocked at her door and waited.

And waited.

And waited.

I knew the game she was playing, and I couldn't do a damn thing about it. There wasn't any point in knocking again. She'd make me wait longer if I did.

Eventually, the door opened, and one of Scarlett's assistants, a petite blonde with pouty lips that had too much collagen pumped into them, greeted me.

Act your ass off, Kingcaid.

I threw out a brilliant smile. "Hi. I'm Blaize Kingcaid, the CEO. I believe Miss Rose has an issue she'd like to discuss with me."

"You sure took your time, darlin'," a Southern accent drawled from somewhere inside the suite.

"My apologies, Miss Rose. I was otherwise indisposed when the call came through."

And I'd like to get indisposed again in double-quick time, fuck you very much.

Scarlett appeared in my sight line, dressed in a sheer negligee and matching robe. "Well, don't stand there in the doorway, sugar." She opened a slim silver box and withdrew a cigarette.

"There's no smoking on board, Miss Rose." I didn't care who the fuck she was or how much groveling I might have to do. Compromising the safety of the passengers and crew on board this vessel was nonnegotiable.

"One little cigarette is hardly going to hurt anyone."

She picked up a lighter. I strode past her assistant and plucked the cigarette from between her ruby-red lips. "A fire on the ship, however accidentally caused, puts the lives of everyone aboard in danger. I'm afraid I'll have to insist."

She stared at me for a second, eyes as cold as a dead fish. Then she let out a girlish giggle and gave my shoulder a friendly pat.

"Relax, angel. I'm just having fun."

Her idea of fun and mine were about as diametrically opposed as kinky and vanilla sex.

"We have a plethora of safe ways to do that on board, Miss Rose."

Reaching out with a long, red-tipped nail, she raked it over the lapel of my jacket. "Oh, I'm sure you do."

Ah, fuck. Really?

Somehow, I kept my smile fixed in place. "I believe you've had some trouble booking a slot at the spa. Please accept my apologies. We've fixed the problem, and your aromatherapy massage begins in"—I checked my watch—"thirty-five minutes. We've assigned our best masseuse to attend to you."

Say, "Thanks," and let me go. I have a restrained woman to return to and a cock that's demanding satisfaction.

"Hmm." Her lips pursed. "I suppose that will have to do."

She picked up a glass filled with clear liquid. Knowing Scarlett's reputation, I doubted it was iced water.

"Won't you join me for a drink?"

"I'd love to," I lied. "But I have a few more guests to see this evening. I'm sure you understand."

"Another time," she murmured, fucking me with her eyes.

Not even if the future of humanity depended on it.

"Have a wonderful evening, Miss Rose."

The click of the door with me on the other side of it sent a rush of relief through me. Scarlett Rose might feature in a lot of men's fantasies. She was a beautiful woman but had a spiteful heart. I couldn't fault her publicist, though. They'd done such a fantastic job with her that everyone thought she was America's sweetheart.

America's fucking nightmare was more like it. Amazing what good PR did for a person.

"Ah, there you are."

I turned to find Nolen and Marlowe making their way down the corridor. Forcing a smile, when all I wanted to do was sprint back to the owner's suite and bury myself in Jill's pussy, I walked toward them.

"Who's the woman?"

I frowned. "Which woman?"

"The woman you strong-armed out of the VIP reception. The same woman I caught you ogling on your phone."

Goddamn my brother.

"I didn't strong-arm anyone. Isn't it time you two started your honeymoon?"

Marlowe grinned. "We already have."

"Ugh." I covered my ears. "I don't want to know."

"You've got a dirty mind," Nolen said.

My brother didn't know the half of it. I wasn't about to enlighten him, either.

"Can I get you two anything? I've got a ton of shit to do."

More lies. I had one thing to do. Over and over and over again.

Marlowe plastered herself to Nolen's side. "No, we're good."

"See you for breakfast?"

"Sounds good."

I walked them to their suite, but as they entered, a thought struck me.

"Where's Aspen? Please tell me she's not stalking that rock star. If she pisses him off, she'll piss *me* off."

"She hasn't. Not that I'm aware of, anyway," Nolen said. "We just left her a few minutes ago. She said she was tired and turning in for the night."

"Good."

One problem put on the back burner for now.

"Night, bro."

He shut the door, and the sound of giggles erupted from inside. I smiled. They were such a terrific couple who'd walked a hard-fought path to happiness.

As I set off for my suite, Nolen's comment about Aspen hit me in the solar plexus.

No. No, no, no.

With the stress of the launch, the unexpectedness of seeing Jill at the reception, tasting her again, and then all this crap with Scarlett, I'd completely forgotten that Aspen had inveigled her way into my private space and taken the second bedroom.

Which meant...

Ah, fuck.

I broke into a sprint.

Chapter 11

Jill

**Well, bugger me.
Talk about embarrassing.**

BLAY COULDN'T HAVE BEEN GONE MORE THAN TEN minutes when I heard the door click open. I breathed a sigh of relief. My shoulders were starting to spasm.

"You're a dead man, Blay Kingcaid," I called out, laughter in my voice. Even though he'd tied me up and left me alone, I couldn't be mad at him. Truth be told, I was turned on, my pussy throbbing and aching for him to finish what he'd started.

"Oh my God."

My head whipped around, my eyes ballooning at the strange woman standing in the doorway to Blay's bedroom. *You have got to be joking.* He had another fucking woman lined up. What did he think was going to happen? A goddamn threesome?

"Who are you?" I demanded, trying my best to sound authoritative despite the fact that I was as helpless as a newborn, tied to a bed, and stark bloody naked. Correction. *Almost* stark naked. I still wore the kitten heels.

"Who are *you*?" she countered.

I ignored her question. "Where's Blay?"

"Blay?" She frowned. "Oh, you mean Blaize. No one calls him Blay."

Arguing from a position of inferiority wasn't helpful. "Can you cover me over and untie me, and then we can talk about who calls whom what?"

"Oh, sure."

She covered me with a sheet and untied me in seconds. I rubbed my wrists, tamping down the horrendous embarrassment that threatened to turn my skin redder than a day in the sun without sunscreen.

"How do you know my cousin?"

My back muscles went rigid. "Cousin?"

"Yeah, Blaize is my cousin." She stuck out her hand. "I'm Aspen Kingcaid."

She said it as if I should immediately recognize the name. Apart from the Kingcaid bit, I'd never heard of her. At least he hadn't organized a threesome. Although, tying me up and leaving me naked when he knew Aspen might appear at any second... I could murder him.

I might murder him the next time he dared show his face.

Despite the downright weirdness of this situation, I shook her hand. "Jill Rowe."

She hesitated, scrutinizing me as intently as a proof-reader going over the final manuscript before publication. A few seconds later, her hand flew to her face, and she made this snuffling kind of noise. Like a horse with its nose in a feed trough. I thought she might be choking. Then her hand dropped, and her eyebrows furrowed.

"J. T. Rowe? The novelist?"

I grimaced. "One and the same. Please don't put this on social media. My career will never recover."

She looked offended by my suggestion. "I'd never do something like that."

"Some people would."

"I'm not some people. Believe me, I've been on the receiving end of my fair share of trolling. I'm not likely to subject someone else to that kind of shit. I am, however, one of your biggest fans. I've read everything you've published." She shook her head, wearing this goofy smile that was utterly endearing. "Goddammit, if I'd known you'd be here, I'd have brought a book for you to sign."

"If you give me an address, I'll send you a whole bunch."

"You will?" Her smile stretched wider. "I'd *love* that."

"There is one condition."

"Name it."

"We both pretend this"—I swung my hand between us —"never happened."

Making a cross over her chest, she dipped her chin. "Deal." She perched on the edge of the bed and hugged me. "I am so *excited* to meet you."

I wrinkled my nose. "I'd kind of like to get dressed. Do

you think you could grab my dress and handbag from the other room?"

"Oh, sure. Of course." She disappeared, returning with my clothes and bag. "Here you go."

I waited for her to leave. She stayed right where she was. I arched a brow.

"Oh, shit. Right. Sorry." She grinned at me again. "I'm being weird. I promise I'm not this strange all the time. I'm just thrilled to meet you."

She scuttled into the living area. I leapt out of bed and dressed in seconds. Still no sign of Blay. Or I should say Blaize, given what Aspen had said about no one calling him by that shortened moniker. Which begged the question of why he'd introduced himself to me like that. Probably all part of his seduction routine. Introduce a little mystery, and bam! Suckered into a onetime deal at thirty-five thousand feet.

Then again... he had seemed awfully pleased to see me.

"Do you want something to drink?" Aspen shouted.

I emerged from the bedroom, clutching my handbag to my stomach as if it were a shield to protect me from further crippling embarrassment. "No, thanks. I should go."

She twirled around with a bottle of gin in one hand and a cocktail shaker in the other. "Not on my account. Please, stay. I'd love to talk about books with you. If you don't mind, that is. Especially as you're on vacation."

"I'm always happy to talk about books." Unless it's the pile of crap I brought with me. God, how was I going to fix that bloody book? I didn't have time to start from scratch, unless a lightning bolt of inspiration hit me and I could knock out eighty thousand words in three weeks. Which I couldn't. I was a clean-first-draft writer, but, these days, a slow one. No, the only solution was to identify the issues—somehow—with the current novel and make it good enough to send to my editor.

Miracles happened sometimes. Right?

Aspen made something with the gin. She handed me a glass. I took one sip. Jesus. I'd be hammered after drinking less than half of that. I put it on the coffee table. Aspen sat beside me, cross-legged, her expression eager.

"What are you working on right now?"

Ah, hell. "Um, a follow-up to *Pieces of Me.*"

"Oh my God! For real? I loved Arton and Kenna. They're getting a second book?"

Supposedly. "Yeah."

I couldn't help but notice that Aspen hadn't asked me why Blay—Blaize—had tied me to a bed and left me here. Perhaps this wasn't all that an unusual occurrence. My stomach cramped at the thought.

"That's incredible. When's it coming out?"

At this rate, never. "That's up to the publisher. I just write the words." Sounded so simple. If only.

"You'll have to message me when you know." She raised her hips and fished a card out of the back pocket of her trousers. "Here are my contact details."

I slipped the card into my handbag. "I'll make sure I—"

The door to the suite opened, and Blay entered. He took one look at the scene before him and blushed hot enough to start a fire.

"Ah, fuck."

Indeed.

Before I could say a word, Aspen sprung off the couch, marched over to Blay, and punched him in the arm. She wasn't gentle about it, either.

"Blaize Isaac Kingcaid, would you like to explain to me what I found when I returned to this suite ten minutes ago?"

Isaac. He didn't look like an Isaac. Then again, he didn't look like a Blaize, either. To me, he'd always be Blay.

"Firstly, ow." He rubbed his arm. "And secondly, no. It's none of your business." He looked over at me with a grimace that appeared to be an attempt at an apology.

"None of my business?" She planted her hands on her hips. "Do you know who that woman is?"

"Are you high? Of course I know who she is. What—?"

"Don't interrupt me. I hadn't finished talking. That woman..." She pointed at me as if there might be a doubt about whom she was referring to. "That woman is J. T. Rowe, the greatest romance novelist in the world."

A nice compliment, but far from true. Good to hear all the same, though. Especially at the moment, given my flagging confidence over the latest shite I'd penned.

"And you leave her naked and tied to your bed?"

I winced at the baldness of her statement. It'd been fun... until she'd walked in. "It's—"

"You're a disgrace to this family. Does Nolen know about this?"

He rolled his eyes. "Yeah, because I go around sharing my sex life with my nearest and dearest all the time."

"Don't come at me with sarcasm."

I raised my hand as if I were in class and trying to get the teacher's attention. "Excuse m—"

"I'll come at you with more than sarcasm if you don't take your nose out of my business."

"Could I just—?"

It was as if I hadn't spoken. Blay made a frustrated noise, glaring at his cousin. "Okay, that's it." He gripped Aspen by the arm and frog-marched her to the door. Opening it, he guided her into the corridor. "Go get a drink or a massage. I need an hour." He glanced over his shoulder. "Make that two."

Shutting the door in her face, he activated the deadlock and combed his fingers through his hair. He pivoted slowly. A veil of unease washed over his face as he slowly lifted his eyes to mine, a sheepish tilt to one side of his mouth.

"I'm so fucking sorry. I got caught up in you, and then having to leave you to go fix some diva's nonissue, it slipped my mind that Aspen was sharing this suite, too. She wasn't even supposed to fucking be here. I'd never have put you in that position if I'd known she'd find you." He palmed his neck. "Say something."

"I tried. Three times. But you and your cousin were far too busy taking chunks out of one another to hear me. She's... feisty."

"Yeah. Aspen's a woman in a man's world. She's been around tough men all her life, and she knows how to handle them better than most." He strode over to me and sat in the seat Aspen had vacated when she'd jumped up to punch him. "I'm surprised you haven't walked."

"Do you want me to go?"

"No! Christ, no. The whole time I was dealing with

Scarlett, I couldn't stop thinking about you and all the things I'd do to you when I got back."

I frowned. It couldn't be... could it? "Scarlett? As in Scarlett Rose?"

"One and the same."

"Wow. I adore her movies. I can't believe I'm sailing with Hollywood royalty."

"More like royal pain in my ass. Don't believe the public image. She's a fucking diva."

"What a dis—" My phone rang. I cursed. "Hang on." Reaching into my bag, I retrieved my phone. Addison's name scrolled across the screen. "It's one of my friends. Can you give me a sec?" Rising from the couch without waiting for an answer, I padded into his bedroom, my stomach clenching at the sight of the ruffled bedsheets. "Hey," I said into the mouthpiece.

"Oh, how disappointing. You answered, and you're not huffing and puffing. I take it you and Mr. Alpha didn't work out? Where are you?"

I couldn't help grinning. "In Mr. Alpha's bedroom."

"Has he fucked you already? Doubly disappointing. Looking at him, I'd have thought he had more staying power than that."

Now wasn't the time to repeat what had happened with Blay tying me up and his cousin discovering me. And knowing Addison's big mouth, there probably wouldn't ever be a time to repeat it.

"We haven't slept together."

"Trebly disappointing."

A laugh fizzed in my throat.

"Well, if you're not getting thoroughly shagged, you might as well meet us for dinner as planned."

"Um..." How did I manage this? "Hang on a sec."

I put the phone on mute and returned to the living room. Blay had poured himself a drink. Something amber. Whiskey or brandy, maybe. He glanced up at me as I appeared.

"You don't have to say yes, but—"

"Yes."

"That's a dangerous response. I could have been about to ask you to sign over your fortune to me."

"I would, as long as you signed over your life to me in return."

I poked my tongue into the side of my cheek. "Smooth. Also a lie."

He hitched a shoulder. "Gotta give me credit for effort."

"Three out of ten."

"Harsh."

"Gives you something to aspire to."

A chuckle vibrated through his chest. "What have I agreed to?"

"Dinner with my friends. And I must warn you, they're a rabid bunch."

His smile lit me up from the inside. "At least I'll have you to protect me."

Chapter 12

Blaize

**Girl's got far too many brains
for an ass like that.**

SEVERAL PEOPLE STOPPED ME AS I WALKED TO DINNER with my arm possessively around Jill's waist. I shared a few words with each one before politely excusing myself under the guise of disliking unpunctuality.

The truth was, I only had eyes for Jill, and every person we met took my attention away from her.

In other words, I was dead to rights on the pussy-whipped stakes.

It wouldn't last.

My brief obsessions never did, although my interest usually waned before the sun kissed the horizon the next morning. I put it down to the fact that Scarlett's demands had interrupted us.

After dinner, I'd persuade her to return to my suite. A night buried inside Jill would slay my thirst once and for all. The ship was big enough to avoid her if things got a little awkward afterward. My instincts told me that Jillian Rowe wasn't the clingy type. She had far too much pride to hold on to a liaison that had run its course.

I put my hand on the small of her back and eased her into the restaurant. The greeter stood up straighter as we approached the podium, but before she could say a word, a squeal of excitement almost punctured my eardrums.

A woman raced over to us and nearly smothered Jill in her ample chest, then released her and gave me a thorough appraisal.

"I gotta hand it to you, Jill. You sure know how to land the hot ones. You don't happen to have a brother, do you, Mr. Kingcaid?"

"Addison," Jill hissed. "Behave."

"Please call me Blaize." Jill gave me a quizzical look, which I noted to ask her about later. "As a matter of fact, I have two brothers, and one is on the cruise. Unfortunately, he's here with his wife. My other brother lives in France and is also spoken for."

Addison pouted. "Ugh. The good ones are always taken."

"Who said they're good?" I arched a brow, squeezing Jill's hip before sliding my hand to her firm ass.

Seriously, the girl had far too many brains for an ass like that.

"Well played." Addison dipped her chin. "Bad ones are much more fun."

Spinning around, she made her way over to a table where two other women were seated, their sharp gazes assessing me.

"Blaize Kingcaid." I stuck out my hand, shaking both of theirs. "Did I pass?"

One of the women, a petite, pretty blonde, hinted at a smile. "Early days. I'm Kelsey, and this is Raya."

She gestured to a dark-haired woman with navy-blue eyes and a friendly smile.

"They're very protective," Jill whispered in my ear.

"I can tell. Should I be concerned?"

"That depends."

I didn't ask "On what?" I didn't need to. It was obvious: on whether or not I treated Jill right.

Out of nowhere, a vortex of unease settled in my stomach.

Maybe this wasn't such a good idea.

If I woke up tomorrow with my usual urge to put as much distance between my conquest and me, I'd make life more difficult than it needed to be.

Avoiding one woman was doable.

Avoiding four, even on a ship this size, wouldn't be easy, especially if they were out for blood.

And something told me that Jill's friends knew how to draw blood. A lot of blood. Enough to require a transfusion.

"Come, sit." Addison patted the seat beside her. "Prepare yourself for a grilling."

I slid onto the circular leather bench. Jill followed, hemming me in.

Too late to escape now.

But as her warm thigh brushed mine, and the smell of her newly applied perfume filled my nostrils, I realized that escape was the last thing on my mind.

As the champagne flowed, her friends relaxed, and by the time the servers brought our entrées, they'd forgotten all about grilling me on my suitability for their friend. Instead, they'd switched their attention to grilling me about Scarlett Rose after Jill had let it slip that she was on board.

The public's fervent interest in that woman astounded me. Then again, she had the best PR money could buy, and they earned every cent. If her precious fans knew the real woman behind the veneer she so expertly painted on, maybe their opinion wouldn't be quite so favorable.

Although... these days, who knew?

Unlike what I'd told Jill about the irrepressible Scarlett Rose, I kept my opinion to myself and remained suitably vague. The arrival of food helped my cause in moving the conversation away from the A-list actress and on to safer subjects.

Jill pressed closer to me with each course and as the last of the dishes were cleared away, she was practically sitting in my lap.

"You're making me hard," I murmured to her, low enough that Addison wouldn't overhear.

"And you're making me wet." Sliding her hand up my thigh, she put her mouth next to my ear. "Shall we go?"

Without waiting for an answer, she rose from the

booth. I almost tripped over my feet in my haste to follow her.

Addison held out her hand toward her two friends and tapped her palm. "Pay up, bishes."

"Pay up for what?" Jill asked.

"I bet you wouldn't last until after coffee, and I was right."

"Fuck off." Jill smiled.

Addison giggled. "Enjoy yourself, kiddos. Remember, stay safe."

"I hate you."

"You love me, and I love you. See you in the morning. I'll have a rubber ring ready for you to sit on."

I couldn't contain my laughter. Addison was one of those women who were both annoying and endearing at the same time.

I slid my arm around Jill's waist, savoring the way her body fused with mine. Brushing my thumb over her hip, I buried my nose in her hair.

"How do you feel about a little delayed gratification?"

She peered up at me, curious. "What did you have in mind?"

I steered her toward the piano bar, an intimate drinking establishment with low lighting, plush, private seating, and a sensual ambience.

It was a place for lovers, for honeymooners, and for horny-as-fuck CEOs who owed the woman they'd devoured on board a commercial jet a taste of seduction.

Despite my one-and-done attitude, I didn't treat the women I banged as nothing more than a hole for my dick. I liked to wine and dine and play footsie under the table. To stare into their eyes over a crisp glass of expensive wine and let my blood fill with lust as I imagined all the things I'd do to them when we were alone.

Jill deserved that, and so much more.

I wanted to give her more than explosive orgasms. She deserved my undivided attention—a chance for me to get to know a little about her and have her get to know the me behind the corporate image.

Jeez, Kingcaid. Who the fuck are you?

The moment we entered the bar, several members of my crew jumped to attention as if the floor had become a furnace that burned their feet.

Some of my business associates loved the power of having others fawn over you, but I'd never enjoyed the sycophantic nature of being rich and holding their careers in my hands. I preferred people to treat me as they would anyone else, even though it was a hopeless yearning. To them, I was the boss, the big cheese, the man who hired and fired at will. As they got to know me over the next two weeks, they'd relax a little, but I'd always garner that "Oh, fuck" reaction.

Comes with the territory, I guess.

"Mr. Kingcaid. Ma'am." The first crew member to reach us bobbed his head. "How can I be of assistance?"

I produced my friendliest smile to put him at ease. "A booth for two."

I scanned the bar, my gaze alighting on the perfect spot, a table tucked away in a dark corner. "That one is perfect."

For so many reasons.

He followed my sight line and nodded, leading the

way. I could tell he was trying his best to stand up straight and not trip over his feet. Jill looked up at me with a "Bless him" expression.

I ushered her into the booth and sat beside her.

"Wine?"

"Sounds lovely."

Without needing to see the menu, I ordered a bottle of mid-priced wine. Jill didn't strike me as the kind of woman who'd demand, nor welcome, a one-hundred-grand, look-how-fucking-rich-I-am bottle.

Once the server had left us alone, I twisted my body to give her my full attention. I tucked a strand of hair behind her ear, grazing the back of my hand along her neck. Goose bumps peppered her skin. It wasn't cold in here. I smiled.

"I hope this is okay?"

Her eyes danced as her lips rose to meet them. "I know what you're doing, and I appreciate it. But you're aware that I'm kind of a sure thing, right?" She laughed before I could answer. "That makes me sound... easy."

"No, it doesn't. It makes you sound like a strong, confident woman who knows what she wants and isn't afraid to go out into the big, bad world and get it."

I continued caressing her neck, my thumb tracking her jawline. She rewarded me with an adorable shiver.

"Let me seduce you a little. Foreplay makes the sexual act that much more explosive."

"I'm not complaining."

"Good."

"Why did you introduce yourself to me as Blay when Aspen said no one calls you that?"

I withheld my answer until the server had set down the

wine and two glasses. I waved him off when he offered to pour. Filling both glasses, I handed one to Jill.

"I'm not sure. Maybe I wanted to forget who I was for a while and just be me. Enjoy the company of a beautiful woman without the baggage that comes with being a member of this family."

"Or..." She tapped her forefinger against her lips. "You thought I might be more interested if I knew you could buy the airline we were flying on." Amusement laced her tone.

"What would 'more interested' have looked like?"

I was teasing her, and she knew it. "Hmm, I might have screwed you right there in the seat."

She didn't mean it, but my stomach somersaulted anyway. "I might have let you."

"Might?" She snorted, and it was fucking adorable.

"You got me."

"Is that really the reason? That you wanted to not be you?"

I nodded. "You saw the greeting we received a few minutes ago. Sometimes, I get the urge to pretend I'm someone else, to forget I'm Blaize Kingcaid, a man with a one-point-five-billion-dollar millstone around my neck."

I meant the comment to come across as flippant and meaningless, but from the concerned look on Jill's face, I'd failed.

"That can't be easy."

"No." I took a sip of wine. "I've had sleepless nights about this voyage, this ship, this entire venture. It has to go well."

Grimacing, I tried for a smile that refused to hold. "I

have no idea why I just told you that. I haven't even told my family how worried I've been. *Am*," I corrected.

"It can be easier to talk to a stranger."

I fiddled with my cuff link. "Is that what you are? A stranger? You don't feel like a stranger."

Her eyes darkened, lust swimming in her hazel irises. My dick responded with enthusiasm.

"You don't feel like a stranger to me, either."

I bent my head, the touch of our lips brief but electric. Jill's brief gasp hardened my dick the whole way. Curling my fingers around her wrist, I placed her hand on my erection.

"This is what you do to me."

"You give me too much credit." She sounded out of breath, as if she'd sprinted up a flight of stairs.

"I respectfully disagree."

Capturing her lips, I kissed her, my broad back shielding her from prying eyes. She kept her hand on my dick, rubbing me through my pants.

I groaned into her mouth. "Carry on like that, and I'll ruin a perfectly good suit."

In response, she upped the pressure. My balls tightened.

"Let's get the fuck out of here."

Blinking at me, she gave me a coy smile. "What happened to seduction?"

"You happened." I rose from the booth and helped her to her feet.

"Should we take the wine?"

"You won't have time to drink it."

I led her out of the piano bar. A groan rumbled

through my chest, this one far from lustful. "What the fuck now?" I muttered.

Marching toward me with her simpering assistant in tow was Scarlett, and she did not look happy.

"Mr. Kingcaid," she hollered. "I'd like a word with you."

"Is that...?" Jill trailed off.

"Unfortunately, yes."

I let go of Jill's hand and made myself smile when what I really wanted to do was toss Scarlett overboard. If only I could off-load her at the first port of call.

If she kept cockblocking me, I might do it, and fuck the consequences.

"Miss Rose. What can I do for you?"

She went into a tirade about overcooked steak and soggy asparagus, and no matter how much I tried to placate her, she tossed another problem at me.

I'd have to be a major-league baseball player to stand a chance at batting them away.

"How can I fix this?" I asked when Scarlett paused for breath.

"I'll tell you how you can fix it. You can come with me right now and demand that your chef make me something edible."

Her plump red lips stretched into a villainous smile, and she ran a crimson nail down my chest. "Before I tell my followers what a shit show this cruise is turning out to be."

Fucking hell.

I caught Jill's eye, an apology in mine.

She touched my shoulder and leaned up on tiptoes to

whisper in my ear. "Focus on your business. Like you said, it has to go well. I'll see you around, maybe."

And with that, she walked away, leaving me with a ranting actress, blue balls, and a niggling feeling that fate had stepped in to save me from myself.

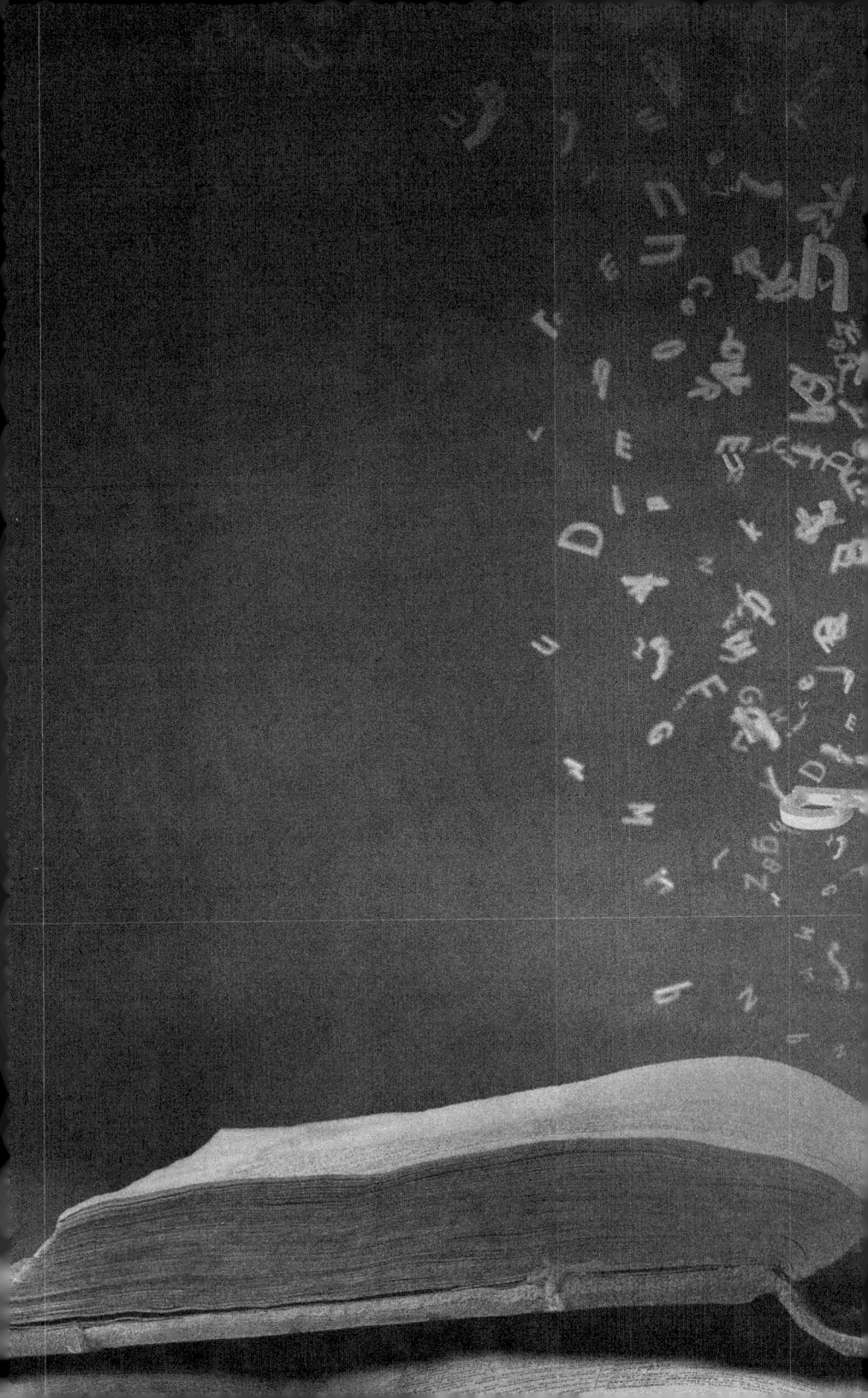

Chapter 13

Jill

A lack of orgasms makes me extra salty.

SCARLETT ROSE WAS OFF MY CHRISTMAS CARD LIST. I'd been a fan of hers, until I'd witnessed what no fan ever should. Peeking behind the curtain was a mistake, especially when it revealed a wailing banshee of a woman complaining about first-world problems that, if I had to guess, were vastly over-egged.

I couldn't see the caliber of chefs on this ship serving up overcooked steak and soggy asparagus. She was clearly one of those impossible-to-please women who lived to complain about pretty much everything.

She'd not only ruined my buzz, as well as the several orgasms that would have come my way if Blay and I had finished what we'd started. But she'd touched him, too. If I saw her prancing around the ship, I'd stick out a leg and laugh as she belly-flopped into the pool.

Ahh, dreams. If only.

With my plans for multiple orgasms thwarted, I made my way back to my suite. The sound of music greeted me before I'd even opened the door. Inside, a party was in full swing. Addison was dancing on the bed with some guy, her boobs jiggling, his eyes out on stalks. Kelsey was making drinks and chatting to another two guys, and Raya was lounging on the couch outside on the balcony with four other men.

"Hey!" Addison blew me several kisses. "What happened to Mr. Billionaire?"

"He had to work." I pretended it didn't bother me.

It bothered me.

Not the work, per se—I knew who he was and the importance of his role—but the reason he'd been pulled away. A fucking stupid reason from a childish actress who needed a slap.

Would you look at that? Seemed being deprived of orgasms made me extra salty. And violent. Who knew?

What really bothered me was the possessive way she'd touched him.

"Boring," Addison sing-songed. "Grab a drink. Kelsey's making cosmos."

On cue, Kelsey thrust a martini glass at me, brimful of sweet cranberry juice and, if I knew Kelsey, included several shots of Belvedere. Addison had progressed to gyrating against her hapless captive, not that he seemed to mind one bit.

"What happened?" Kelsey asked me before taking a huge gulp of her cocktail.

"Scarlett Rose. Who are all these people?"

"Scarlett Rose? As in the actress?"

"One and the same."

She whistled. "Wow, is she as pretty in real life?"

"Yeah, gorgeous." I jerked my chin. "I didn't know you'd planned a party."

"It's not a party. It's a gathering." She nudged me. "And if Mr. Billionaire is off sucking up to the Hollywood elite, maybe you should bag yourself a backup."

She'd misunderstood what had happened, but that didn't stop the sharp edges of anxiety from digging into the lining of my stomach. What if, instead of sucking up to Scarlett, she was sucking up to him? Or rather, sucking him. I mean, he had form, right? He'd freely admitted he wasn't into relationships. And men who didn't do relationships didn't do monogamy, either. Just because he'd been about to take me to bed did not mean he wouldn't find himself tempted by Scarlett. She might be a complete bitch, but she was a beautiful, sultry, temptress bitch. What heterosexual man wouldn't have his head turned by a beauty such as her?

I'm pissing myself off. I wasn't the jealous kind. Or I thought I wasn't, anyway I glanced into the mirror behind the minibar. Phew. No green tinge to my skin. That was something, at least. Now all I needed was the pressure on my chest to bugger off.

Come on, Jill. This was supposed to be a vacation, not a funeral. *Save that for the disaster of a book you've penned.*

I downed half the cosmo. "Let's get this party started."

Kelsey linked arms with me, and we strolled onto the balcony, where most of the party guests had gathered. Raya took one look at my face, read me as easily as a large-print paperback, and gave me a comforting squeeze.

"Plenty more fish in the sea," she whispered.

"And you've amassed quite the shoal, it seems."

She giggled. "Don't blame me. This is all Addison."

"Color me shocked."

I ended up in conversation with a guy called Greg, a midthirties stockbroker from New York. I tried to look interested in the conversation, but between his constant jabbering about yields and return on investment and checking my phone in case Blay had messaged me to come rescue him from the wicked witch, I failed miserably. Meanwhile, Greg was oblivious to my drifting attention, but when he moved on to bear markets and bid-ask spread, I feigned a yawn.

"Sorry, it's been a long day. Would you excuse me?"

I turned to join another group. He clasped my elbow. "Where you going, sweetcheeks?"

Sweetcheeks?

"Um, a refill." I brandished my almost empty martini glass.

"Allow me." Before I could protest, he took the glass from me, gripped my hand, and led me inside. When I tried to wrestle my hand from his, he held on tighter, almost crushing my fingers.

"Would you mind letting go?" I asked as politely as I could muster.

"I'm never letting you go, sweetcheeks." He leered at me. I responded with one of my renowned cold stares.

"I'm afraid I'll have to insist."

"Aw, come on, baby." He put down my glass, leaving his other hand free, which he wasted no time in slipping around my waist. "I only want to have some fun."

I scanned around for my girls. Addison had her tongue down her captive's throat, and Kelsey and Raya were in the middle of a group of guys, their backs to me. Great. Down to me, then. This joker didn't worry me, though. It wasn't as if I were in any danger, not with a room filled with people, three of whom would cut off this guy's balls if he didn't play nicely.

"Have it someplace else." I freed my hand at the second attempt, and as tactfully as I could, I removed his other hand from my waist.

"Are you with someone? Is that why you're not interested?" He accompanied his inappropriate question with a pout. Jesus. We'd only met, like, ten minutes ago.

"No, I'm not with anyone." Even though I wished I were. If Scarlett Rose hadn't turned up when she had, I'd be naked with Blay right this second. Disappointment flooded my tongue, and it tasted like fermented eggs. What was it with guys? They were either hard to pin down or all over me like an acute case of the measles. "And I'm not interested because you're not my type."

"Oh yeah? Who is your type?"

An image of Blay flashed before me, his head between my legs, his mischievous smirk as he'd tied me to the bed with the belt from a robe. The sheepish, apologetic expression when he'd discovered his cousin had found me naked and restrained. The hesitancy and worry that had appeared briefly when he'd talked about the weight of responsibility on his shoulders, showing a vulnerability that I'd wager was a rarity for a man like him.

Why hadn't he at least texted me?

"Someone who knows how to take no for an answer." I smiled sweetly.

"There's no need to be a bitch. I'm only trying to be friendly."

Okay, now this jerk was pissing me off. I crossed my arms.

"First of all, call me a bitch again and you'll leave here with your dick in a sling. And second, no, you're not being friendly. You're harassing me."

"*Harassing* you?" He sneered. "Maybe you shouldn't use words you don't understand, sweetcheeks."

Ohhh. That did it. I marched over to the door and wrenched it open. "Out."

"Aw, come on, honey. Just one kiss." He made a move. I skipped out of his way, picked up a glass containing a vile green liquid someone must have thought better of, and tossed it in his face. His expression turned thunderous.

"Why, you fucking—"

The music halted. Addison inserted herself in between me and the guy with green liquid dripping off his chin.

"You heard her. Out. In fact, all of you, out. Party's over." She stepped up close to him and jabbed him in the chest. "You'd better hope I don't see you around this ship, buddy, or you'll find yourself swimming back to Miami."

I loved how Addison had stepped in, even though she'd known I could easily handle this guy by myself. These girls were my family. My ride-or-dies. We stood beside each other through thick and thin.

Unlike my birth family...

"Yeah, and she knows the CEO, so you might find yourself off-loaded at the first stop," Kelsey interjected.

I elbowed her. The last thing I wanted to do was share this debacle with Blay, who *still* hadn't called me.

"Frigid bitch," Greg muttered as he walked down the hallway.

"At least I'm not a boring twat," I shouted after him.

The rest of the guys filed out, a couple murmuring apologies for their friend. As the guy Addison had been snogging left, he moved in to kiss her. She stepped back. "Blame your buddy," she said. He shrugged and left. Addison slammed the door behind him and locked it.

"Well." I grinned. "Who said we can't throw a great party?"

Chapter 14

Blaize

Sexting is fun.

By the time I'd placated Scarlett and extricated myself from her clutches, thirty minutes had passed.

Thirty minutes I could have spent in bed with Jill.

My feelings about the beautiful author swung like a pendulum from "Not a good idea to entangle myself in a relationship, however brief" to "Fuck, I want her, and I'd damn well have her, too."

The problem was that I didn't know where she'd gone when she'd left me behind with Scarlett. Nor did I have her cell phone number. Lucky for me, I had loose morals and the right contacts. In seconds, my team had furnished me with her suite number and her phone number.

After removing my phone from the inside pocket of my jacket, I changed my mind. This called for a personal visit.

I made my way down the stairs to her deck, but as I approached her suite, music seeped through the door. It sounded like a party in full swing. I lifted my hand to knock on the door, but something stopped me. What was it she'd whispered in my ear? *See you around.* Not *Call me,* or *I'll be waiting,* or anything resembling an invitation to turn up at her suite, unannounced, and drag her away from her friends.

Again.

No. I'd leave her to it. Better to keep things casual. By coming here, I was signaling a greater interest than intended. I had more than enough on my plate without embroiling myself in what would probably turn out to be an unholy mess.

I didn't do seconds.

The rule had kept me out of trouble more times than I could count, and given the forced proximity situation I found myself in, it was even more important to hold fast to that decree.

I'd had her. It was wonderful. And it was over.

As I made my way back to my suite, an ache spread throughout my chest. Probably indigestion from having to play nice with Scarlett when what I'd much rather have done was pitch her overboard.

And the worst of it? This was day fucking one. If this carried on, by day fourteen, they'd have to put me in a padded cell.

I entered my suite to Aspen pacing, phone jammed to her ear, barking orders rapidly into the speaker. She barely acknowledged me, too busy giving whoever was on the other end of the phone an earful.

Poor bastard.

Most of the time, Aspen was sweet and fun and easy-going, but piss her off or cross her and she'd rip out your throat. As the only daughter in an extended family of eight sons, she was the biggest ballbuster of us all.

She knew it, too.

I disappeared into my bedroom, shutting the door behind me. Pulling off my tie, I shrugged out of my jacket and unfastened the top button on my shirt. The digits on the clock beside my bed read 10:15—the middle of the day for me. I might as well work. It wasn't like there was anything else to do.

Or *anyone* else to do.

Perhaps I should have knocked on Jill's door. Then again, if she'd wanted me to join the party, she could have texted. And she hadn't.

Because she doesn't have your number, dickhead.

No, but I had hers.

Kicking off my shoes, I flopped onto the bed. A faint crack ran from the middle of the bathroom door to halfway across the ceiling. I let out a heavy sigh and sent a message to the maintenance team. One fucking thing after another.

I rubbed the back of my neck, squeezing the tight muscles. I pulled up an empty text, adding Jill's contact details to the recipient box. The curser blinked at me, taunting, daring me to send her a message.

Fuck it.

Me: I'm sorry about before, Tilly.

Jesus Christ. Talk about lame. Is that really the best I can do?

> Me: I enjoyed our night.

No better, dickhead.

> Me: Until we were interrupted, that is.

A message in reply remained stubbornly absent, which should have been my cue to leave it alone. But I wasn't a quitter. Jill could tell me herself if she wasn't interested.

> Me: Do you want to come over?

> Me: I'd like you to come over.

> Me: Strike "over" from that message.

Finally, three dots appeared. I held my breath, cursing when they disappeared, cheering when they reappeared. The reply, when it came, was not at all what I'd expected.

> Tilly: I see you've added stalking to your resume. Also, sending multiple messages one after another is the most annoying habit. Can you not just send one containing everything you'd like to say?

I grinned.

Me: I'm sorry about before. I enjoyed our night. Until we were interrupted, that is. Do you want to come over? I'd like you to come over. Strike that. I'd just like you to come. On my face, preferably.

Her reply took eons to arrive.

Tilly: A litany of short sentences one after the other makes for difficult reading.

My grin widened. She was truly magnificent.

Me: Once an author...

Tilly: Is there an end to that sentence?

Me: Yeah. Once an author... came on my face.

Tilly: I think you're trouble, Blaize Isaac Kingcaid.

My stomach turned over. She'd remembered my full name.

Me: To you, I'm Blay. And to me, you're Tilly. Let's be those people, if only for a little while.

Tilly: To me, you're the guy who chose someone else. Twice.

Me: You're making me work for it? Seriously?

Tilly: You call this work? I haven't even started yet.

Me: And for the record, I didn't choose Scarlett.

Me: Come to my suite. I'll make it worth your while.

Tilly: Oh yeah? What does "worth my while" look like?

I palmed my dick. Even talking to her over text message turned me on.

Me: Multiple orgasms until you beg me to stop.

Tilly: You mean until Scarlett calls.

Me: You're vicious.

Tilly: I don't stroke egos.

Me: I'm fine with not having my ego stroked. My dick, on the other hand...

Tilly: It's late, and I've hardly seen my friends. I'm not one of those women who dump their gal pals the second a sexy guy appears on the scene.

Me: You think I'm sexy?

Tilly: Now you're fishing.

My cheeks hurt from grinning so much. I could do this all day. I mean, I'd rather have her here, beside me. Naked, writhing, pussy clenching around my dick, but as a backup, it wasn't half bad.

> Me: Have I caught anything?

> Tilly: You did, but then you let it go. Such a shame.

> Me: I'm never letting you go, Tilly.

We were only flirting, and I didn't mean a word of it, but simply typing those words made my chest tighten, the feeling reminiscent of a noose that I knew would choke me, yet couldn't help sticking my neck through. At the end of the cruise, I'd happily let her go, but for the next two weeks, I wanted her to be mine.

Hell, she *was* mine. She just didn't know it yet.

> Tilly: Good night, Blay. If you're not too busy schmoozing up to Hollywood A-listers tomorrow, then come find me. Maybe I'll let you buy me a drink.

Disappointment mingled with awe. She was utterly magnificent. I hadn't been turned down since... since... fuck, I couldn't remember. It was true what they said about the male species. The chase spurred us on.

> Me: Good night, Tilly. Sleep well. I'll dream of you.

A crash, followed by a frustrated scream, came from

the living room of my suite. I climbed off the bed. It could only be Aspen, and she sounded furious.

"What's wrong with you?" I dashed forward, plucking an expensive vase from her clutches before she smashed it on the floor. She'd already smashed one. Jagged pieces of porcelain lay strewn across the silk rug.

"Asshole rock stars, that's what's wrong with me." Red tinged her cheeks, and her eyes had that vengeful sparkle.

I groaned. "Not Joz Raynor." The last thing I needed was an onboard political incident between my fiery cousin and one of the world's most famous—or perhaps infamous—musicians.

"No. I haven't caught up with him. Yet."

"Then who's pissed in your bed?"

She scrunched up her nose. "Ew, Blaize. If you're going to use metaphors, please choose ones with less ick factor."

A smirk tugged at my lips. I saluted. "Gotcha." I poured her a brandy. "Here. Drink this. And calm down."

She chugged half, wincing as it went down. "Why did my family put me in charge of this sector of the firm?"

I arched an eyebrow. "Put you in charge? My darling Aspen, as I recall, you muscled your way into a board meeting the day you graduated and announced that you were the new CEO of Kingcaid Music."

She pouted. "Do you have to remember *everything*?"

Sliding a hand around the back of her neck, I drew her to me and kissed the top of her head. "It's an affliction. Now tell me what's happened. I might be able to help."

It was past midnight by the time I'd calmed Aspen down from the PR disaster caused by one of Kingcaid's newest signings trashing a hotel room and causing fifty grand's worth of damage. I kissed her good night and retired to my room. The first thing I did was check my phone to see if Jill had texted me back.

She hadn't.

Chapter 15

Jill

OMG! It's Hugh Hefner reincarnated.

BLAY HAD NOT SOUGHT ME OUT THE DAY AFTER OUR night of texting. All day I'd kept my eyes peeled, my body feverish and horny after our sext-a-thon, but I hadn't caught sight of his tall, muscular back or those electrifying green eyes that appeared to undress me each time he laid them on me.

To say his absence had disappointed me would be under-egging the pressure on my chest, the way my lungs had constricted, restricting my breath. It was so silly, if I thought about it. I barely knew the guy. Sure, the interlude on the plane had repositioned my idea of what good sex was, and he'd reaffirmed that with the all-too-brief encounter in his suite, but that was all it was. Sex. He owed me nothing, and the same went for me. As he'd made clear, he was a busy guy with high-pressure responsibilities. I couldn't expect him to be at my beck and call. Unlike me, he wasn't enjoying a holiday. He wouldn't have the same amount of free time as I did. Or any free time, if truth be told.

I rose on Monday morning as soon as the sun broke the horizon, painting the sky in a deep orange. Donning one of Kingcaid Serenity's complimentary bathrobes, I quietly opened the patio doors and slipped onto the balcony. All around, the deep blue waters of the Caribbean Sea greeted me.

Tomorrow, we'd dock in St. Maarten for our first stop. When Addison had initially suggested a cruise for our girl's trip, I'd feared that I'd get itchy feet, knowing I was stuck on the ship without the ability to disembark whenever I chose. Instead, I'd discovered it was more of a floating city, one I hadn't yet begun to explore. Maybe I'd do a little of that today. It beat sitting around pining for a glimpse of the fascinating, gorgeous CEO.

"You were moaning in your sleep last night." Addison appeared to my right, yawning as she stretched her arms overhead. "Someone's feeling frisky."

"I was *not* moaning." An indefensible defense, a bit like an ex-boyfriend who'd insisted he didn't snore, until I'd recorded him one night and presented the earsplitting, sleep-depriving evidence.

"You were, too. And writhing like a horny bish. Why don't you message him? Put your vagina out of its misery."

I rolled my eyes. "My vagina is perfectly happy, thank you. As is the rest of me."

"Tell your face that. You're mooning."

"So I'm frisky and mooning, and have a miserable vagina?"

"Pretty much sums it up, yeah." Addison flashed me a grin. "Come on, let's get ready, grab some breakfast, and then we can set about Project Cheer Up Jill's Vagina."

I couldn't help laughing. "You shower first. I'll make some coffee."

Thirty minutes later, we knocked next door for Kelsey and Raya, and the four of us headed to the Galleria for breakfast. Despite my best efforts not to keep my eyes peeled for Blay, they hadn't gotten the memo. The slightest glimpse of a tall, dark-haired guy in my peripheral vision raised my pulse, and when it wasn't him, my stomach dropped to the floor.

Seated at an outdoor table with the smell of salt in the air and a warm breeze lifting the hair at my nape, I felt myself relax. Pushing thoughts of Blay to the back of my mind, I perused the menu. As I gave my order to our server, Aspen approached. My heart stuttered, my eyes drifting past her to see if Blay was with her.

She was alone.

"Do you mind if I sit with you guys? I've had the shit-tiest thirty-six hours, and I need to be around normal people right now, not an asshole rock star who gives me a PR headache and then sails off on his yacht with six of his harem, leaving me and my team behind to clean up his mess."

"That sounds... not fun." I grabbed a chair from the table next to ours and put it beside mine. I liked Aspen, even if she had caught me in a compromising position. There was something inherently trustworthy about her. I listened to my instincts until they were proved false. Somehow, I didn't see Aspen Kingcaid falling into the dishonorable category.

"It wasn't. I mean, I've fixed his shit, but I could have done without the hassle, you know?"

I didn't, but I nodded anyway.

"My poor cousin hasn't had a good time of it, either. The Kingcaids are taking a beating right now."

My ears pricked up. "Oh?" I couldn't bring myself to ask outright what was wrong. Addison had no such issues.

"Is that why he blew off my friend yesterday?"

I kicked her under the table. "Addison! He did not blow me off. There was no formal arrangement."

"Jilly, he spent Saturday night fawning over you like a neglected lapdog, and then yesterday, nada."

"Like I said. We hadn't arranged to meet." I kicked her again for good measure. She shifted her legs out of my reach and stuck out her tongue.

"He had a security issue to attend to. It took him all day, and then he had meetings with the family for most of last night." She put her hand over mine. "He likes you. Trust me."

Butterflies took flight in my chest. "He's a busy man. I'm on holiday. He isn't."

Addison opened her mouth. I silenced her with one of my resting-bitch-face glares and changed the subject, but my mood improved drastically. Blay hadn't avoided me. He'd had urgent priorities to attend to. That was all.

Today was going to be a magnificent day.

K

Famous last words. Today *might* have been magnificent if I hadn't decided to gut up and tackle this disaster of a manuscript. Armed with a red pen in one hand and the book in the other, I got to work. There was so much red ink that it resembled the literary version of a bloodbath.

Angling the parasol to shade me from the sun before I turned into crispy bacon, I scrawled through another pitiful sentence.

"I know you'll refuse, but I am happy to take a look if you want." Kelsey lowered her wide-brimmed sun hat and flipped the top on a bottle of sunscreen. "Just a couple of chapters. Three, tops. You might be seeing things that aren't there."

"I don't know, Kels..." Addison caught my eye and waved from the jacuzzi where she and Raya had spent the last half an hour giggling with a couple of guys and drinking copious amounts of champagne. Thankfully, their companions were not the guys at the party the other night. With any luck, they weren't VIP guests and therefore couldn't access the exclusive sundeck.

"As a friend, not as an editor. I'll be gentle, promise."

I was about to take her up on her offer when a loud, booming voice on my left drew my attention. I turned to see who was making the racket. So far, the VIP deck had been an oasis of tranquility.

Standing at the bar, wearing a dressing gown and a captain's hat, was an old guy in his midseventies at least. Maybe eighty. Snow-white hair, leathery skin that had seen too much sun, and a well-fed, rounded stomach. He had his arms around two gorgeous, leggy brunettes young enough to be his granddaughters.

"It's Hugh Hefner reincarnated," Kelsey half whispered, half giggled.

I nudged her even though the same thing had occurred to me.

"—not happy with the rules on this ship, young man."

I tuned in to his complaint. The guy gave me the creeps, but if a paying customer wasn't happy, I'd rather know, so I could tell Blay—if I ever saw him again.

Shut up. You'll see him again.

"In what way, sir?" the bartender queried.

"It's too strict," he boomed. "No topless bathing. No bottomless bathing. All these beautiful women are far too covered up for my liking." He leered at his companions.

Nausea flooded my stomach. What a fucking creep! I looked over at Kelsey. Her jaw hung open. Good thing Addison was out of earshot. If she'd heard this dude, she'd probably slam his face into the marble bar.

The bartender muttered a reply, but it was too low for me to catch what he said. Whatever it was, the old guy guffawed and wandered away with the two women in tow. I turned to Kelsey.

"What the fuck?"

"I know. Oh my God. Dirty old bastard."

"Who's a dirty old bastard?" Addison flopped down beside me, peppering me with drops of water.

I relayed the conversation we'd overheard. Addison's jaw dropped farther than Kelsey's had, and her eyes widened until I could see the whites all the way around.

"Ugh." Addison's gaze locked on the old man in the jacuzzi on the other side of the sundeck. "I should go over there and drown the fucker. Do the world a favor. In fact..."

She half rose from her seat. I dragged her back down. "You can't do that."

"I like to think anything goes on my cruise ships. What is it you want to do, Addison?"

My head snapped up, my eyes homing in on Blay. Despite the heat, he wore a smart suit, a brilliant white shirt, and a crimson tie. He looked... beautiful. I broke into a smile, and my insides turned to mush.

"I—"

"Did you know you have a fucking creep on board?" Addison interjected before I could greet him.

I groaned. Great.

Blay's jaw flexed, and he stood up a little straighter. "Pardon me?"

"Him." Addison pointed. Blay's eyes tracked to the old guy, who, fortunately or unfortunately, paid us no attention. He was too busy sticking his tongue down one of the girl's ears. I almost brought up my breakfast. Pukesville.

"Ah, Mr. Sloan. Yes, he's one of our more... eccentric penthouse guests."

"Eccentric? He's a sleaze. Tell him what he said, Jill. Go on."

She nudged me into action. I gnawed my lip and considered the best way to word it. Penthouse. That meant he'd parted with a lot of greenbacks, as well as probably being a man with power and influence. Blay's commentary about needing this voyage to be a success twanged the edges of my memory. He had enough on his plate with the diva-ish Scarlett Rose without adding to it the vile Mr. Sloan.

"Um... he seems to prefer a kind of... natural approach to sunbathing."

Blay's eyebrows furrowed. "Natural? I don't follow."

"He thinks—"

I shut Addison up with a glare and a toe poke. "He... well, he thinks the women are... overdressed. Top and bottom."

A flush of red crept up Blay's neck as my meaning hit home. A muscle throbbed in his cheek, and he scissored his jaw.

"Is that so?"

"Yeah. Just ask your bartender." Addison couldn't keep quiet a second longer. "He was the one Mr. Disgustington spoke to."

Blay glanced over at the bartender, who looked as if he'd rather chow down on cockroaches for the rest of his life than get involved in this fiasco.

"Excuse me," Blay said, beelining for Sloan.

I launched to my feet. "Don't." I put a hand on his arm. "He's not worth it, and you said yourself how important it is that your VIPs are kept happy."

"Happy, yes. Treating my cruise ship as his personal Pornhub is not acceptable."

"He's a creepy old man who probably can't get it up, and being disgusting is how he gets his kicks. Leave it. Please. Addison was born outraged. Don't let her coax you into making more of a fuss of this than there needs to be."

His nostrils flared. He shifted his gaze between me and

Sloan, his eyes narrowing. "Okay. But if anything like this happens again, I want you to tell me."

"It's good to see you." I purposely avoided answering his demand. For me, it depended on the situation. I didn't want to be at fault for this voyage failing to be the roaring success Blay deserved it to be.

His frown turned into a smile. "You, too. I'm sorry I didn't get to see you yesterday. I had a clusterfuck to deal with." He rolled his eyes. "One of many."

"Aspen told me. It's fine. Your business is your priority."

He lowered his head until his lips were inches from my ear. "I'm an expert juggler."

A shudder spilled down my spine. "I look forward to a demonstration."

He kissed my cheek. "I'll come find you tonight." Spinning on his heel, he walked over to the bar and tapped on the counter. "Kamal, these ladies are my special guests. Give them anything they want."

Kamal dipped his chin. "You got it, Mr. Kingcaid."

Blay saluted my friends. As he passed me, he lowered his head once more. "But you're the most special of all."

Chapter 16

Jill

Oh, look. Mr. Disgustington is back.

THAT NIGHT, WITH MY SKIN GLOWING AFTER A DAY IN the sun, I gave myself a final once-over in the mirror. My skin wasn't the only thing glowing. My eyes sparkled, too. In fact, my entire demeanor was buoyant, despite the shit-show novel I still hadn't plucked up the courage to give to Kelsey. She was a brilliant editor, and that was half the problem. Because despite her saying she'd be gentle, her professional training would take over, and I wasn't sure my dented confidence could take any more knocks.

"You look positively fuckable." Addison hugged me from behind. "He won't be able to resist."

"He's done a pretty fine job of resisting me so far."

"Pfft." She shook her mane of curls. "I saw the way he looked at you up on the VIP deck earlier today. Bet he had a boner for the next several hours." She dabbed her glossy pink lips with a tissue and spritzed perfume on her neck and between her boobs. "Lucky bitch."

Looping her arm through mine, she towed me next door. We picked up Raya and Kelsey, and the four of us took the elevator down to the Crown restaurant on deck seven. A steakhouse with a Michelin-starred chef in charge of the kitchen. It was the top restaurant on board Serenity, so popular, in fact, that we'd had to book it weeks earlier. Luckily, VIP guests were given first dibs on restaurants and activities.

The greeter showed us to our table, but as he seated us, I spied Aspen walking in, alone. I waved to her, beckoning her over. She beamed, beelining for us.

"Thank God." She hugged me as if we were old friends. The funny thing was, I felt far closer to her than I should have, especially as I hadn't known her for long. Maybe it was the fact that she'd seen me stark naked and tied to Blay's bed that had sped up our friendship. My cheeks heated at the thought, doubt crawling from the corners of my mind. Would I ever get the chance to sleep with Blay again, or would the fates conspire to keep us apart?

Screw that. I was a modern woman in a modern world. The next time I saw him, I'd take control. Life was too short to wait for opportunities to land in our laps. Sometimes, taking the initiative was the best course of action to get what we wanted.

And I wanted Blay. No bones about it.

"Blaize is on yet another interminably long conference call," Aspen piped up as if she'd read my mind. "And my other cousin, Nolen, is having an intimate dinner for two with his wife." She huffed. "Guess I can't blame him. It *is* his honeymoon, after all."

"You're more than welcome to join us for dinner." I made the offer without consulting my friends. I already knew they wouldn't have a problem with it. "Although, it's only a table for four, so we might have to squish up a bit."

The greeter looked decidedly uncomfortable. He motioned to us to wait, bustling over to the other side of the restaurant, where he had a frantic, whispered conversation with another man. Seconds later, he returned.

"Please follow me, ladies. We have a table for five ready for you."

Surprise must have shown on my face, because Aspen grinned and blew on her fingernails. "Perks of my surname, Jill."

Once seated, and our drinks and food choices made, I turned to Aspen, sitting on my left, unable to help myself from asking after my current obsession.

"So Blay's busy with work again, huh?" I tried to sound nonchalant, even if my heart had kicked up a notch—or seven.

Aspen snickered. "It's so funny to hear you call him by that name. He's always been Blaize to his family, and to every woman he's ever dated. And he's dated a lot."

I suppressed a wince. Not well enough, it seemed.

"Fuck, sorry. That was crass of me."

"Not at all. We barely know each other."

"Sure, sure. Positive strangers." Her eyes twinkled. I blushed furiously, knowing what she referred to. She nudged me gently. "I'm just teasing you. Forgive me. I couldn't help myself. And to answer your earlier question, yes. He's hardly stopped for two days. He gets like this sometimes, engrossed to the point of exclusion of pretty much everything. Hopefully, whatever's got his panties in a twist will untangle itself soon and he might get an hour or two of downtime."

I could do a lot in two hours.

"I can read minds, you know. And yours is filthy."

Aspen winked at me. I ducked my head to hide another flush of heat blooming in my cheeks. Fortunately, she took pity on me and turned her attention to my friends. "Ladies, I have a favor to ask." She produced a few business cards, handing them around. "I just recruited you to my 'Find Joz Raynor' project. I've waited long enough, and he can't hide out in his penthouse forever. If you spot him, night or day, call me, and I'll make sure you get VIP tickets to the show of any star on the Kingcaid Music label."

Kelsey's eyebrows touched her hairline. "Joz Raynor? *The* Joz Raynor is on this ship?"

Aspen had said the magic words. Joz Raynor was Kelsey's dream man. Long, wild hair, an unkempt beard, tattoos covering most parts of his body. The complete opposite of what I found attractive. If Aspen wanted to find Joz Raynor, then she'd recruited the ideal person in Kelsey.

"Yep. I heard he's unhappy with his label, and I plan to exploit his dissatisfaction. If I can find the reclusive bastard, that is."

Kelsey clutched Aspen's business card to her chest as if it were a winning lottery ticket. "I'm your gal, Aspen. I got you, sweets."

Aspen beamed. "Excellent."

The conversation moved on. As our steaks arrived, a loud voice drew my attention. I glanced over my shoulder and groaned. The repellent Sloan was seated right behind us, still wearing his bathrobe and that ridiculous hat. This time, he had three girls with him, the two from earlier and one I hadn't seen before. I should feel sorry for the sad old jerk, but he repulsed me too much. Whatever their reasons for choosing to be with him, I hoped those women were bleeding him dry.

I twisted back to my friends. Addison jerked her chin and rolled her eyes. I grinned, nodding in agreement.

My steak melted on my tongue, and the accompanying sauce was thick and glossy and delicious. Now and then, Sloan's booming laugh drifted over to our table, but for the most part, I tuned him out. Or so I'd thought.

"You like to suck on my big, fat cock, don't you, baby?"

My stomach roiled, and I stopped eating mid-chew. *Did I just hear what I think I heard?* I checked around the table. Everyone was busy chatting, and no one paid any attention to the disgusting man sitting at the table behind ours. I pricked up my ears as he spoke again.

"I can't wait to take a photograph later of my huge dick in your mouth."

I fucking heard that. I fidgeted in my seat, my fingers twitching. I curled my hand around my steak knife. Not the best idea, considering the vividness of my imagination.

"You'd like that, wouldn't you? My perfect little slut. One for the wank bank for when I've bled your pussy dry."

Okay, enough.

Springing from my chair, I spun on my heel. Two striding steps brought me to the edge of his table.

"I would appreciate it if you kept your disgusting thoughts to yourself. I'm trying to keep my dinner down, not hurl all over the table. What you do in private is up to you, but I do *not* want to be subjected to the details."

By the time I'd finished, Addison stood beside me, her arm brushing mine. "What's going on?"

Mr. Disgustington's vile gaze slid over me. I had a violent urge to strip the skin from my body.

"You can join us if you like." His lips peeled back, revealing small, white teeth. "The more the merrier. You look like the type who could use a little loosening up."

Addison bristled. "The fuck you say to her?"

I felt for her hand, squeezing it. Rage ignited in my stomach, but it wouldn't do Blay any good if we broke this loathsome man's nose. The guests at the tables on either side of Sloan had put down their silverware and were now paying attention to us. Aspen joined me on my other side.

"Is there a problem, Mr. Sloan?" she asked sweetly, but I sensed the tone. She abhorred this prick, too.

"No problem. I was inviting your friends to a party. That's all."

"Party?" Addison snorted. "More like a fucking orgy."

"What is going on here?" Blay put his hand on my lower back. I jumped at his unexpected arrival. The warmth from his palm soothed my ire, and I leaned into him.

By this time, Raya and Kelsey had joined us. Sloan leaned back in his seat, smug and unapologetic. I shook my head. Power, money, and ego were a cocktail of entitlement. Men like Sloan thought they could do and say anything without challenge or recourse for their actions.

"I'm under siege, Kingcaid." Sloan laughed. "Time to put the mutts back in the cage." He slapped the thigh of his nearest companion. She flinched and rubbed her leg. My jaw ached. I clenched it that tightly.

Aspen whispered something in his ear. Whatever she said made his body vibrate. His nostrils flared and his face hardened. He raised his arm and crooked a finger. Seconds later, another man joined us.

"Reynolds, please accompany Mr. Sloan and his companions back to his penthouse. He's decided to finish his meal in private."

I wanted to kiss him. Sloan's response was entirely the opposite. He spluttered, rising to his feet. His robe gaped open. I considered bleaching my eyes to rid myself of the sight.

"Are you throwing me out? After what I paid for this trip."

Blay didn't respond. Several servers approached and picked up dinner plates and glasses brimful of wine. They looked at Blay. He nodded, once. They bustled out of sight. Blay turned his attention back to the apoplectic Sloan, motioning with his hand.

"After you."

Spittle gathered at the corners of Sloan's mouth, his face redder than was healthy for a man of his age. The entire restaurant was agog, following the events without knowing the details of what had brought about this kerfuffle.

"This isn't over, Kingcaid," Sloan said as if he were a mafia boss in a B-movie.

Blay didn't engage him, nor did he respond to his attempted threat. He followed Sloan and the man he'd called over, who, I guessed, might be security. My shoulders sagged. I took a step to go after him. Aspen put out her arm, stopping me.

"Let him handle it."

"I don't want to cause trouble for him. He told me how important it is for this cruise to be a success."

"Blaize won't tolerate that kind of behavior, regardless of the consequences. Besides, everyone in the know is aware of what a pathetic old man David Sloan is. His opinion won't carry much weight."

"I can't believe people like that exist." I shook my head. "Why would Blay let him on the ship?" My comment came out more accusatory than I'd meant it to.

Aspen looked at me as if I were a baby fawn witnessing the realities of the world for the first time. "We can't discriminate against people just because we don't subscribe to their preferences. Sloan is a sleaze, but his companions are all over twenty-one."

She had a point, even if I didn't like it. "Ugh."

Addison grabbed a passing server. "A round of margaritas. And make them strong ones."

I counted every minute that passed until Blay reappeared, his expression unreadable as he moved through the restaurant toward our table. I rose to greet him, an apology on my face. If I hadn't made a fuss, then I wouldn't have forced Blay's hand into dealing with a difficult situation.

"I'm so—"

He placed a finger over my lips, silencing me. "Excuse us, ladies." Gripping my elbow, he steered me out of the restaurant.

"What happened?" I asked as we entered the elevator.

He pushed the button for deck nineteen, one above where my suite was located. My heart constricted, and prickles crept along the back of my neck. He was taking me to his suite.

"Mr. Sloan will be leaving us when we dock in St. Maarten in the morning."

I gaped, my mouth forming the perfect "O" shape. "You're throwing him off the ship?"

He nodded. "I warned him about what he said to the bartender this afternoon, and—"

"I told you not to do that."

His lips twitched. "I like the idea of you ordering me around, but you should know I'm not the obedient type. You might need to... punish me." He curved both hands around my neck and pressed his forehead to mine. "I made my expectations clear, and Sloan ignored them. What he does behind closed doors is not my concern, but I will not tolerate that kind of behavior in front of my guests, and especially in front of you. He's fortunate I didn't throw him overboard for what he said."

Blay hadn't done this solely for me. He'd done it to secure the reputation of his business. But that didn't stop me from pressing my lips to his.

"Thank you."

His eyes twinkled. "If it's gratitude you'd like to give me, I have the perfect idea."

Chapter 17

Blaize

Strawberries and cream, and Jill.

My heart rate hadn't dropped below one ninety since the altercation with Sloan. I couldn't remember a time when I'd let anger consume me to the extent it had when he'd called Jill, her friends, *and* my cousin mutts. The only thing that had stopped me from smashing his face against the wall was the likelihood that such actions would lead to my downfall. Far better to exercise control, regardless of how difficult, and use other avenues of retribution. Hence the decision to off-load Sloan at the first opportunity.

I'd preempted the potential PR disaster with a call to the department that handled such things, as well as calling Dad and updating him. He'd agreed with my decision to kick the fucker off my ship. Not that I'd had a doubt he would, but it was good to hear it from the old man directly. I had a security detail stationed outside Sloan's penthouse, and the second we docked at seven o'clock in the morning, a team would escort him onto dry land.

Good fucking riddance.

His companions could stay if they wished, but I had a suspicion they'd leave with him. Still, I'd extended the offer. What they did with it was up to them.

There was another reason my heart galloped. The beautiful woman walking beside me, her hand encased in mine, our steps in perfect synchronicity. The height of my desire for her both concerned and excited me. No matter how hard I thought about it, I could not come up with a single woman I'd wanted more in my entire thirty-one years of life.

It wouldn't last. I felt sure of it, but as long as lust filled my veins, I'd drink from the well of desire until I'd quenched my thirst. At least Aspen wouldn't plan to spend the night in my suite. She'd read the room and crash at Nolen and Marlowe's pad tonight, or maybe she could sleep in Jill's suite.

Jill wouldn't be using it.

The moment I had her inside, I kicked the door shut and hooked my hands under her ass. Using the closed door to support her, I smashed my lips to hers. Unless the fucking ship was sinking, the first person to disturb me tonight would enjoy a one-way ticket back to Miami courtesy of Princess Juliana International Airport on St. Maarten the second we docked in the morning. I didn't give two shits who it was. Scarlett Rose, or the president of the United States. Nothing was getting in the way of my cock and Jill's pussy.

I carried her to the bedroom, still kissing her, my tongue wrapping around hers with a sensuality I wouldn't have thought myself capable of. She tasted delicious, of sin and strawberries and alcohol.

Settling her on the bed, I pushed her thighs apart with mine, resting in between her spread legs. Her dress rode up, revealing acres of golden skin. The urge to taste every inch overwhelmed me. I dipped my head, tracing circles with my tongue, peppering her skin with kisses, making my way north. Burying my nose in her pussy, covered only by a thin layer of lace, I breathed deeply.

"I'm going to wreck you in the best of ways and the worst of ways." Using my teeth, I tugged down her panties. She raised her ass. I had them whipped off and on the floor in seconds. I feasted on her. She made these sounds, half moan, half cry, that did things to me no woman had ever done. I swirled my tongue around her clit, sucking the nub of sensitive nerves between my lips.

"I can't..." She gasped as I used my teeth, sliding two fingers inside her. "God, Blay."

Flicking my tongue back and forth, I worked her from the inside. I knew I'd hit the right spot when she screamed my name, a violent release tearing through her. Every part of her shuddered through her climax. She gripped my shoulders, digging her nails into my skin hard enough to draw blood. I didn't care. I'd bleed for her if it meant I got to watch her come undone again and again. And again.

I left her lying there, still lost in the aftereffects of her orgasm, and went into the living room. When I returned holding a plate of fruit, a tub of cream, and a bottle of whiskey, she hadn't moved a muscle. Her legs were still spread wide, her pussy glistening with her cum, and she wore this look of bliss and satisfaction that made me feel like a fucking king.

As I set the items on the nightstand, her eyes opened. Her gaze went from the fruit to me and back to the fruit.

"What's that for?"

"I'm hungry. I haven't eaten yet. Well, other than your pussy, of which I intend to enjoy seconds and thirds, and maybe fourths, before the night is out."

I reached for a strawberry, pressing it to her lips. She opened without question, and the strawberry disappeared.

"Good?"

She nodded, her eyes bright and filled with wonder. "So good."

I jerked my chin at her. "Get naked."

A flush of pink colored her cheeks, but it wasn't from embarrassment. She pulled her dress over her head, unclipped her bra, and threw both items on the floor, then lay back with a hint of challenge in her expression.

Smiling, I plucked a second strawberry from the plate and put it over her belly button. I proceeded to choose different berries, laying them in a circle around the strawberry. Raised up on her elbows, she watched in fascination, her eyes tracking every move I made. Once I was satisfied with the arrangement, I picked up the jug of cream.

"Is there anything better than berries and cream?" I poured a trail of cream over her breasts and her abdomen, coating the fruit. But I didn't stop there. I continued south, drenching her pussy. She gasped when I lowered my head and licked the cream off her left breast, biting her nipple before moving on to her right.

"It's dripping onto your bed." She groaned when I bit her right nipple. "You'll get cream on your suit."

"I don't fucking care."

"I'm naked and you're still dressed. It's unequal."

"It is." I lapped up the cream, working my way to her belly. "But I'm busy right now." I dined on the fruit and cream, and Jill. She tasted the best of all. Drinking every drop of cream from her pussy, I shoved my tongue inside her. The sound of her moans spurred me on. I gripped her hips tight enough to leave a mark. My cock rubbed against my zipper, begging for freedom. I unzipped myself and pulled it out. Taking hold of Jill's hand, I wrapped it around my shaft. She tightened her grip, then tugged me hard. Once, twice, three times. I groaned.

"That's it, Tilly. Be rough with me. I need it."

She took me at my word, rubbing me furiously, gripping my balls with her other hand, twisting them, taking no fucking prisoners. Just how I liked it. She paused only when a second orgasm took her, her legs jerking and a sheen of sweat coating her skin.

I was close, too close. Gripping her wrist, I tried to get her off me. Instead, I found myself lying on my back with Jill crouched over me. Before I could take a breath, she sucked my cock into her mouth, taking me right to the back of her throat.

"Holy Christ. Fuck!"

She did the same thing again, except this time, she swallowed. I came so fucking hard that stars exploded behind my eyes, and I'd swear in a court of law that I blacked out for a second or two.

"Don't move."

I blinked, my vision blurred. As I waited for my sight to dial in, I felt something cold on my dick.

"My turn to feast on you."

I raised myself up as Jill poured the rest of the jug of cream over my cock and balls. She licked me from root to tip. Tingles erupted all over my body, and my dick perked right back up, three-quarters hard before she'd taken a second lick.

What was it about this woman that defied logic? I shouldn't be able to get hard so soon after she'd already ripped an almighty orgasm out of me.

She licked every drop off me, then grabbed the hem of my trousers, arching an eyebrow in a silent command. I tilted my hips, and she pulled them and my boxers off in one go. I went for the buttons on my shirt. She stopped me.

"Don't. It's hot. Like a hidden prize I have to work for."

I flipped her over, landing between her legs. I rolled on a condom and nudged my cock against her entrance. "What are you doing to me?" I murmured as I pushed inside.

She answered by pushing my jacket off my shoulders, removing my tie, and unfastening my shirt. Her warm hands roved over my chest, her eyes flicking down to where we were joined. Propping herself up on her elbows, she watched as I thrust in and out.

"We look great together."

"We really fucking do."

"I don't think I can come again."

"Want to fucking bet?" I growled, angling my hips so that every time I buried my cock in her, I grazed her clit. "Twist your nipples for me."

She did as I asked without a murmur of dissent. Fuck. She was goddamn perfect. A low groan sounded in her throat.

"Feel good, baby?"

"So good." She gasped as I shifted position. "God, yes. There. Do that again."

I did, earning another one of her groans that made my cock ache and my balls beg for release. They'd have to wait because there wasn't a chance I'd come before I proved to her that she could orgasm a third time.

My shirt ended up on the floor. I wasn't sure if I'd shrugged it off or if Jill had removed it, but from the feel of our naked bodies grinding together, our joint moans and gasps and cries of pleasure echoing off the walls, I lost it. As the first spurt of cum shot out of me, Jill thrust her hands into my hair and muttered, "Jesus Christ," hotly in my ear. Her pussy vibrated along my shaft, milking every drop out of me.

I nestled my arms underneath her and lay there for a second, holding most of my weight back. *What just happened?* I'd never had a sexual experience like that in my life, and I'd had a lot of sex. Some great, some good, some forgettable, but that... I wasn't sure my soul was still inside my body.

Sweat poured out of me as I withdrew. My balls still tingled with the aftermath of my second orgasm, and my dick twitched at the sight of Jill beneath me, her eyes sated, her hair mussed, her lips swollen and deliciously pink.

"Fuck me," I rasped, rolling onto my back.

"I think I just did." Jill coiled onto her side, her palm resting on my stomach. Even that faintest touch jolted my dick to life.

I was officially screwed. This woman, this *vixen*, owned me from the top of my head to the tip of my cock. For now. There was no forever. Not for me.

"I think you just rocked my world."

"You think?" She gave me a teasing grin, her irises sparkling with a mischief that imprisoned me. "I need to up my game."

I went for her waist, tickling her. "I never took you for the egotistical type."

She squealed, kicking out with her legs and slapping at my hands. "And I never took you for a corpse, which you will be if you *ever* tickle me again."

"Threats directly after three orgasms." I tapped my lip. "Duly noted."

She grinned. "Does that mean I'll only get two next time?"

I arched a brow. "You're pretty confident there'll be a next time."

"I rocked your world, remember?"

Moving fast, I caged her beneath me. Her pussy still glistened with the evidence of what we'd spent the last hour doing. An urge to go bareback, to watch as my cum dripped out of her, hit me squarely in the chest. I never went bareback. *Never.* But for this woman, I'd make an exception—if she'd allow it.

I froze, an uncomfortable feeling spreading from my core. What the hell was happening here? I'd met Jill on

Thursday. Today was Monday. Five fucking days and I was already thinking about barebacking?

Chill. In all likelihood, it was the combination of a release of the enormous amounts of stress I'd carried around for months after the launch had gone off without a hitch, and the company of a beautiful, funny, intelligent woman who was my equal in every way that mattered.

"What's wrong?" She lifted her hand and pressed it to my cheek. "Are you okay? You've gone a little pale."

I shook off my inertia and stole a kiss. "I'm good. Just..."

"Wondering how things could be this good between two people who, until five days ago, had never set eyes on each other?"

"Yes!" I shifted to the side again, holding her waist and staring into her eyes. "That's it exactly."

"And it's freaking you out?"

"I never said that."

"You didn't need to. It's right there in those come-to-bed eyes."

This woman. She had me dead to rights. No one read me that easily, not even members of my family. "'Freaked out' is a little extreme, but I won't disrespect you by lying and making out that I'm blithe about what I'm feeling."

"Which is?"

I traced her cheek with the back of my hand. "I'm thirty-one years old, and I've never invited a woman to my bed for a second time, nor accepted an invitation into her bed. I've always explained my behavior away by pointing to my career and how absorbing it is. And that's true. I don't have the spare time to cultivate a relationship. Yet with you..."

I trailed off. The actual words didn't need saying. She understood.

Jill confirmed with a nod. "I'm the same. Writing and marketing and the gazillion other things an author needs to do monopolize every minute of my day. Plus, when I'm deep into my characters' heads, nothing breaks through. There could be a nuclear explosion, and the first time I'd realize it was when I turned into ash. I don't have time for a relationship either, yet with you, I want to make the time."

I waited for panic to set in. It didn't.

"Perhaps it's our busy professional lives that unite us. We understand how engrossing they are and how little time they leave for other pursuits." I bit my lip. "I can't promise you longevity. After this cruise is over, I expect we'll go our separate ways and this will become a happy memory we take out of the box and enjoy from time to time. If that's acceptable, then I'd like to spend as much time with you as I can spare on this cruise."

I held my breath. If she declined, it would gut me, and not because I was used to getting what I wanted, but because I wanted her that badly.

"Is taking happy memories out of the box and enjoying them a euphemism for masturbation?"

A laugh burst out of me, one that came from deep in my belly. Freeing and joyous and all Jilly Tilly Rowe. "You're magnificent."

She glanced down. "And you're almost hard again. Shall I take care of that?"

Without waiting for a response, she crawled down the bed, taking my throbbing cock into her mouth for the second time.

I raised my arms overhead, a contented sigh spilling from my lips. It wouldn't be easy letting this woman go at the end of the cruise.

But let her go, I would. I didn't have time for relationships.

Chapter 18

Jill

I have the best friends in the world.

"Barbados, baby!"

Addison grabbed me from behind, squeezing the air from my lungs. We'd chosen this cruise for its destinations, and Barbados had been at the top of all our lists. I'd loved St. Maarten, and Antigua, and Dominica, but there was just something... enticing about Barbados. Magical.

Plus, Rihanna was from here. It didn't get much cooler than that.

"I know. I can't wait."

We'd booked a catamaran cruise that offered snorkeling and promised free-flowing rum. Sounded like a dangerous combination to me, but the company had been in business for over twenty years, so I guessed they had to know what they were doing.

Fingers crossed.

"Are you sure Mr. Sex-on-Legs can spare you for a day?" Addison clutched her chest, dancing around. "Oh, Jilly, my darling Jilly, I'll pine for you. Every second you're gone will be a stake to my heart."

I laughed. "A stake? He's not a vampire."

"That hickey on your neck says otherwise."

Instinctively, I touched the spot Addison referred to. Last night we'd gotten a little carried away. I'd given Blay three love bites, as we Brits called them. A blush crept over my cheeks.

"You are so adorable." Addison hugged me again, then leaned back, scrutinizing me. "What's that look for?"

She knew me far too well. I'd come on this cruise to spend time with my three best friends, and I hadn't abandoned them, per se. We'd toured all the islands we'd stopped off at together, but I had spent a lot of my evenings with Blay, and staying over most nights, and I couldn't help feeling guilty about it.

"I hope you're not regretting inviting me on this cruise."

Addison's head jerked back, her eyes widening. "What the fuck are you talking about?"

"Blay. I've left you alone in this suite most nights, and I feel bad about it."

"Oh, babe." I got a third hug in a row. "Who says I'm spending my nights alone?" She waggled her eyebrows. "I'm eating from the fucking buffet, and it is tasty as hell."

I should have known. "I haven't caught you with anyone."

"That's because I kick them out before you show up."

I laughed. "You are the best."

She nodded. "I am the best."

We met up with Kelsey and Raya and headed to breakfast. I had the same conversation with both of them separately and received the same reassurances—that they were happy for me, glad I was having fun and decompressing after a tough few months. Kelsey made the offer again to look at my manuscript, but my mind had been whirring for days, and my confidence was creeping back. I felt certain I could turn around the hot mess it currently was into something my editor wouldn't puke over.

Maybe all the orgasms had unclogged the block in my brain. Whatever the reason, I wasn't complaining.

I spied Aspen on the far side of the restaurant and waved. She waved back but didn't come over. I hadn't seen much of her these last few days. I'd asked Blay where she was sleeping, because it wasn't in his suite, and he'd simply shrugged and said that Aspen was resourceful and wouldn't exactly be sleeping on deck.

"Did you guys ever spot Joz Raynor?" I asked. Seeing Aspen had reminded me of her quest.

"No." Kelsey pouted. "I'm so disappointed."

"There's still time." I patted her arm.

"Why come on a cruise if you're going to spend it all in your room?"

"A penthouse suite on this ship is hardly a room." Addison rolled her eyes. "It's, like, three thousand square feet or something. And I bet he has a butler tending to his every need."

"I'd tend to his every need, given half the chance," Kelsey muttered.

"Come on, eat up." Addison gestured to us. "I have a hot captain to seduce."

"How do you know he's hot?" I asked.

"Duh. I Googled the company. He's hot. Trust me."

"He's also responsible for his passengers."

"Don't worry. I'll make sure my ass doesn't knock the stick, or whatever it's called, when he's banging me on the bridge."

I shook my head. Addison was a free spirit, a woman who careered through life determined to make the most of every day. I envied her sometimes-reckless-but-always-joyous attitude to life. I worried far too much. About everything.

"Morning, ladies." Familiar hands gripped my shoulders, and the smell of Blay's cologne tickled my nostrils. "Do you have everything you need?"

"We do." Addison smiled up at him, blinking rapidly. "Do you?"

Blay chuckled. "That depends."

I twisted to look up at him. "On what?"

His thumbs grazed my nape. Goose bumps peppered my skin.

"On whether your friends will forgive me if I steal you from them for the day."

Blay knew I had plans with my friends for today. I'd told him all about the catamaran trip last night during one of our catch-our-breaths moments. He hadn't mentioned spending today together.

"I know you have plans, but I wondered if I could tempt you to change them."

I scanned my friends' faces. Every single one nodded. I

had no clue what I'd done to deserve these women, but I was never letting them go.

"I'll have to weigh up my options. What did you have in mind?"

Blay pulled over a chair from a nearby table and sat. He draped an arm over the back of my chair. "I have a house here in Barbados. I thought you might like to see it."

"Hmm." I tapped my finger against my lower lip. "A house. Or a catamaran trip with, according to Addison, a hot captain. Decisions, decisions."

"Erm, a hot captain whom I've already claimed," Addison corrected. "You have one hottie. You can't claim two. Greedy bitch."

Blay chuckled again. "That is tough competition. But I'm sure I'm up to the task."

"I'll bet you are," Addison said in her usual too-loud voice.

I glared at her, willing her to shush for once. "As long as it's okay with my friends, then that sounds lovely."

"It's fine by us," Raya said, grinning.

"Yeah. Go get some." Addison winked, adding, "More."

Laughing, despite my determination not to, I stood. "Okay, handsome, lead the way."

Catcalls and whistles followed us as Blay took me by the hand and led me from the restaurant, a smile stretching across his face.

"Are you smiling because of my crazy friends or because you got your own way?"

"A little of both, maybe."

"Appreciate the honesty."

His arm slid around my waist, and he kissed the top of my head. "I will always give you that."

He gave me so much more, but I kept reminding myself that this wasn't for keeps. It was a blip in the history of time, a dalliance, a holiday romance that, in seven days, would end. I'd return to England to fix my cataclysmic manuscript, and Blay, well, Blay would crack on with building the next superliner, or whatever his future plans were.

I tried not to focus on the tight band around my chest at the idea of not seeing him again once the cruise ended. That way led to trouble, and I couldn't afford to fall for a man who'd made it clear his number one priority was his business empire.

Besides, *my* priority was *my* business empire. It might not be as large as his, nor as lucrative, but it was no less important to me. Whatever was happening between us, I needed to remind myself regularly of its temporary nature. To treat it as a bit of fun, and one that I could look back on when I was old and gray with fondness.

"Are you planning to wear that suit all day?" It must be at least ninety degrees outside.

"No, but I don't like to wander about the ship in anything other than business attire. My passengers expect a certain look. Don't worry, you'll see my bony knees soon enough."

"I've already seen them."

His lascivious grin made my toes curl. "So you have."

We swung by my suite first to pick up the beach bag I'd already packed for the catamaran trip. I opened it, peering inside.

"Do you have anywhere to swim, or should I leave the bikini behind?"

His eyes traveled over me, slowly and with filthy intent. "I have a swimming pool and a private beach, and skinny-dipping is positively encouraged."

"I should imagine burnt nipples are uncomfortable."

"So's a burnt cock, but I have sunblock, too."

I laughed. "You have an answer for everything."

"Not quite everything." Concern drifted across his features, but as I was about to ask what the matter was, his expression brightened. "Bring the bikini. I'll have fun removing it."

As we disembarked, a golf cart was waiting for us at the bottom of the gangplank. Although, it was bigger than a normal golf cart, with six seats and a space at the rear for luggage. Blay put our things in the back and took my hand, helping me inside. The cart sped away, overtaking excited passengers on their way to enjoy the delights of Barbados.

"Will we have time to see the island?"

Blay looked at me. "You've never visited Barbados?"

I shook my head. "First time."

"In that case..." He tapped the driver on the shoulder. "Miguel, give us your best tour."

Miguel saluted. "You got it, Mr. Kingcaid."

Chapter 19

Blaize

I've officially lost my mind.

JILL'S ENTHUSIASM FOR AN ISLAND I KNEW WELL WAS contagious. I couldn't take my eyes off her. She rattled off dozens of questions for Miguel, listening intently to his answers, and asked him to stop at various places, snapping photos on her phone, then showing me the pictures. We pulled over at a hut by the side of the road and drank cocktails out of scooped-out coconuts and pineapples. We paddled in the sea, holding hands and pausing to kiss every few feet.

The normalcy of it was addictive. I pondered whether I could get used to this freer life, one without the weight of responsibility on my shoulders. Yet even as I asked myself the question, I already knew the answer. While this was great for a few hours, a day, a week even, I craved the adrenaline rush of running a multibillion-dollar business. I'd slowly wither without the frenetic pace of my life.

"I can't believe you own a home here," Jill announced as we climbed back into the golf cart, sand in our toes and salt in our hair. "You're so lucky." She immediately shook her head. "No, not lucky. Fortunate. I'm not a believer in luck."

"Neither am I. We make our own luck in life. Yes, I'm fortunate to have been born into a wealthy family, but if I didn't pull my weight, my father wouldn't hesitate to oust me from the business. And you're fortunate that you have a talent for storytelling, but if you didn't work hard at your craft, then you wouldn't have seen the success you have."

She wrinkled her nose. "Your father would fire you?"

"If I didn't put the work in, yes. In a heartbeat."

"Hmm. Well, if he does, I'll hire you as my PA."

My lips twitched. She truly was adorable. "I'll bear that tempting offer in mind."

Satisfied that Jill had seen everything she wanted to, we arrived at my home at fifteen minutes before one. We didn't have to be back on the ship until seven, leaving us plenty of alone time.

Time I planned to use wisely.

"Wow!" Jill spilled out of the golf cart and stared up at my house, a plantation-style white property with a wrap-around porch, an infinity pool, and lush vegetation. I'd purchased it from a Hollywood producer that my cousin Roman, who headed up our film studios business, intro-duced me to. It had been in his family for two generations, but his new, far younger wife preferred Hawaii.

His loss, my gain.

"This whole thing is yours?"

I nodded. Compared to my Miami home, this was on the small side, but from the way Jill's voice held a hint of incredulity, to her, it must have seemed enormous. I guessed it was an impressive-looking house. Historic.

She squinted at me. "You really are filthy rich, aren't you?"

Snaking my arms around her waist, I pressed my forehead to hers. "I'm filthy rich, yes. Filthy in other ways, too."

"Are your... do you... do you keep your toys here?" She kept her eyes on mine, but I could tell she wasn't used to talking about such things, let alone using them in the bedroom, regardless of the joke she'd made at Miami Airport about her suitcase being full of vibrators. It surprised me that she'd remembered what I'd said, never mind bringing it up.

"A selection, yes." I waited for Miguel to drop off our bags and depart. He'd return for us later today. The ship wouldn't sail without me, but it wouldn't be a good look for our late departure to be caused by the CEO of the company's tardiness. "Are you curious?"

"Maybe." Her voice wavered with uncertainty.

"Lunch first, then a swim, then we can... play. If you want to, that is. There's no pressure or expectation. Especially if your sexual experiences lean toward vanilla."

"Nothing wrong with vanilla."

I grinned, running my gaze over her, lingering on the way her top showed off her cleavage. "Absolutely nothing. It's delicious." I took her hand and led her inside. Ten minutes later, after a tour, and a quick change into more suitable attire—for me—we emerged onto the porch where my housekeeper had set out our lunch. As instructed, she'd left immediately afterward. As discreet as my staff was, I wanted it to be just us.

Directly in front of the porch was the pool, sparkling in the sun, and beyond lay the golden sands and crystal-clear waters of the Caribbean Sea.

"See that path?" I pointed to a stone walkway that disappeared into green foliage.

Jill followed my gaze. "Yeah."

"It leads down to the beach. If you like, after we've eaten, we can go down there. Or swim up here in the pool if you'd prefer."

"Or both."

"Ah, a woman who wants to experience it all."

"Life is for living." She sighed. "And I haven't been doing very much of that before coming on this trip. I made a promise that I'd use this time to try new things, to make memories I hope will see me through the dark days ahead."

A shadow crossed her face, one I yearned to erase permanently. "The book?"

Her chest rose and fell with another deep sigh. "The book."

"Tell me something." I reached across the table for a goat cheese and pesto canapé, eating it in two bites. "What happens if you return to England without figuring it out?"

She'd spoken about this on the plane, but I wanted to explore her fears in a more relaxed environment. Jill thought that one mistake would set her career on fire, but I didn't believe a single mistake had the power to crush our livelihoods other than when actions involved a heinous criminal act. But simply struggling to meet an editing deadline with a publisher, no matter how cutthroat the industry was—I didn't buy it.

"Erm, my publisher drops me."

"And you have evidence of that? In writing?"

Squinting, she helped herself to a vegetarian bao bun. Taking a bite, she moaned. "These are delicious."

My dick hardened. If she moaned like that again, I'd fuck her where she sat. "Answer the question."

She licked her fingers, and this time, I moaned. "Are you trying to distract me from this line of questioning on purpose?"

A smile stole across her face. "Is it working?"

"Too fucking well."

"Men are such simple creatures when it comes to sex."

"Guilty as charged, and not even remotely apologetic. And I'd wager that if I wanted to distract you from something and used sex as my weapon of choice, it wouldn't take long for you to capitulate." I stuck my finger in the hummus and held it out to Jill. "Suck."

She didn't hesitate, as I'd known she wouldn't. Her lips closed around my finger, her eyes on me, lust darkening her hazel irises to a deeper brown. I shifted my position to give my cock a little more room and silently thanked the designer of these shorts for making them spacious enough for horny guys.

"Case in point." I withdrew my finger. My dick protested. Too bad. This was more important. There was plenty of time for sex.

"Aren't holiday romances supposed to be all sex and no chat?"

Something shifted in my chest, an alien feeling that felt

too much like regret for my liking. In seven days, we'd return to Miami, and Jill and I would go our separate ways. That was the deal we'd made. Yet the more the inevitable crept toward me, the greater the ache inside me grew.

"Stop procrastinating."

"Ugh." Her head flopped against the back of her chair, and her cheeks puffed out as she expelled air from her lungs. "I'm a writer. Procrastinating is what we do."

I chuckled and stayed silent. A well-trodden business technique that had many uses outside the boardroom. A few seconds passed, and as I'd anticipated, Jill caved.

"I have no evidence that they'll drop me if I deliver late or if I tell my editor how much I'm struggling." Her eyes narrowed. "But you knew that already, didn't you?"

"I mean..." I shrugged. "I could have been wrong." A hint of a smile lifted my lips.

"Double ugh. Smart and beautiful."

I reached for her, taking her hand in mine. "Right back at you, gorgeous. Now, please, stop worrying, take the bull by the horns, and email your editor and tell her what's going on." I released her, staring pointedly.

Her eyes flashed open wide. "Now?"

I popped an eyebrow. "Why not?"

"Because... because it's... it's *stupid.*"

A laugh rippled through my chest. "Or maybe, just maybe, it'll take some of the pressure off you, allowing you to enjoy the rest of your vacation without a dark cloud of unproven worry hanging over your head."

Jill chewed the corner of her mouth. I waited for her to mull it over, sampling a salmon skin roll in the meantime.

"Okay, I'll do it." Reaching into her bag, she removed

her phone, her fingers trembling as she typed out an email. Two minutes later, she tossed her phone onto the table. "Done. God, I feel sick." Bending over, she curled her hands around her abdomen.

"Come here." I rose from my chair and took both her hands, helping her up. My arms encircled her waist. "Well done."

"If this goes pear-shaped, I'm holding you entirely responsible."

"If this goes pear-shaped, I'll buy the fucking publishing house and publish you myself."

Shock stirred behind her eyes. "You wouldn't."

"Oh, I would."

A ping sounded from her phone. She froze. "Shit. Do you think that's her reply?"

I let her go, pressing my fingertips to my temples. "Hold on. I'm just tuning in to my psychic abilities."

A flash of amusement registered in her eyes. "Such a comedian."

"Jill." I sighed. "Check your goddamn phone. The sooner you do, the sooner I can undress you and fuck you in the pool."

"With charm like that, no wonder you're fighting women off."

I flattened my lips. "You're procrastinating again. I swear, I'll knock that out of you if it's the last thing I do."

"Seven days, baby." She shot me a grin. I forced my lips to respond, although the knife buried in my gut made it a challenge. Seven goddamn days, and work would interfere with a majority of that time.

Interfere? Jesus. Who was I becoming? Work had

always occupied positions one, two, and three priorities in my life. It was my entire reason for avoiding relationships. I craved a healthy amount of sex, as any guy my age would, but the whole putting someone else first was something I consciously avoided.

Until now.

Until her.

"Check your phone," I repeated.

Her ragged breath spoke to her anxiety. I squeezed her shoulder.

"Goddammit." She snatched up her cell. "It's from her."

"Rip off the Band-Aid, Tilly."

She took in another shuddering breath. Her eyes traveled across the screen, her teeth continuously grinding against her bottom lip as she read the message.

The moment I knew it wasn't bad was when her shoulders sagged and she briefly closed her eyes. "She's fine. She understands. She told me to enjoy my holiday and when I get home to England, we'll figure it out together."

I didn't say "I told you so." This wasn't about one-upmanship. It was about taking away the pain from someone who'd unlocked a piece of me I hadn't realized was shuttered tight. I couldn't bear the thought of never seeing her again after we docked in Miami. An idea forged in my mind, growing at an exponential rate. And you know what? It didn't scare me. It fucking energized me.

"Hey, Jill. Here's an idea."

"Always listen to Blaize Isaac Kingcaid?" She wove sarcasm into every syllable.

A grin stretched my lips wide. "Well, that's a given, but no. That's not what I was going to say."

"Spit it out, then."

There she is. My magnificent woman.

I faltered. *My woman.* How could that be? We'd met nine days ago, not nine months ago, yet I couldn't deny the depth of my feelings. I wasn't in love with her, far from it, but an intended second bite of the cherry had led to something deeper, something instinct demanded that I explore.

"What if we don't say goodbye in Miami?"

Startled eyes fixed on mine. "How would that work?"

"I don't know yet. If you feel the same, we can iron out the details later. What I do know is that I don't want this to end. I have no idea what 'this' is." I air-quoted. "But every part of me is insisting that I hold on."

She gave me a look layered with uncertainty and elation. It resonated on a cellular level.

"Say something," I urged.

A whisper of breath carried her words. "I think I'd like that very much."

Chapter 20

Jill

This has gotten awfully serious, awfully fast.

BLAY MOVED WITH THE SPEED OF A CHEETAH streaking across the prairie, it's prey in its sights.

My heart cartwheeled as he picked me up and spun me around. The joy on his face shifted something inside of me. It had no name, but intuitively, it felt important.

Exciting.

Scary.

I'd vowed to take risks on this holiday, and Blay felt like the biggest risk of all, yet one with the biggest payoff.

I hadn't dared admit to him, or even myself, how the thought of never seeing him again made me ache. It amazed me how close we'd gotten in such a short amount of time. My parents had married after knowing each other for only three weeks, but they were hardly bastions of a happy marriage. Despite their pious doctrines, their relationship had all the hallmarks of a couple kept together by their religious beliefs rather than a fervent desire to be with one another.

But as I reminded myself often, I was not my parents.

Thank God for that.

Kelsey had asked me once if I missed them and my sister. I'd taken my time to think about her question before answering with a resounding no. In a way, my mother's ultimatum had set me free.

"Where'd you go, Tilly?"

I blinked. Blay's brows dipped together, concern swimming in his eyes as he lowered me to the ground.

Talking about my parents wasn't something I did often, and if Blay hadn't suggested an extended relationship past the holiday romance we'd both envisaged, then I wouldn't talk about them now. But he had, and, oddly enough, I wanted to tell him.

"Just thinking about my mum and dad."

His gaze roved my face as if he'd picked up on the dull tone in my voice and was trying to get a bead on the reason.

"You're not close?"

"I haven't seen them, or my sister, since they discovered I write romance novels. Porn, my mum called it. She gave me an ultimatum: her and my dad, or my career." I smiled wryly.

"Fuck. That hardly feels like a fair choice."

"My parents don't care about fair. They care about God, and in my mother's eyes, He wouldn't admit me into heaven as long as I penned that 'dreadful smut.' Her words, not mine."

"Ah."

"Indeed." I hitched a shoulder. "It doesn't matter. Truly. I have a family. They're called Kelsey, Addison, and Raya. They love me for the person I am, not the person they think I should be. Plus, I have many author friends, readers, my advance team, my street team. Those people are my family now."

"Space for one more?" His crooked smile hit me in the chest, goose bumps peppering my skin.

"This has gotten awfully serious, awfully fast."

He bobbed his head. "It has. Does that scare you?"

"A little."

Brushing his lips over mine, he murmured, "Me, too. But if what we're doing doesn't scare us, it isn't worth pursuing."

He deepened the kiss, driving his tongue inside my mouth as his hips circled, his cock grazing exactly where I needed it.

Urgency burned through my veins. I pushed my fingers into his hair, driven mad with all-consuming desire. I didn't feel him pick me up, nor the movement of us gliding across the patio. The first sign we'd moved at all came when the water lapped at my feet. Blay plunged us, fully dressed, into the pool.

I gasped, the water chilly against the blazing sun. "Oh my God. You're crazy!" I splashed him with water.

"Guilty as charged." Wrestling with my soaking sundress, he tugged it over my head. My bra followed. I pulled down my knickers, kicking them away, my eyes locking on Blay's T-shirt. The way it clung to his skin, outlining every ridge of muscle.

I licked my lips. "You'd win a wet T-shirt competition, hands down."

He fought to remove the sopping wet item of clothing, growling in frustration. "I did not think this through. It was supposed to be romantic."

"It *is* romantic." I joined in his attempt to take off the shirt, then moved on to his shorts. "But this habit you've got of ruining my lingerie is becoming expensive."

"I promise to recompense you in the form of several orgasms and an entire dresser filled with the best La Perla has to offer."

"Deal."

His hands encased my waist, and he hoisted me up onto the side of the pool. Pushing my thighs apart, he trained his eyes on my pussy.

"We didn't finish lunch." My voice sounded raw, filled with anticipation.

His pupils dilated. "You're my favorite thing to eat, Tilly."

Air hissed through my teeth as he licked me in one lazy sweep. I braced my forearms on the warm stone and leaned back, spreading my legs as wide as they'd go.

Fuck, I hoped whoever had laid on lunch wasn't spying on us from an upstairs room. If they were, they'd cop an eyeful. Funnily enough, now that I thought about it, I didn't care.

Blay propped my ankles on his shoulders, and from that moment on, conscious thought vanished, leaving a fiery heat that concentrated in a singular spot between my legs.

That tongue.

Those fingers.

His dark eyes locked on mine, watching for every reaction, adjusting the speed and pressure depending on what he saw.

I lost myself, sucked into a swirl of desire until I was falling, falling, my entire being fixated on this moment.

Blay had studied giving head. He must have. No one was that accomplished at something they hadn't done many times before.

The stray thought made my stomach clench, and not in a good way. He might have proposed a continuation of our arrangement, but a man who didn't date the same woman twice wasn't capable of switching just like that.

Was he?

"Hey, come back to me, Tilly."

He flicked his tongue over my clit, sliding two blunt fingers inside me, getting me *right fucking there.*

"I'm here," I gasped.

"Yeah, you fucking are."

He did something, I couldn't even say what, and I shattered. My toes curled, my calves cramped, my pussy pulsed and throbbed, clenching around his fingers.

"Jesus Christ." I squeezed my eyes closed as tiny sparks of pleasure continued to rip me apart.

"Come here." Blay lifted me into the pool, hooking my legs around his waist. He slid inside me, the water, or maybe how wet I was, making it frictionless.

"Fuck, Tilly."

He buried his head in my neck, the buoyancy of the water supporting me as he pulled out before slamming back in. His lips found mine, and he kissed and kissed and kissed me, his tongue mirroring his thrusts.

"I can't... I... fuck." He groaned, peppering my cheeks and lips and forehead with his soft lips. "Shit, God, I'm sorry. I can't hold on."

With a final drawn-out moan, he came, his dick jerking inside me, his large hands squeezing my arse, mashing me closer to him. He stilled, his breaths gradually slowing. I cradled his head, holding him to me as he withdrew.

Setting my feet on the bottom of the pool, he looked at me, his eyes brimming with apology.

"Blay, it's okay. In fact, I'm flattered. God, what a turn-on, making a guy like you lose control. I swear, it's the sexiest thing I've ever seen."

He shook his head. "I'm not apologizing for not making you come again, although I'm not happy about it."

"Then what?"

He cupped my face, his thumbs brushing my cheeks. "I didn't use a condom."

"Oh." I wrinkled my nose, tackling the difficult subject head-on. We were both culpable here. We'd both forgotten. "Are you worried you might have something?"

"No. Christ, no, that's not it. I'm clean. I fucking swear to you. I'd never risk your health like that—yours or anyone else's. It's just... I want you to know that if I just put a baby in you, I will stand by you and our child every step of the way." He grimaced. "I never have unprotected sex. Ever."

"Ah." I smiled, pecking his lips. "You're pretty darned wonderful, you know that?" I kissed him again. "I'm on birth control. You're good. But if I get an itch down there in a couple of days' time, I warn you, I will throw you overboard."

A laugh rumbled through his chest. "Noted."

"And while we're on the subject of unprotected sex, I'm clean, too. In fact, before you, I can't remember the last time I had sex."

"But you remember every time since, right?"

I narrowed my eyes. "An ego the size of Jupiter is an unattractive quality."

"Just as well. Mine's only the size of Saturn, then, isn't it?"

Before I could formulate a response, he picked me up and threw me at least five feet. I went under, coming up for air, spluttering.

"You are dead."

I pushed sopping-wet hair out of my face and launched. I climbed on his back and ducked him under. He emerged from beneath the water, a grin puffing his cheeks. But by then, I'd already swum to the opposite side of the pool.

He cut through the water with the grace of a dolphin, determined and focused. I hoisted myself out of the pool, sprinting toward the house. I paused outside the double doors that led into the enormous open-plan living area.

"Hold it, mister." I put my arms in front of me. "Unless you want chlorine drips all over your pristine floor, you'll concede the battle to me."

One shoulder lifted in a "don't care" manner. "It's only water."

He made a grab for me. I skipped out of his way,

running into the house. Bracing myself on the other side of the kitchen island, I planted my hands on top and grinned.

"Whatcha gonna do now, stud?"

My stomach did several somersaults just from the predatory look on his face. I wouldn't have guessed I'd enjoy the chased-by-your-lover game, but the fluttering in my chest and the way my thighs trembled in excitement told me everything I needed to know.

Yep. I bloody well loved it.

As easily as a cat climbing a fence, Blay leapt onto the counter and down the other side and had me in a tight hold before I'd blinked.

"To answer your question, Tilly"—he hooked one arm underneath my knees, put the other around my shoulders, and lifted me into his arms—"I'm going to take you to bed, and if you're good, I might let you play with my toys."

"If *you're* good, I might let *you* play with them."

Grinning, he carried me toward the stairs that led to the upper level, when his phone rang.

He cursed. "Sorry, I told my staff I wasn't to be disturbed unless it was urgent."

"Then it must be urgent."

I waited for him to put me down and go answer his phone, which he'd left on the side before we'd gone out to the pool.

"Make sure it's not a video call." I pointed my chin at his semi-hard dick.

He grinned, but his smile fell when he looked at his phone. "Goddamn, what the fuck does she want now?"

"Who?"

"Scarlett 'Diva' Rose."

He answered it, transforming from playful lover to pissed-off CEO in the time it took me to blink.

"Miss Rose, what can I do for you?"

He listened intently, his eyes hardening in response to whatever she was saying.

God, I hoped this wasn't bad.

He had more than enough on his overflowing plate, and from what he'd told me about Scarlett, she appeared to have the ability to turn a minor gripe into a major catastrophe for him.

"I'll have someone come by your penthouse." He shifted his weight. "No, I'm afraid I can't do that. I'm otherwise engaged." His eyes drifted over to me.

I mouthed, "We can go."

His lips flattened to a thin line, and he shook his head vigorously. "I understand that, and of course you're one of my most important customers, but I'm not on the ship right now. I—"

He stopped talking. She must have interrupted him. I couldn't make out a single word, but there was an undeniable increase in the volume and speed of her voice.

I should get dressed. He had more important things to deal with.

I headed toward the pool, where I'd left my beach bag. Blay snapped out a hand as I passed. He wrapped his free arm around my waist, holding me against him, my back to his front.

"I'll have someone come to see you immediately, and I will stop by when I return to the ship later. I'm afraid that's the best I can do." He dropped a kiss on my shoulder. "Goodbye."

I twisted in his arms, grimacing. "It's fine if you want to go back. She's important to your business."

He snorted. "Not nearly as important as she thinks she is. And I have no intention of returning to the ship early. If it were a real issue, I'd have already called Miguel and had him come pick us up, but it's nothing. Just Scarlett being her usual overbearing and demanding self. She needs to understand that I am not her personal fucking servant."

He tapped out a message, hit Send, and then tossed his phone onto the kitchen counter.

"I couldn't stand having to be nice to people like that all the time. I don't know how you do it."

"With great difficulty. But Scarlett has spent most of her life surrounded by sycophants, and she isn't used to people standing up to her. I mean, the woman tossed her husband to the side as soon as he'd outlived his usefulness."

"He was her manager, too, right?"

I vaguely recalled reading something about it online, although I couldn't count myself among the gossip lovers. I left that to Addison, who hoovered up celebrity shit like it was her favorite flavor of ice cream.

"Yeah. That's how they met. Ten or eleven years ago, if I recall the briefing my team gave me about her."

"Your team briefed you about her?"

"They briefed me about every one of our penthouse guests. As the CEO, I'm expected to know these kinds of details in case they're pertinent."

"Wow."

His eyes lowered to my boobs pressed against his chest.

"Let's forget about prima donna celebrities. We have much more important things to do."

"Yeah? Like what?" I teased.

He caught my bottom lip between his teeth. "Each other."

Chapter 21

Blaize

What a goddamn nightmare.

MIGUEL TURNED THE GOLF CART ONTO THE QUAYSIDE, giving me a perfect view of Serenity's majesty rising from the gentle swell of the Atlantic Ocean. Pride inflated my chest. I rarely stopped to celebrate successes, always with one eye on the horizon looking for the next thing to make leaving a warm bed in the morning worthwhile.

I'd done this. Me. Sure, I'd had help. A ton, but it'd been my vision, my determination, that had brought this magnificent sight to fruition.

All those worries, the countless sleepless nights before sailing, had come to nothing. Apart from the odd gripe here and there—which was to be expected—and Scarlett's waspish complaints, the cruise could only be described as a resounding success.

As we crept closer, though, a mist of cold sweat touched my forehead. Why were all these people standing in line, using bags and linen jackets to shield them from the relentless sun? Why weren't they boarding?

"Long lines at both embarkation points." Jill gave me a nudge. "Do you have a secret entrance?"

She grinned. I didn't. Something wasn't right.

"Miguel, stop here," I barked, hotfooting it onto the quayside before the golf cart had come to a complete halt. I barreled ahead, past the lines of disgruntled passengers waiting to board, the odd complaint reaching me as I swept by.

God-fucking-dammit. What the hell was going on?

"Is there a problem?"

The security guard skipped a tired glance my way, as if he'd been asked the same question a hundred times. He did a double take the moment he recognized me.

"Mr. Kingcaid." He stood up straighter. "Sir, I'm afraid the badge scanners are down."

Jill appeared to my right. She brushed my arm. My stomach knotted. I felt for her hand, clasping it. The badge scanner had gone down before we'd set sail. I'd had cast-iron guarantees from the maintenance team that they'd fixed it. Obviously fucking not.

Jesus Christ.

Of all the things that could go wrong, this was up there as one of the worst. Without being able to security-check people, we couldn't let them board. And without the badge scanner, there was no way of knowing who was a Serenity passenger and who wasn't.

What a goddamn nightmare.

Despite the raging inferno charring my insides, I schooled my expression and took control. I beckoned to a nearby staff member.

"Have bottles of water brought out for the passengers and bring a few chairs for our older guests." A woman in her eighties who was near the front of the line gave me a grateful smile. "And umbrellas for shade. It's baking out here."

"Yes, sir." He raced inside the ship.

I got on the phone and put in a call to the captain, stepping far enough away from the passengers to ensure they didn't overhear my conversation. "John, what the fuck is going on?"

"Kris is working on it. He's assured me he'll have it fixed soon."

Kris was my head of IT. "Soon isn't fucking good enough. I have passengers out here at risk of sunstroke. Not to mention the reputational damage this will cause. Why the hell didn't someone call me?"

He hesitated. "That's my fault. I felt certain we'd have it fixed before any passengers arrived back."

"And when that failed to occur, you didn't think to call me then?"

"What could you have done, Blaize? You're not an IT expert."

I fumed. "No, but I'd have had fucking shade and water and fucking seats out here to ensure our passengers suffered minimal inconvenience until we could get them onboard."

He went silent. I rarely lost my temper, but this was an overstep I wasn't willing to accept. I was the fucking CEO of this ship, not John.

"I screwed up. I'm sorry."

His willingness to apologize quelled my anger. My fist unclenched. "Tell me we've at least got some passengers on board; otherwise, we're about to have a fucking great puzzle to solve."

"Most returned already. We're missing three hundred."

I'd guessed that, given we were only forty minutes from our scheduled departure time. Glancing at the lines, I'd estimate most, if not all, of those three hundred were here already.

"Thank Christ for small mercies. We'll talk when this shit show is fixed."

I hung up and called Kris, who said the same to me as he'd said to John. I pressed for a time. He wouldn't give it to me.

"I'm going as fast as I can" was all he'd commit to.

Fucking marvelous.

Within ten minutes, my customers had access to water, shade, and, for those who needed it, somewhere to sit. I walked the lines, chatting with the passengers and reassuring them we'd board soon, while praying I wouldn't get caught in the lie. The relentless heat from the sun beat down. I'd never rued my stupid, self-imposed rule to wear business attire when in public more.

"It'll be okay." Jill led me a short distance away, almost as if she recognized how close to the edge I was.

"Will it? If we don't get the scanner fixed, no one here is getting on board. We'll have to find accommodations for three hundred people, not to mention missing our departure slot, meaning we won't make it to our next destination." I raked both hands through my hair. "It's a fucking nightmare."

She gnawed at her lip. "I hadn't thought of that."

"Jill!" We both turned our heads as Jill's friends approached. "What's going on?"

"There's a bit of a technical hitch, which means we can't board yet," Jill said, which resulted in a snort from me. Technical hitch? More like a clusterfuck. "But it'll be fixed soon."

"We hope," I muttered.

Oh, look. It seemed I'd reverted to being a child.

I gave myself a metaphorical kick in the ass. Infantile responses wouldn't help anyone, least of all my passengers.

"Well, not to worry," Addison said. "If we can't board, we'll have a party right here on the quayside and sleep under the stars." She fired a grin at me. "Chill, gorgeous. It's no biggie. Shit happens. It's how we react to it that counts."

If I weren't falling for her best friend, I'd have kissed Addison.

Wait. What?

What?

My phone rang, distracting me. Aspen. I answered. "Yeah?"

"You know there's a bunch of people who can't board."

"Yeah. I'm out here with them."

"Oh. Everything okay? Can I do anything from in here?"

"You seen Nolen and Marlowe?"

"Yup. We had lunch together, then they sloped off to their suite and, to the best of my knowledge, haven't emerged since."

"Good." Barbados wasn't a stranger to my family, so it didn't surprise me that they hadn't disembarked to explore. Marlowe must not have been interested in the whole tourist thing either. If she wanted the moon, Nolen would lasso it for her.

"Mr. Kingcaid." The security manager motioned to me. "We're good to go."

I gave him a curt nod. "We're boarding. Talk to you later."

I hung back with Jill and the rest of the girls as the passengers finally filed on board. Only when the last one had trudged up the gangplank did I enter my ship.

"Here." I gave Jill the fob for my suite. "Will you wait for me?"

"Of course." She raised up on her tiptoes and kissed my cheek. "Take all the time you need."

"Ooh, party at Blaize's pad. Cool." Addison swiped the fob, waving it in the air. "I hear it's rad."

I rolled my eyes but smiled, too. "Have at it."

"Awesome." She skipped off with Kelsey and Raya in tow, Jill bringing up the rear. She glanced back as she entered the elevator, blowing me a kiss. I didn't have time to blow one back before the doors closed.

Taking the staff elevator down to deck four, where Kris's office was located, I marched along the corridor, entering without a courtesy knock. Kris had a few of his team surrounding him, each one frowning as they stared at his screen. Something about their body language was off.

The knot in my stomach tightened as several pairs of eyes snapped to me.

"Can you give us a minute?" I held the door open, my message clear. They filed out, heads bowed, muttering a greeting as they passed me. I closed the door behind the last one, my eyes locking on Kris.

"What happened?"

"I think... I *think* the code was altered."

I rested my hands on my hips. "What does that mean?"

"It means that someone, or multiple someones, found a back door to the system and altered the coding, which took the badge scanners offline. Problem is, they've covered their tracks so well that I can't find a trace."

I jabbed a finger at him. "This is your only priority. Find out who did this and make sure, the second you do, I'm the *only* person you tell."

"You got it, Mr. Kingcaid."

My heart lodged in my ribs as I rode the elevator up to deck nineteen. There was only one reason I could think of for someone to meddle with the badge system. I put in a call to my head of security and demanded a full sweep of the ship before we left port.

If someone was on board who wasn't supposed to be, I'd smoke that fucker out and ensure the police threw the fucking book at him—or her.

On the way to my suite, I passed Scarlett's penthouse. I paused. As much as I despised playing nice with the woman, she was a VIP, and there was a high possibility I had some ruffled feathers to smooth after palming her off on someone else earlier today.

I pressed the bell. "Miss Rose?" I announced myself

because, knowing Scarlett, she wouldn't answer the door. "It's Blaize Kingcaid."

Silence greeted me. I shrugged. She either wasn't there, or she was sulking. Either way, I had more important things to do. A security breach was a big fucking deal.

A boulder-sized worry sat squarely across my shoulders, and talking it through with my brother might take some of the weight off. Jill wouldn't mind. She had her girls with her, and there was enough alcohol in my suite to keep them entertained if Addison went ahead with her threat to throw a party.

I was about to leave when a noise came from inside. I paused.

Unless I was mistaken, that sounded like a muffled scream. I pressed the bell again.

"Miss Rose. It's me. Blaize Kingcaid. Are you all right?"

This time, I heard nothing.

But my instincts had fired up. I fished out my wallet and removed a card, one I hadn't had cause to use on this or any other ship. It allowed me to access every room.

I hesitated.

If this was nothing, I was about to piss off an influential customer with a vindictive streak longer than her career in showbiz.

I held the card to the badge scanner until the door clicked. I pushed it open.

It took a second for me to grasp the situation.

Scarlett's assistant lay on the floor, a gash on the side of her head. Scarlett was tied to a chair, gagged. And a man in a hoodie and scuffed jeans was ransacking the safe.

"What the—?"

The man whipped around.

Scarlett's muffled screams increased.

He pointed a gun at me and fired.

Chapter 22

Jill

This is a living nightmare.

TWENTY MINUTES EARLIER...

"This place is so rad!" Addison poked her nose into every room. "No wonder you're not sleeping in ours, Jilly." She fired a grimace at Aspen, who'd had us descend on her unexpectedly and had taken it in stride. "Sorry. That's not to say our suite isn't gorgeous. Because it is gorgeous. But this..."

"Yeah, Blaize designed it himself. He wanted a comfortable space the family could use."

"Your cousin is multitalented." Her eyes went to mine, and I braced myself. I knew exactly what was coming.

"Come on, Jilly. Tell us about your day. I mean, you can still walk, so the man has work to do."

I pointed my chin in Aspen's direction and glared at my best friend. "Later."

"Don't hold back on my account." Aspen grinned. "Although, maybe skim over some of the more... vibrant details."

"I'm skimming over *all* the details because we are not having this conversation. Get your own sex life, Addison, and stop focusing on mine."

She beamed, unoffended by my rebuke. "My sex life is motoring along nicely, thank you very much. That doesn't mean I can't steal ideas from yours."

I shook my head. Addison was like a ten-ton truck. Once she got rolling, it was almost impossible to stop her.

"Why don't we make some cocktails?" Aspen got up off the couch and crossed over to the bar. "Cosmos all round?"

"Ooh, yeah. I'll help." Addison joined Aspen, grabbing the cocktail shaker.

I mouthed a thank-you. Aspen dipped her chin ever so slightly. Minutes later, drinks in hand, the conversation moved on to a fresh topic that didn't involve my sex life. That Addison would return to the subject was as certain as the sun rising tomorrow morning, but I'd gotten a reprieve for now. I shivered every time I thought about sex in the pool and all the stuff we'd done afterward. I wasn't exactly innocent, but the sheer array of toys Blay owned and the orgasms he'd given me with them had opened my eyes to a whole new world of sex.

"A toast," Aspen said, raising her cosmo in the air. "To new friends and exciting exper—"

A loud bang echoed in the hallway, immediately followed by a second one. I jumped, spilling my drink. My heart rate spiked. "What was that?"

"I don't know." Aspen put her drink aside, advancing to the door. She gingerly opened it, peering outside. "Hey, you. Wait!"

She ran into the hallway. I hurried after her, catching sight of a man in scruffy clothing disappearing into the landing where the stairs and lift were located. I shifted my gaze.

"Blay!"

I raced to him. Aspen beat me to it. She crouched beside him. My knees crashed to the carpet. Footsteps echoed behind me, and passengers began emerging from their cabins.

"What the hell happened?" I scanned his body, lying half in, half out of Scarlett Rose's penthouse. Fuck. Blood everywhere. I couldn't catch my breath. Gasping for air, I traded glances with Aspen. Her eyes were wide, and fear flooded her face. "Help, please! Somebody. Somebody help!"

"Move!" a voice bellowed, pushing aside the crowd that had gathered around us.

"Nolen, thank God." Aspen clasped his arm. "He's breathing, I think. I don't know. Shit, shit."

"Marlowe, untie her, and check the woman on the ground. Blaize, hang on. Medics are on their way. Keep breathing for me, buddy."

Untie whom? What woman? My mind whirred. I

couldn't process, couldn't think. Everything moved slow and fast at once. How was that possible?

"Blay." I bent over him, pressing my lips to his forehead. He was cold, clammy. A fist squeezed my heart, my chest collapsing. "God, please. Please don't die."

His eyelids fluttered, and he groaned.

"Don't move, bud." Nolen put a hand on his shoulder. "I'm gonna tie up your leg, okay? This might hurt a bit."

I followed his movements. Oh God. Oh God. Oh God. His leg... his leg. So much blood. Nolen slipped a belt underneath Blay's right leg, above his knee. As he tightened it, Blay screamed.

"You're hurting him!"

"I have to stop the bleeding. I think the bullet hit an artery."

Bullet? What bullet? Guns weren't allowed on the ship. We'd had to put everything through a scanner. I didn't understand.

"What's happening?" Faces swam into one another. I braced a hand against the wall. Hands clasped me, lifting me. I fought them off. "No. I want to stay with Blay."

"Let the medics get to him, Jilly."

Addison. I spun into her arms, clinging on. She stroked my hair. "It's okay, love. He'll be okay."

My two other friends crowded in. I let them comfort me for a few seconds before shaking them off. There were three people tending to Blay now. Two medics and his brother Nolen. How was he so calm when I was losing my shit? I sought Aspen, her face as pale as mine must've been. Shot. Someone had shot Blay. Who? Why?

A stretcher appeared. The medics loaded Blay onto it.

I froze as they wheeled it down the narrow hallway, past the groups of passengers gathered in the doorways to their penthouses.

"Come on, sweetheart." An arm went around my shoulder. I peered at Blay's sister-in-law, Marlowe, through blurred eyes. Blay had introduced us a few nights ago, and I hadn't seen her since. Her voice calmed me somewhat, although my skin was clammy and cold and terror ran riot through my veins.

"Where are they taking him?" I allowed her to propel me forward.

"To the hospital. There's an excellent private facility on the island. They'll take great care of him."

"Is he...? Will he...?"

"Let's go, shall we?" Her gentle coaxing without answering my question was a testament to her worry. I glanced over my shoulder at my three friends gathered at the spot where Blay's blood had soaked into the carpet. As I did, another woman was stretchered out, Scarlett Rose by her side, holding on to her hand. Her eyes briefly cut to mine, then away.

Marlowe bustled me into a car waiting on the quay-side. Aspen climbed into the other side. Blay was nowhere to be seen. Nor was Nolen. He must have gone with Blay. The compression in my lungs reduced my breaths to a shallow wheeze. I rubbed a fist against my chest.

"I don't understand what happened."

"Neither do I. One thing at a time, though, yes?" Marlowe rubbed my arm. Aspen looked shell-shocked, her skin the color of alabaster. I bit my lip, staring out the window. Not all that long ago, we were out here, waiting to board the ship. And now... and now...

Tears broke free, streaming down my face. I let them fall. Marlowe handed me a tissue. I took it, plucking it to shreds. She handed me another one. I managed a grateful smile.

"Blaize is tough. Trust me. I've known him most of my life, and if anyone can survive two bullet wounds and come out the other side, it's him."

"Two?" I'd clocked the wound to his leg. Where was the other one? Oh God, not his heart. Or any other vital organs.

Marlowe bit her lip. "He took one to the shoulder."

"Whoever did this..." Aspen's bitter voice snapped through the air. "I'll see them in hell."

The fifteen-minute journey from the port to the hospital was the longest trip of my life. I stumbled out of the car before the driver brought it to a complete stop, and ran into the building. Aspen and Marlowe ran after me. Marlowe went up to the reception desk and found out where they'd taken Blay. Nolen rose to his feet as we arrived in the waiting room. He wrapped his arms around his wife and kissed her forehead. The moment of intimacy made my chest ache. I'd known Blay for less than two weeks, yet our connection was just as strong. Would he ever hold me like that again? Would he kiss my forehead and encase me in his arms?

"He'll be fine." The icy rage on Aspen's face had dulled, but her eyes burned with a desire for vengeance. I understood her feelings all too well. "What did the doctors say?" She directed this question to Nolen.

"He's in surgery."

"Did they give a prognosis?"

Nolen shook his head. He grimaced as he looked at his wife. "They said he's lost a lot of blood."

My knees gave way. I stumbled to a chair and sank into it. Nausea swirled in my stomach. I doubled over, clutching my abdomen, breathing through my nose to quell the sickness.

"Here." Nolen handed me a bottle of water. "Take small sips."

I couldn't manage a smile. Unscrewing the top, I did as he suggested, and it helped a little.

"Have you called your parents?" Marlowe asked.

"Yeah. They're on their way, but it'll take them a few hours to get here. I called Kadon, too. He headed straight for the airport." He sat beside me. Marlowe took the seat on his other side. Raking his hands through his hair, he left them there.

"Did he say anything in the ambulance?" I was glad Aspen had the presence of mind to ask questions, because I couldn't manage a single one.

Nolen shook his head. "He was pretty out of it. They gave him something. No idea what."

I stood and began pacing. Sitting felt redundant. Walking felt like I was doing something, even if there was nothing I could do. On my tenth turn, Addison, Kelsey, and Raya barreled toward me. They surrounded me, just as they had back on the ship.

"We brought you your phone, in case you needed it." Kelsey handed it to me. "We can go, or stay. Whatever you want."

Tracie Delaney

"Stay," Aspen answered before I could. "The more support he has, the better."

Despite the love in this room, I felt alone. Alone and desperate and so very frightened. The feelings I had for Blay had crept up on me with the stealth of a panther, but they were undeniable. The possibility of losing him had fast-tracked me to where I now was. Facing up to the reality that I'd fallen in love with a man I'd known for less time than most family summer holidays.

Would I ever get the chance to tell him? I doubted he felt the same way, but the scent of death in the air was a leveler. To love a man like Blay made me luckier than most, and whatever his feelings for me, he deserved to know.

"The police are here."

I jerked at the sound of Nolen's voice. It had been a while since anyone had spoken. He rose to greet them. I did the same. Aspen joined us, too. Preliminary inquiries, they said, but wanted to know if we had any information to share. Aspen told them about the man we'd seen running away. I was glad she'd seen him, too, so the weight of giving a description hadn't fallen only on my shoulders. I backed up what she'd said as the police officer took notes. After we'd finished, Nolen led the police officer to one side, away from me and Aspen.

"What's that about?" I queried.

She shrugged, sitting down. Nolen returned a few minutes later. He whispered something to Marlowe, then resumed the same position as the rest of us. Waiting. Hoping. Praying. If I'd thought the fifteen-minute drive to the hospital had taken forever, then the interminable wait for news was a torture I wouldn't wish on my worst enemy.

Night fell, and still we waited. I didn't believe in no news being good news. Not in cases like this, anyway. No news meant the surgeons were having to work longer and harder. What if his heart stopped, and his brain didn't get enough oxygen? The vibrant man I'd fallen in love with reduced to someone who depended on medical care for the rest of his life.

What if he didn't make it?

My hands shook like an addict craving a fix. I jammed them under my armpits, my stomach turning over and over. Addison must have sensed my growing panic because she put her arms around me and hugged me, whispering comforting words in my ear.

Nolen shooting to his feet alerted me to the doctor approaching us, his mouth grim. Sweat trickled between my breasts, despite the efficient air-conditioning. I slurped a lungful of air, holding it. Slowly, in case my legs didn't hold, I stood up.

"Blaize Kingcaid's family?"

Why had he asked? He must have known we were.

"Yes," Nolen replied. "Just tell us, Doctor. We're straight shooters."

He might be. I wasn't sure I was. Addison clasped my hand. I held on to her, and the breath I couldn't seem to let go.

"It was touch and go for a while. We had to give him several bags of blood, but he finally pulled through."

"Oh, thank God." I sagged against my best friend.

"But I'm afraid we couldn't save his leg."

What? What did he say?

"We had to amputate below the knee. I'm very sorry."

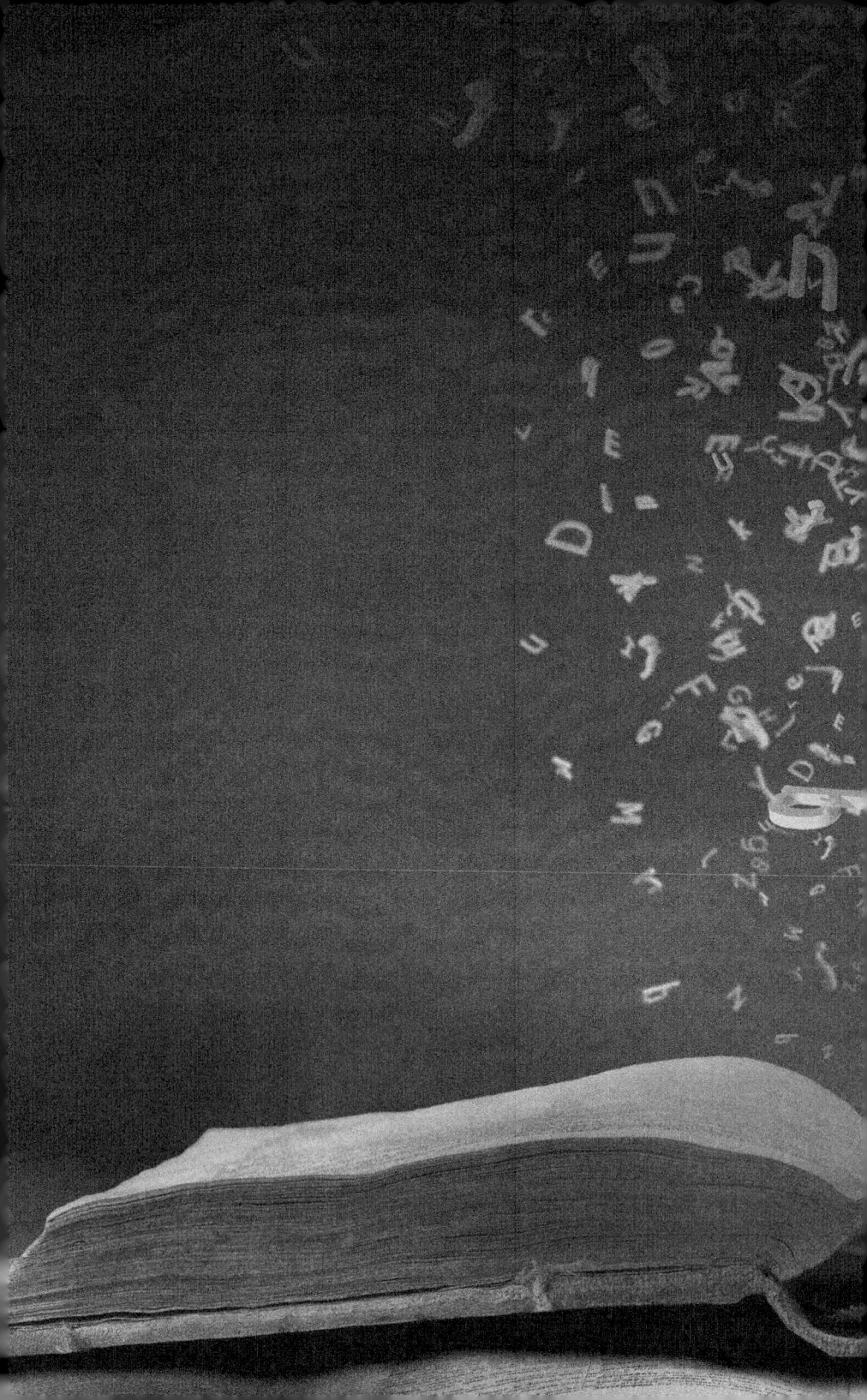

Chapter 23

Jill

Hey knife, meet heart.

FIREWORKS EXPLODED IN MY EARS. I COULDN'T HAVE heard correctly. Amputate? No. No, no, no. I looked at Nolen for reassurance. He had his shit together. He was calm and in control. He'd have listened properly, unlike me.

I'd never seen a man look sicker.

Oh God. It was true.

"Can we see him?" Nolen asked.

"Shortly. He's heavily sedated, and we'll keep him that way for a while longer. I'll have a member of staff take you to him. A maximum of two at a time, though."

I shut out the rest of the conversation. Blay. A vibrant, funny, kind, beautiful man was about to face the battle of his life. Try as I might, I couldn't imagine being robustly healthy one moment, and then the next... the next...

I clasped both hands to my chest, squeezing my eyes closed. The pain was so intense, so sharp, that I struggled to breathe. My lungs cut off the air they desperately needed. My head swam. I screamed but didn't emit a single sound. The screaming was all in my head.

"Mom, Dad." Nolen's strangled voice jerked me to the present. He strode down the corridor, meeting his parents halfway. The three of them hugged. Embraces followed for Marlowe and Aspen. "Kadon's on his way. He should be here in the next few hours. You just missed the doctor."

"And?" his father asked.

"They had to take his leg."

His mother paled, and his father had to prop her up. I couldn't even begin to imagine how she felt. My agony made it hard to stay upright, but her pain must have been on an entirely different level. She'd carried him, raised him, loved him his entire life. Thirty-one years. I hadn't even known him for thirty-one days. Not even half of that.

"We'll all have to rally," his father said grimly. "I won't allow this to destroy my son. He'll need our support, and every damn one of us is going to give it."

"Do you even need to say that, Dad?"

His father's face crumpled. "No. No, I don't."

Nolen patted his shoulder. "It's okay. We're all in shock."

"I want to see him." His mother squared her shoulders. "I want to see my son."

"The doctor said he'd come get us when we could see him."

"I want to see him now." She took hold of her husband's hand, and the two of them strode away.

Nolen gave a crooked grimace. "Poor doc had better prepare himself. He's about to come face-to-face with the indomitable Sandrine Kingcaid. We should send help."

Somehow, Aspen managed a grin. "Yeah, when Aunt Sandrine gets going, everyone ducks for cover."

The Kingcaid in-family jokes circled around me. I'd never felt like more of an outsider than I did right then. They didn't mean it, but I felt it all the same.

"Maybe... maybe I should go. Leave you all to it. You're his family."

Aspen's eyes flashed open wide. *"Excuse me?* You do know my cousin is in love with you, right? Even if he is a distance away from being able to admit it to himself. But that's Blaize. An asshole at times. Make no mistake, though. That man is deep, deep, deep in love with you. Which means you have as much right to be here as any of us do."

The unexpectedness of her statement shook me to my core. She had it wrong. She had to. Blay didn't love me. He lusted after me, liked spending time with me. We enjoyed each other's company. But love? No. He'd made it clear that relationships were a distraction, and while he'd tentatively broached the subject of us continuing to see each other after the cruise was over, I doubted he'd meant in a boyfriend-slash-girlfriend scenario. More of a "Hey, you're in town. Fancy a hookup?" kind of thing.

"I-I..."

"Jill." Aspen clasped my upper arms. "Blaize is going to need us. *All* of us. Especially you. I'm sure it hasn't escaped your notice what a self-sufficient, confident man he is. That he's lost a limb is going to hit him hard. If you leave now, what does that say to him?"

Horror struck me in the chest. She thought I was looking for a way out because Blay had lost his *leg?* "Wait a minute... That's not why I said what I said."

"I know that, you silly girl." She gave me a little shake. "Good God. Do I have to bash your head against the wall?"

"I'd rather you didn't," I muttered.

She smiled then, far more genuine than the one she'd summoned for Nolen. "I know you don't believe he loves you. It's written all over your face, which means he hasn't told you yet. And maybe he isn't even aware of how deeply he's fallen. But I know my cousin. He needs you, now more than ever." Her face grew serious. "What you have to answer is whether you're in this for the long haul, or, for you, if this was just a fun interlude, a holiday romance, if you will."

It had started out like that, but now? No. *What was the moment it changed?* I couldn't pinpoint it. The days had blended into one another, a seamless stretch of time.

"If I'm welcome, then I'm staying."

"You're more than welcome." Aspen turned to look at her family. "Right?"

"A hundred percent," Nolen said.

Marlowe nodded. "Absolutely."

"And my aunt and uncle will feel exactly the same." Aspen kissed my cheek. "Welcome to the Kingcaid family. Buckle up, buttercup. It's a hell of a ride."

"You can go in now."

Legs trembling, I got to my feet, acknowledging Nolen with a small dip of my chin. Rightly, I'd waited until his mum and dad and Nolen and Marlowe had spent some time with Blay, although Aspen had given up her place in the line to me. I'd protested, but she'd insisted that it was what he'd want. Blay's other brother, Kadon, still hadn't arrived from France, where he lived.

The clock on the wall showed that eighteen hours had passed since Blay and I had reboarded the ship after an idyllic day spent in Barbados. Eighteen hours in which everything had changed.

My heart hammered my rib cage as I made my way toward the intensive care unit. I wasn't sure what to expect, or how I'd react, but whatever happened, I had to hold it together. Breaking down wouldn't do me any good. I needed to draw on my reserves of strength and put on a brave face no matter how desperate the circumstances.

He was alive. That was all I cared about.

The challenge would be making *him* see that.

When the doctors brought him round, I expected he'd be confused, in pain, struggling to comprehend how he'd ended up in the hospital. But when reality set in, I could only imagine the shock. I watched a documentary recently about a sports star who had an accident and ended up paralyzed from the waist down. During the hour-long program, told over a period of a year, he'd gone through all five stages of grief, ending, eventually, at acceptance of his new reality. But it had been tough, on him *and* on those who loved him. We were all in for a rough ride.

The nurse tending to Blay glanced over at me as I entered. She gave me a tight smile, then retreated to a chair in the corner of the room. Blay was hooked up to various machines, the constant beeping something of a reassurance. As long as the machines made that repetitive noise, then Blay was okay.

Tented sheets covered his legs, and his shoulder was bandaged from his other gunshot wound. I still couldn't get my head around it. A gun. To a Brit, the concept was alien, and while guns were far more prevalent in the US, cruise ships were one of the safest places in the world. The security was so tight, and every passenger was checked on and off the ship, as well as having to put their bags and jackets through a scanner, similar to an airport.

I pulled a chair closer and sat, holding his hand. He was so *warm*, so *alive*.

"Hey, you." I bent my head and pressed a kiss to the back of his hand, then rested my cheek on top. "So, everyone's here. Your mum and dad, Nolen, Marlowe. Aspen, too. Kadon is on his way, too." It felt odd to talk about people I hardly knew, and in Kadon's case, I'd never met, but if there was a chance Blay could hear me, I wanted to reassure him, to provide some continuity and familiarity. A one-way conversation wasn't easy. In the end, I pulled out my phone and opened my e-reader app, choosing a thriller I thought Blay might like. I'd gotten through the first chapter when a tap came at the door, and a tall, blond-haired guy with a chin dimple poked his head inside the room.

"Hey, I'm Kadon. Do you mind if I...?" He trailed off, his eyes going to Blay. They narrowed, and his mouth pinched around the edges. "I don't want to intrude."

He spoke as if he was the outsider and I was the gatekeeper. There was something about his demeanor that made me want to give him a hug. I pointed to a second chair. "I'd love the company, unless you'd rather be alone with him."

Kadon shook his head, edging farther into the room, his steps slow and tentative. Eventually, he reached the chair and sat down.

"I can't fucking believe it." He raked a hand through his shaggy hair, grabbing a fistful.

"I think we're all struggling with that one. I'm Jill, by the way." I stuck out my hand. He shook it.

"Yeah, my folks told me. According to Aspen, you're the woman who finally made Blaize Kingcaid fall." He flashed a dazzling grin but struggled to hold it, almost as if he thought smiling was disrespectful to his brother.

"I don't know about that." My eyes drifted to Blay, then back to Kadon. "But when he wakes up, you can guarantee I'm asking him if that's true."

Kadon gave a low, brief chuckle. "You should know that when the Kingcaid men fall in love, they fall hard. There's no escape now. He'll chase you to the ends of the earth." His eyes filled with sorrow as he realized what he'd said. "Fuck. You know what I mean."

I touched his arm. "I know." Sighing, I returned my gaze to Blay. "This is so strange for me."

"How so?"

"I don't know any of you, and if I'm truthful, I hardly

know Blay. Yet I feel as if I've known him all my life, and your family has been so welcoming and understanding under terrible circumstances."

"But?" Kadon coaxed.

How did he know there was a but? Was the entire Kingcaid clan a family of mind readers or something?

"There's an inner voice that keeps telling me I'm intruding. That, in times of crisis, family is what's important."

Kadon said nothing for the longest time, even when I looked at him, waiting for an answer.

"My brother is thirty-one, and do you know how many females have passed through his life since puberty?"

I winced. Jesus. Was he punishing me for something?

"A lot."

Hey knife, meet heart.

"The key phrase here is 'passed through.' Blaize is the consummate playboy. Or, I should say, *was* the consummate playboy. Yet from the brief conversation I had with Aspen, which Nolen backed up, ever since the ship set sail, my brother has glued himself to your side."

"Not quite," I murmured. "He's had a few issues to deal with."

"But he made time to spend with you." Kadon's lips lifted to one side. "My brother doesn't date, Jill. Not really. I figured that out years ago. It was the reason I never bothered to learn the names of any females on his arm. I'd only see them once, so what was the point? What I'm trying to say is that you have as much of a right to be here as any of us. Almost two weeks with Blaize? That's like... twenty years in most people's books. Trust me." He touched my hand. "He wants you here."

I placed my hand over the top of his, feeling oddly connected to a man I'd only just met.

"Thank you."

"No." His eyes crinkled with a smile. "Thank *you*."

Chapter 24

Jill

You're a Kingcaid now.

THE ONLY THING THAT MADE ME LEAVE BLAY'S SIDE was an urgent need to pee and a raging thirst. I left Kadon sitting beside his bed and went in search of a bathroom. On my way back to the ICU I caught sight of Nolen talking to the police. What were they doing back here? Had they found out what had happened? I rushed over, Nolen's red face and fisted hands sending prickles racing along the back of my neck. Whatever the police were saying, it had infuriated him. Marlowe stood on his other side, her hand at his elbow.

"What's going on?"

The police officers glanced at me, then back at Nolen. "We'll be in touch, Mr. Kingcaid," one of them said. They spun on their heels and made their way toward the exit.

"What is it?"

His face contorted with rage, his eyes like balls of fire. "Let's find somewhere private." He beckoned to Aspen. "Go get Kadon so I only have to say this once."

The hair at my nape lifted, and goose bumps covered my arms. "Is it bad?"

Nolen grimaced. "It ain't fucking good. Wait here. I'll find a private space for the family to talk."

Unsure of whether that included me, I crossed over to where my friends were sitting. They'd stayed here the entire night. As much as my heart ached for Blay, it burst with love for these women.

"What's going on?" Addison asked, straightening from where she'd slumped in her seat. She looked as exhausted as I felt.

"I'm not sure yet. But listen, you should go and get some rest." Would they be allowed back on the ship? It'd be a crime scene, wouldn't it? And if so, where would everyone stay?

"You need rest yourself," Kelsey said.

"I'll rest when Blay's awake. There's nothing you can do, though. Go get something to eat and have a break. Really. I'll only worry if I know you're here hanging around when there's nothing you can do."

"You sure?"

"Positive."

Kelsey nodded, nudging Addison and Raya into standing. The three women individually hugged me, and then we had a group hug. Addison glanced over her shoulder as the three of them walked away. Making a phone signal with her thumb and little finger, she mouthed, "Call me."

I nodded. My heart squeezed as they disappeared through a set of double doors.

"Jill?" Nolen cocked his head, beckoning to me. "You coming?"

Guessed it included me after all. I trudged after the five of them. Nolen waited for me to enter the room he'd secured, then shut the door.

"Before I start, what's said in this room goes no further. We have enough press nosing around trying to dig up dirt without one of us letting something inadvertently slip and giving them a fucking gigantic payday."

"Dude," Kadon said. "We hardly need a lesson on how to zip it."

"I think he means me." Nolen opened his mouth, possibly to refute what I'd said. I held up my hand, smiling. "It's okay. If I were in your shoes, I'd feel the same. You've been kind enough to include me, but you don't know me. Not really. It's smart to proceed with caution. And in case it needs saying, if there's a leak, I guarantee it won't have come from me."

He nodded curtly. "The police arrested the man you guys saw running away from Scarlett's penthouse. He came clean pretty quickly. Turned out he'd been hired by Jeremy Herdson to steal Scarlett Rose's jewelry."

I frowned. "Who's Jeremy Herdson?"

"Scarlett's ex-hubs," Aspen said.

My eyebrows shot up. "Why would he do that?"

A muscle pulsed in Nolen's cheek. "Scarlett cut off Jeremy's alimony, and, well, let's just say he was pissed about it. So he decided he'd help himself to what he believed she owed him. He knew her well enough to guess she'd have some of her most expensive pieces of jewelry on a cruise. I'd wager that she had her home in LA sewn up, preventing him from getting within a mile of the gates. But he couldn't do it alone, which is when he devised a plan to get someone past security and on board to commit the crime. He found out that one of Serenity's IT technicians had run up a large gambling debt with the wrong people. They were demanding their money back—with a sizable interest percentage on top. Jeremy swooped in with a solution. He'd pay off the debt if this technician took down the badge scanners long enough to smuggle someone on board and past security."

"Which he did, obviously." Aspen looked as if she was close to murdering someone. The technician was probably first in line. If she didn't murder him, I might.

"Yep."

"Do we know who the technician is?" Blay's dad asked.

"We do. The police have him in custody."

"What about Jeremy?" Aspen's fisted hands drummed against her thighs.

"Los Angeles police should have picked him up by now."

"Good." I ground my teeth. "I hope he gets a good long stretch in jail."

"There's more bad news, I'm afraid." Nolen locked eyes with his dad. "The lowlife Jeremy hired shot three people as he ran off the ship. A security guard and two passengers. Two of them died. The other one has a shattered arm, but other than that, she'll be fine."

My hand flew to my mouth. "Oh, no." A person just doing their job and a passenger enjoying a well-earned holiday. Two innocent lives snuffed out through no fault of their own.

"Fortunately, Scarlett and her assistant are okay. A little shaken up, but that's all. We'll need to prepare a statement, Dad."

Nolen's father nodded, his jaw flexing. "I'll call Eric."

I didn't know who Eric was. Probably PR. God, what a mess.

Something Nolen had said on the ship came back to me. *"Marlowe, untie her."* He must have meant Scarlett Rose. God. As much as I wasn't fond of the woman, no one deserved that. She must've been terrified. That whole time was a blur in my mind. It kept coming back to me in snatches that made no sense, the only clear vision one of Blay lying on the ground, critically injured.

"Would you excuse me for a moment?" I brushed past Nolen, past Marlowe, past them all, dashing toward the hospital entrance. I needed air. I couldn't breathe in there. The walls closed in on me. I'd suffocate if I stayed here a second longer.

I burst through the doors and into the brilliant sunshine. An ambulance whizzed by, its sirens blaring. I stared after it, biting my lip. Another family or friends of a loved one were about to go through hell. A bench nearby called to me. I slumped into it and let my head fall into my hands. My heart galloped too fast. I took several deep breaths through my nose, letting them out slowly. My heart slowed, and the sense of panic faded. It'd be okay. He was alive, and he'd make a full recovery. He had to.

"Hey."

I twisted my head. Aspen approached, her steps

cautious. I tapped the space next to me. She sat and put her arm around my shoulders. "It's a lot, isn't it? Especially for you. Not exactly what you signed up for, I guess."

I couldn't tell if she was testing me or if she was being genuinely sympathetic. "There are lots of things we don't sign up for, but life is filled with challenges, and it's how we respond to them that matters. I'm going nowhere."

A myriad of emotions traveled across her face. Her eyes softened, and she reached out to clasp my hand. "You're a keeper, Jill."

"I hope Blay thinks the same."

She chuckled. "It still throws me off when you call him that."

"I guess I kind of like being the only one who uses it."

"I don't mean to play know-it-all here, but I do think there's something I should explain, to help prepare you for when Blaize wakes up."

Prickles raced along the back of my neck. "Okay."

"My cousin is a proud man. Honestly, our entire family has way too much of the pride gene. We're also 'blessed,' if you can call it that, with oodles of self-confidence and a healthy amount of competitiveness."

"Your point being?"

"When Blaize wakes up, he's going to have a hard time coming to terms with what's happened."

"Who wouldn't?"

"True. But for him... if it were Nolen or Asher, then I wouldn't be as worried. But Blaize is going to *hate* having to depend on people for the most basic of needs. I mean, sure, they'll fit him with a prosthetic, and knowing my cousin, he'll work his ass off until he's back to being as close to the man he was before as possible. But on that journey, he's going to get frustrated and angry, and he'll probably hit out at those he loves the most."

I'd kind of expected all this. Even though I hadn't known Blay all that long, I *knew* him. I couldn't explain it, but it was as if we'd met in a previous life. We'd clicked from that very first meeting, and we'd only gotten closer as each day had passed. Of course he'd be angry and frustrated and sad. Losing a limb would push him into the grief cycle. But eventually, he'd come out the other side and accept his new reality. I planned to be there every step of the way.

"You seem so confident that he loves me, yet he hasn't said he does."

"Honey, I don't think he knows himself. And even if he does, he'll rail against it. Blaize is a playboy, a grazer, a one-and-done kind of guy. Or at least he was. Until you. So it wouldn't surprise me if he's in complete denial. But trust me. He's fallen hard." She patted my arm. "You might have to wait longer than you would have for him to admit it, given what's happened. You mark my words, though. That man is a goner."

I leaned over and kissed her cheek. "Thank you for being a friend."

"Like I said, you're in the bosom of the Kingcaid family now. We take care of our own. I'm here for whatever you need." She got up, cocking her head. "How about a bite to eat? They have a passable cafeteria, from what my uncle Jameson told me. Gotta keep your strength up."

I wearily rose to my feet. "Guess so." I linked her arm, and we trudged inside.

Chapter 25

Blaize

Why am I getting a bad feeling about this?

Fuck me.

Pain. Sharp, hot, unrelenting.

I forced my eyes open. A light flickered overhead. My lids fell shut. I shifted my weight and groaned.

"Blaize."

A hand touched mine, fingers curling in a gentle grip. I opened my eyes again, moving my head toward the voice.

"Mom." I tried to smile. Not sure if I managed it or not, but Mom smiled back.

"You sound like you've smoked forty cigarettes straight."

She rose from her chair and brushed a strand of hair out of my eyes. Funny how it didn't matter how old I got—Mom's tender touch always took me back to my childhood.

"Your dad's here. He's just gone outside to get me a cup of coffee."

I licked my lips. "Thirsty."

"Nurse?" Mom looked over her shoulder. "He's thirsty. Can he have something to drink?"

A straw appeared, nudging at my lips. I gulped down the water. She pulled it away too soon.

"Do you remember what happened?"

"Yeah. I got shot." I tried to lift my left arm. A searing agony exploded in my shoulder. "Fuck."

"Try to stay still. Everything's still raw."

"How long was I out?"

"About forty hours. You kind of came around earlier this morning, but you went right back to sleep."

I had no memory of that. "Christ." I let my head sink further into the stack of pillows. "What about the ship?"

"Darling." Mom's head angled to the side, her eyes filled with reprimand. "There's plenty of time for that."

"I want to know. I *need* to know."

"Your dad will explain when he gets here. Nolen, Marlowe, and Kadon are outside. Aspen, too." She took my hand again. "And Jill. I do like her, Blaize. You chose well." A hint of a teasing smile lifted her lips. "Took you long enough."

"Jill's here?" I croaked.

"She's stayed by your bed most of the time, but they only allow two of us in here at once. We often have to crowbar her out of here."

I swallowed. My throat was so damn raw. "I want to see her."

The door opened, and my heart rate spiraled, but

instead of my girl walking through the door, a doctor entered instead.

"Mr. Kingcaid. How are you feeling?" He shined a light into my eyes. "Welcome back."

"I'd feel better if you didn't burn my retinas with that thing."

The doctor chuckled. "Good spirits. That's helpful." He beckoned to the nurse. "Can you take his vitals?" He looked at Mom, then at me. "And then we can have a chat."

Mom nibbled on her bottom lip. "My husband isn't here yet. And I'd like the rest of my family to be here if that's okay?"

I frowned. *Why am I getting a bad feeling?*

"Of course."

Mom rose to her feet. "I'll be right back, sweetheart."

"Mom, wait."

She paused midstep, then pivoted. "Yes, darling?"

"What's going on?" I tried to sit up, almost passing out as pain ripped through my shoulder. "Shit, that fucking hurts."

"Blaize, lie down. I'll be two minutes."

I let her go, mainly because I didn't have the energy to fight her. I felt weak, helpless, and I didn't fucking like it. So many questions fired through my mind.

Who was the guy who'd shot me?

Was Scarlett okay?

How the fuck did this happen?

I needed answers. Not knowing was driving me crazy. A cage was over my leg, the covers draped on top. I guessed the bullet had shattered a bone. Damn. I hoped they'd managed to pin it back together again. Fuck only knew how long that'd take to heal. Six weeks, two months, longer?

The door opened again, and my stomach did several backflips.

"Jill." I held out my right hand, gesturing to her. "There's my girl."

Her eyes glistened. "Your mum said to come in. She's gathering everyone else together." Sitting in the chair my mom had vacated, Jill rested her forehead against my hand. "I thought you were dead."

Pain was etched in every word. I wanted nothing more than to take it away. "Tilly. Look at me."

She sat up. Fat tears clung to her eyelashes, a couple falling as she blinked.

"It'd take more than a bullet to tear me away from you."

More tears fell. She dashed them away with the back of her hand, almost as if she was embarrassed to let me see her cry. Before I could reassure her, the rest of my family filed in. Mom, Dad, Nolen, Marlowe, Kadon, and Aspen.

Goddamn, it had to be bad because they all looked as if they were attending a wake. Their worry couldn't be about me. I was fine. Sure, my shoulder hurt like a motherfucker, and my leg was killing me, too.

At least I wasn't dead.

My business, on the other hand... Christ, I hoped and fucking prayed it wasn't irrecoverable, that my worst fears hadn't come to fruition.

"Mr. Kingcaid, I wanted to talk to you about your injuries and your prognosis." My family parted to allow the doctor to stand closer to me. "Are you in any pain?"

"Yeah, my shoulder hurts like a bitch, and my leg feels as if someone's run over it with an eighteen-wheeler."

Mom averted her gaze, and I couldn't help but notice she felt for Dad's hand. I cast a glance around the rest of my family. Nolen had his poker face on, as did Kadon. Marlowe smiled kindly, and Aspen looked worried.

As for Jill, she kept her eyes trained on me, her fingers entwined with mine.

"Which leg is that?" the doctor asked.

Odd question.

"Which do you think? The one the bullet hit. The right one. Jeez. Are you okay, Doc?"

Nolen and Kadon traded a glance. Mom tightened her hold on Dad's hand. Aspen suddenly found the floor far more interesting. Marlowe's smile remained in place as if she were frozen.

Everything in my chest shifted. I looked at Jill. "Tell me."

She transferred her gaze to the doctor.

"No. Don't look at him. Whatever the fuck is going on, I want *you* to tell me."

"Blay, please. The doctor can explain it better than I can."

Fuck. This was not good. Not good at all.

Prickles raced over my skin, and my pulse skittered. I snapped my eyes to the doctor.

"No bullshit. Give it to me straight."

The doctor nodded. "The bullet went right through your shoulder, but it didn't hit any bone. You've got a fair amount of soft-tissue damage, but it'll heal in time."

"And my leg?"

His lips thinned, and he stood up a bit straighter. "Despite the tourniquet your brother applied, when we got you into surgery, we couldn't stop the bleeding. Added to that the catastrophic damage to your tibia and fibula, I'm afraid it left us with only one choice."

"Which was?" *Christ, it's like twenty fucking questions.*

"We had to amputate your right leg, below the knee."

"Right." I waited for panic to hit me. It never came. "So what happens now?"

Mom's eyes flitted between me and Dad and back to me. "Blaize, did you hear what the doctor said?"

God bless Mom. She clearly thought because I wasn't throwing things and screaming bloody murder that I hadn't absorbed what he'd said. I'd absorbed it fine.

I only had one leg.

But I was here. Alive. Ready to fight on. Ready to save my fucking business from total collapse.

It was just a leg. I could afford the best prosthetic money could buy.

"Yeah." I reached out for her hand, squeezing it. "I heard. It's fine, Mom."

"We can arrange for you to talk to a therapist," the doctor said. "What's happened to you is life changing. In my experience—"

"No need for a therapist," I snapped. "I'm perfectly fine."

"Blaize." A round tear clung to Mom's lower lashes, then dripped down her cheek. "Think about it."

"Aww, Mom. Don't cry. I don't need to spill my guts to

a therapist. I'm alive. That's all that matters, right? Could have been far worse."

Aspen traded looks with Nolen. Kadon scrutinized me with narrowed eyes.

I turned to Jill, who gnawed on her lower lip. "I'm not in shock. I'm completely coherent."

"It's a lot to take in." Jill touched my undamaged shoulder.

"I know. But I'm okay. Sure, I'll have to adjust, and it'll be fucking hard, but if they hadn't taken the leg, I'd be dead. Better alive with three limbs than dead with four."

My family all looked at one another as if I were ready for my padded cell.

"Guys, stop. I'm not faking it. I can buy a fucking new leg."

"Oh, Blaize." Mom's tears came faster now, one after another tripping down her face and spilling onto the hospital bedsheets. I ran my thumb over her hand, my intent to reassure. All that did was make her cry harder.

"Dad, why don't you take Mom outside for a bit of fresh air? In fact, why don't you all go?" I clasped Jill's wrist. "You stay. And Nolen. I want to know what happened."

"Okay, son." Dad moved forward and kissed my cheek. "Don't worry about the business. I'm taking care of everything."

My chest collapsed. Having Dad swoop in and clean up the mess I'd made was ten times worse than losing a leg. I'd rather lose both legs and keep my father's faith in me.

I painted on a smile, even as my insides shriveled.

I'd let Dad down,

I'd let the Kingcaid name down,
I'd let *myself* down.

A man had gotten on my ship with a firearm. Was I the only one who'd been injured? Had he shot Scarlett after me? What about her assistant lying on the ground? Was she dead?

"Thanks, Dad. You're the best."

"Just get well. That's your only job for the foreseeable future."

He couldn't have said anything worse, and still I kept that fake smile in place.

"Sure thing."

I waited until they'd all filed out, then my eyes snapped to Nolen. "Talk."

"Blay, are you sure you want to—?"

"I want to hear everything." I didn't shift my gaze from Nolen. "Everything. Don't fucking treat me like an invalid. This is still my fucking business, and I want to know how badly fucked it is."

Disbelief stirred in his eyes. I flattened my lips.

"I know you think I'm in some sort of denial, and who the fuck knows? Maybe I am. But right now, my focus is Kingcaid Cruises. All I remember is visiting Scarlett to smooth things over after I ignored her latest attempt to make me jump through hoops to satisfy her demands. I almost walked away when her assistant didn't answer the door, but I heard something that made me use my access card to gain entry. The next thing I remember was a white-hot pain in my shoulder, and then my leg went from underneath me. After that, it's all hazy or nonexistent. Is Scarlett okay? What about her assistant?"

"Scarlett is fine. A little shaken up but unharmed." Nolen pulled up a chair and sat. "Her assistant has a concussion, but she'll be fine, too." He chewed the inside of his cheek, and my mouth went dry. He had bad news to impart. I fucking sensed it.

"But?" I coaxed.

"The guy who shot you also shot a security guard and two passengers as he made his escape. One passenger survived, but the other one and the guard didn't make it."

"Fuck." I let my head fall against the pillows, staring at the ceiling.

People were dead.

Dead.

I'd expected bad news, but this was a disaster. The business would never recover from an incident where people lost their lives. It was over. Everything I'd worked for. Gone. The medics had saved my life, only for me to face a new nightmare. A worse nightmare.

But my nightmare was nothing compared to those families'. A cry of agony crawled into my throat. I swallowed it down. I didn't deserve to eject the poison. I deserved to let it eat me from the inside.

"It was the badge scanners, wasn't it? That's how he got on board. That's why they went down that day?"

Nolen nodded. "The man behind it all is Scarlett's ex-husband."

My eyes flew wide. "What?"

"She stopped paying alimony, so he decided to take what he thought she owed him. He blackmailed a member of our IT team who took down the scanners and helped the guy Jeremy hired to carry out the robbery get on board without passing through security."

"Jesus Christ." I swept a hand over my face. "This is bad, Nolen."

"I won't lie. It isn't great. But if anyone can smooth it over, it's Dad."

Dad. Right. Not me. Not with my missing leg and busted shoulder stuck in this godforsaken hospital for fuck knew how long. Not me, who'd fucked up so badly that two people were in the morgue rather than safely tucked up in their beds.

Jill hadn't said a word the entire time. I turned to her now, faking a yawn. I needed them both to go. When I fell apart, I didn't want witnesses trying to placate me when I deserved to feel everything. "I'm tired. Think I'll get some shut-eye. It's a lot to take in."

Her soft eyes bathed me in affection. I felt only numbness combined with a dark cloud that closed in, pulling me under. I barely acknowledged her lips touching my cheek or the slight pressure she applied to my hand as she stood.

"I'll be right outside."

I forced a nod, but a smile was beyond my capabilities. Nolen put his hand on her lower back and eased her outside. The door closed, and I breathed a sigh of relief. I craved the space and time to process the horrific events.

This was all my fault. I'd ruined my business, disappointed my father, lost my leg. But worse than all those things was that I had blood on my hands. Families were grieving because of me. I'd never forgive myself.

And Jill... what use was I to her now? A cripple who couldn't pick her up and carry her to bed, who couldn't step in to protect her. We barely knew each other. She hadn't signed up for this. The kindest thing would be to let her go.

Except I couldn't.

And that might be my biggest sin of all.

Chapter 26

Blaize

A clusterfuck of epic proportions.

THE SOUND OF THE DRAPES SCRAPING AGAINST THE rail forced me to open my eyes. Sunlight burst into my hospital room, bathing the clinical space in warmth.

"Rise and shine." Mara, the nurse my father had hired to take care of me here in the hospital and when I returned to Miami at some point today, hit me with a beaming smile. "It's release day."

"You make it sound as if I'm in prison, and I'm getting early parole for good behavior."

She smiled wider, although how that was possible was anyone's guess. Mara had a permanent grin on her face. I'd never come across someone so happy in their work. She should bottle that shit and sell it. She'd make millions overnight.

"We both know there've been times when your behavior was anything but good."

I cringed. "All right. No need to rub my nose in it."

Two fucking weeks I'd been holed up in this hospital. Two fucking weeks where I'd traversed a whole range of emotions, some so dark I'd scared myself. The nightmares were the worst, though. Mara reassured me they'd eventually fade, but the masochist in me wasn't sure I wanted them to. Hell, I didn't deserve them to.

News of the funerals of the two people who'd died had reached me a few days ago. That had been one of my worst days. I'd spent hours on my iPad trawling news sites for every shred of information, barking at anyone who'd interrupted me. The security guard had left behind a wife and three daughters. The passenger, a twenty-eight-year-old newlywed on her honeymoon, had left behind a devastated widower. They'd never celebrate their first wedding anniversary, never feel the joy of their first child. Never grow old together.

I felt myself spiraling. I gripped the covers and took a few deep breaths, and after a minute, the iciness coating my skin vanished. Mara set a tray in front of me. Overcooked scrambled eggs, undercooked bacon, limp toast. Coffee that was a crime to caffeine lovers everywhere. I pushed it away.

"Tell the hospital cook his food still sucks. You'd think after the number of times I've given him feedback, some of it would stick."

She chuckled. "I think he made it extra dreadful for you today. A celebration of your last day."

"Lucky me." I gazed out the window. Jill would be

here soon. She hadn't missed a single day since I'd arrived here, unconscious and bleeding. My parents had gone back to Seattle, mainly so Dad could clean up my mess, and Kadon and Aspen had pressing work issues to deal with, so they had left once they were certain I wouldn't try to off myself. Nolen and Marlowe had stuck around for a week, but on our scheduled arrival date in Miami, they'd had to return to Vegas.

Lives moved on. Apart from the two people who'd died. They didn't get to move on.

"Hey." Mara flicked my arm. "I know that face. Quit it."

"Quit my face?" I screwed up my nose. "How the fuck do I do that?"

She rolled her eyes. "Jesus, I deserve a medal for taking this job."

"You can pack it in any time you want to."

She grinned. "The very fact that you'd enjoy that is the one reason I won't do it."

I smiled in response, although it felt weird to perform an action meant to show happiness when my insides were rotting day by day. It was impossible to offend Mara. Hell, I'd tried. Not on purpose, but I'd run the entire gamut of emotions during my stay in the hospital, and Mara had been around for most of them. I preferred her to Danesha, who worked here on a permanent basis. She was one scary motherfucker. Even I didn't dare to cross her.

"Knock, knock." Jill poked her head inside my hospital room, wearing a bright smile. She'd tried so fucking hard to keep up my spirits, and yet I couldn't stop the thoughts running through my mind that she deserved better than

251

this. Better than being stuck with a cripple she hardly knew. For selfish reasons, I hadn't broached the subject with her yet. I needed her even if I hated that I did. I couldn't bear to face the next few weeks alone.

If she lasted that long, given my foul mood swings. If *I* lasted that long without fucking it up.

"Hey." I forced a smile. They used to come so easily to me. Not now. I felt like a fake every time I lifted my lips. "I'm so glad you're here." That wasn't a lie. She grounded me. "Dad messaged earlier. The jet is fueled and ready to go as soon as this dragon organizes my release papers." I jerked my head toward Mara.

"Careful. I have a mean right hook."

"You love me."

She looked over at Jill. "At least I only have to put up with him until he's back on his feet. You, sweetcheeks, are stuck with him for life."

Jill laughed. "I can handle him." She knitted our fingers together, and I stole her warmth, her goodness, her *wholeness,* bringing them to my lips to kiss them.

"Let's get you up and ready, then. No point in you taking up a much-needed bed any longer than necessary." Mara peeled back the covers. I avoided looking at the space where my leg once was.

"You're all heart."

The entire time Mara helped me dress, I kept an eye out for signs of pity from Jill. There wasn't a single one. I couldn't love her more. I'd never deserved her less. A less self-centered man would do the kindest thing and let her go. I couldn't bring myself to do it.

Having two burly guys carry me up the steps to the

company jet was the single most humiliating experience of my entire life. That Jill was there to witness it only made it worse. By the time they had me settled in a plush leather seat, my mood was in the shitter. How could a single car journey and being carried from a car to a plane exhaust me? I hadn't been this tired after running the Boston Marathon. Was this how it would be from now on? The smallest activity resulting in having to take a nap?

I couldn't bear it.

"You okay?" Jill's hand landed on my uninjured shoulder. "Can I get you anything?"

"A new leg?" I flashed a grin. Pain leached across Jill's face, and she winced. "Too soon?"

"Maybe a little."

She took the seat opposite while Mara wrapped a blood pressure cuff around my bicep and clipped a pulsometer to my forefinger. Satisfied that I'd passed the bar she'd set, she removed them, then retreated to a seat across the aisle. I closed my eyes, only vaguely aware of the taxi ride to the runway, and by the time the engines roared ready for takeoff, the undeniable pull of sleep dragged me under.

"We're here."

I forced my eyes open. Jill was standing over me, her beautiful face bathed in light. I blinked, yawned, and rubbed my eyes.

"Good. I'm ready to get home."

Being carried down the airplane steps to the Escalade waiting at the bottom of the stairs was just as mortifying. The sooner I got a fake fucking leg and learned how to use it, the better. Unfortunately, I had to wait for the stump to heal before the doctors could fit even a temporary one.

Stump. What a vile word that was. Surely medics should be able to come up with an alternative. I might have to invent one just so I didn't cringe every time it popped into my head.

How the fuck had this happened to me? What a clusterfuck of epic proportions. The media had mostly been supportive and kind. Some of the online comments were less so, but that was to be expected these days. Online trolls loved nothing more than to nail an already severely wounded man in the balls.

As the car sped through the gates and up to my sprawling Miami mansion, a sense of relief washed over me. Home at last. I couldn't help but think, though, that this wasn't Jill's home. Hers was an entire ocean away, and who knew how long she'd stick around once reality set in? So far, she'd remained resolute, determined to stay despite owing me two-fifths of fuck all. I took nothing for granted. Not her feelings, or my own.

Things changed in the time it took a butterfly to flap its wings. Jill could realize her loyalty to me had vanished at the same time my leg had and was only sticking around because the optics of the alternative didn't look good.

Renata, my housekeeper, stood by the front door, her rosy cheeks puffed up from the big smile she wore. The familiarity should have soothed me. It didn't. It just reminded me of what a mess I'd made of everything. The car drew to a halt. Mara climbed out of the front seat and brought a wheelchair around to the rear. She opened the door and gave me one of her don't-mess-with-me smiles.

"Home sweet home. Here, give me your arm."

"I can manage," I growled, gripping the arms of the chair and hoisting myself into it. All those pull-ups and tricep dips at the gym had come in far handier than I'd ever have thought. I had good upper body strength, and if I was to haul around my two-hundred-pound frame of pure muscle, I'd need it. Probably one ninety now that I was missing half a leg.

I laughed internally at the dark thought. Using humor as a defense mechanism wasn't part of my pre-accident MO, but it sure as fuck had become part of me now. Whatever got me through the day, right?

Jill walked alongside me as Mara pushed me toward the house. Renata bent to kiss my cheek.

"Welcome home, Blaize."

I squeezed her arm and managed a smile. "Thank you, Renata." I took Jill's hand. "This is Jill."

Renata shook Jill's hand. "You must both be hungry and exhausted after your trip. I made your favorite." She winked at me.

Thank fuck she was behaving as she always had. I didn't expect everyone who'd known me when I was a complete man to do the same, and I was prepared for it. Prepared to rip them a new fucking asshole.

"Paella?" Renata made the best seafood paella outside of Spain.

She nodded.

"You know the way to my heart, Renata. If you weren't

already married, I'd marry you in a heartbeat."

She blushed, casting a nervous glance at Jill as if she was expecting a standoff, which was actually pretty funny, considering Renata was old enough to be my grandmother. See? I could still find humor in shit, despite being a leg short.

"Oh, shush. Let's get you inside and fed."

Renata loved to stuff food down people. I swore it was one of the main reasons my family visited. They knew they'd leave with full stomachs. I reached for Jill's hand as Mara pushed me inside. My house looked different from down here. I felt small, vulnerable, fucking helpless. The humor I'd congratulated myself on fled, a cloud of doom descending as my eyes went to the sweeping staircase leading to the second floor. Would I have to install an elevator just to get around my own fucking house? The mere thought sent me spiraling into depression.

"You okay?" Jill squeezed my hand.

I forced a smile I didn't feel. "Peachy."

Her brow furrowed, but she said nothing as Mara wheeled me into the kitchen. Renata had laid on a feast, but as the smell of chorizo and prawns and spicy rice wafted over, my stomach roiled.

"Y'know, I am pretty tired. I think I'll take a nap."

"We've converted the room next to your study into a bedroom," Renata announced, beaming as if it were good news.

It was the worst fucking news. I knew it'd be like this, but faced with the reality, I felt as if someone had walloped me in the face with a baseball bat. In the hospital, I could pretend that it'd all be fine. It wouldn't be fine. My life had irrevocably changed, and there was nothing I could do about it.

"I'll take him." Jill moved behind me. "If you can just point me in the right direction."

"Down the hall and to the left," I said, my voice as gloomy as my thoughts.

Jill didn't speak as we traversed the marble flooring, the wheels of my chair moving with ease. At least I didn't have carpeting throughout the ground floor. That would make it easier to move about. I did not plan on being pushed everywhere. Not a fucking chance. As we passed my study, I held up a hand. "I've changed my mind." Grabbing the rails on the sides of the wheels, I twisted my head to glance up at Jill. "I can take it from here. I have work to do."

I needed to call the families of the deceased. I'd wanted to do it in the hospital, but they'd had enough to cope with in managing their terrible grief and the accompanying funerals. But I had a duty of care, and regardless of my health problems, I intended to carry it out to the fullest.

"Blay." She crouched beside me, much as one would to a child. "I'm worried about you."

My face felt frozen, as if I'd been Botoxed to within an inch of my life. "Don't be." Wheeling myself inside, I pushed the door shut behind me harder than I'd intended, slamming it in Jill's face. I'd caught her crumpled expression moments before the thick oak wood had separated us.

A twinge of guilt twanged my insides. The very last person who deserved my ire was the woman I loved. The woman who'd stood by me despite knowing me less than a month. The woman who'd been nothing but kind and caring and a fucking angel throughout this entire shit show. The woman I still hadn't confessed my feelings to. But nor had she confessed hers to me. It was as if we were both walking a line, unsure of which way to jump and determined to keep our options open.

I maneuvered myself behind my desk and booted up my computer. While I waited, I phoned Carly. My assistant answered on the second ring.

"Blaize. I'm glad you called. Are you home now?"

I'd hardly talked to Carly while in the hospital, preferring to text. She knew me too well, and I'd been afraid she'd see through my "I'm fine" charade to the gut-wrenching fear that threatened to overwhelm me every time I thought about the future. Not just my personal challenges, but also my business. On each occasion I spoke to Dad, he glossed over the problems that had arisen, assuring me all was well and being handled. By him, not me.

I'd failed on such a spectacular level that business degrees would add my fuckup to their curricula. *How Blaize Kingcaid destroyed a cruising empire* would be a subject studied for years to come.

"Yeah. A few minutes ago. Listen, I need the phone numbers for the family members of those who died."

"Oh." She hesitated. "Why?"

My jaw flexed. "Because I fucking said so." In all the years she'd worked for me, I couldn't remember a single occasion where I'd snapped at Carly. It didn't feel good, and yet I couldn't help it. Was this the way it would be now? Me taking out my shitty moods on those who didn't deserve it?

"Right. Sure. Hang on."

I bit my lip, knowing I should apologize. Somehow, though, the words wouldn't come. She reeled off the phone numbers.

"You should know, though, Blaize, that your dad already called them on behalf of Kingcaid Cruises."

Of course he fucking did.

"That doesn't let me off the hook. I'm the CEO," I snapped.

"Who's had his own issues to deal with," she replied softly.

I rubbed a hand over my face. "Look, ignore me. I'm not feeling like myself."

"Blaize." She sighed. "I'm your assistant and, I hope, your friend. If you want to yell, scream, and curse, that's okay with me. I'm here for whatever you need. You're grieving, whether or not you realize it, and you have every right to your feelings. Just do me a favor and don't bottle them up. If you don't feel you can talk to those closest to you, then I'm your girl."

A lump formed in my throat. "Thank you," I rasped. "I'll bear that in mind."

I hung up before I lost control and blurted out how desperately sad I was, how angry and confused, and infuriated. How I felt as if I'd failed in all the things that mattered.

My emotions were all over the place, a pendulum that swung from determination to overcome the challenges that lay ahead, to wanting to shut out the world and become a recluse.

I heaved a sigh, picked up my phone, and made the most painful phone calls of my life.

Chapter 27

Jill

**Near-death experiences have a habit
of changing people.**

"Scarlett Rose is here."

Blay's head snapped up, his eyes narrowing. Since we'd
arrived in Miami two days ago, he'd barely left his study to
eat or sleep, and despite my gentle coaxing, he hadn't even
ventured outside to get some sun on his skin.

After two weeks holed up in a hospital room, I'd have
thought he'd yearn to breathe fresh air, but no. Every time I
suggested it, he did little more than grunt at me, most of the
time not even bothering to look up from whatever had
grabbed his attention.

I kept reminding myself it was early days. He had to

travel the full grief cycle, and he was at the very beginning. I'd gone through something similar when I'd walked away from my parents, even though they'd been completely in the wrong and I wouldn't even say we'd been all that close. I'd still grieved. And despite what some people believed, the feelings you get when dealing with loss weren't on a continuum. They didn't happen in order, moving seamlessly from one to the other.

For me, a year after I'd walked out, leaving the only family I had behind, I'd thought I was over it. Then I'd passed my mum in the street, and she'd looked right at me —or rather, through me—as if I were a stranger instead of a child she'd carried for nine months.

That singular event had undone twelve months of hard work.

"What does she want?"

I hitched a shoulder. "No idea. She's at the front gate. Do you want me to have Renata tell her you're not up to having visitors?"

He considered it, his forefinger rubbing his bottom lip. My stomach tilted. There had been flashes of intimacy while he'd been in the hospital, the odd kiss and cuddle here and there, but since returning home, he treated me almost like one of his staff, barking orders one minute and ignoring me the next.

But however he treated me, I still loved him.

I couldn't stop.

And even if that was possible, I didn't want to stop. I knew abandonment, and I'd never do that to a friend, let alone the man I'd fallen deeply in love with.

"It's fine." He gestured dismissively.

I gave Renata the message, hovering in the foyer like a bloody butler. A minute later, Renata answered the door and in walked Scarlett, accompanied by two burly bodyguards and what I guessed was an assistant, a different woman from the one who'd accompanied Scarlett on the cruise. I couldn't blame her for being overly cautious after what she'd endured.

"Hi." I moved forward, hand outstretched. "I'm Jill. Blaize's girlfriend."

It felt odd to call him Blaize, but Blay was my name for him. A private name. Ours. Just like Tilly was his for me.

"I remember you from the cruise."

Scarlett appeared to have lost all her swagger. She was pale behind her professional makeup, and her hand trembled the tiniest bit as she shook mine.

"I'm so sorry to intrude, but when I heard Mr. Kingcaid had returned home, I had to come. I won't take up much of his time."

Yep. Definitely swagger-less. A near-death experience had the power to change everyone, I guessed.

"He's in his study. If you'll follow me."

Scarlett took two steps, which her bodyguards and assistants mirrored. She stopped, turning to them. "I don't need shadowing. I'm perfectly safe here. You will wait for my return."

A small smile touched my lips. *There's the Scarlett I remember from my brief encounters.*

I led her to Blay's office, knocking once before entering. He'd moved from behind his desk, positioning his wheelchair in front of the sofa lining one wall of his study.

"I'll leave you to it," I said, backing out.

"No, stay." Blay gestured to the couch. "Please sit, Miss Rose. It's nice of you to come."

"It's Scarlett." She blushed a little, adding much-needed color to her pale complexion. "Thank you for seeing me."

Blay leaned forward in his chair. "How are you doing?"

She startled, as if the question had surprised her. Or maybe it was the soft tone he'd used.

Either way, her eyes widened. "Me? I'm fine. It's you I'm concerned about." She shook her head. "I am so very sorry. This is all my fault."

"Nonsense," Blay said.

I wouldn't have been so generous. She might not have pulled the trigger, but she was the one who'd cut off her ex, setting in motion a chain of events that had ended with two people losing their lives and Blay losing his leg.

Not to mention the reputational damage to his business, a worry he'd chosen to share with me.

My face hardened. Scarlett side-eyed me, paling further.

"No. I have some culpability here. I should have known Jeremy wouldn't just accept me cutting him off like that. And while there is no way I could have known the lengths he'd go to, and the horrific outcomes of his actions, I have to shoulder part of the blame."

"Correct," I muttered.

She half smiled at me, then returned her attention to Blay.

"I've learned a rather harsh lesson in humility, Mr.

Kingcaid. I used my fame and fortune as a stick with which to beat people, behaving in a manner diametrically opposed to the way I was raised. In other words, I was a complete bitch most of the time."

She smiled again, tucking her chin to her chest. "It's true what they say. Power corrupts. Except you seem to have escaped its clutches. From now on, I shall try to follow your example, and act with far more class than I have in the past."

She fiddled with the strap on her handbag, running her thumb and forefinger over the soft leather.

"None of us know the ripple effect of things we say or do, Miss Rose. We can only try to do our best. Please try not to let what happened overly burden you. I don't hold you in any way accountable. You were a victim of what happened just as much as I was."

Blay's compassion was far more generous than she deserved. If the roles had been reversed and she'd lost her leg, I doubted she'd be nearly as understanding.

In fact, she'd probably have sued him through every court in the land.

"You're too kind."

Couldn't have said it better myself.

She rose to her feet, sliding the strap of her handbag over her shoulder. "If there is anything I can do, please call me." She handed him a business card. He took it, setting it on the edge of his desk.

I got up, too. "I'll show you out."

"Thanks for coming," Blay said, his lips forming a smile for her he rarely had for me these days.

A twinge of jealousy pinched my insides. "Please follow me, Miss Rose."

I ushered her to the door, glancing back at Blay as we walked through it. His head was turned toward the window, a pensive expression on his face.

I closed the door with a quiet click, a hollow feeling in my stomach.

After Scarlett left, I returned to Blay's office. I didn't knock this time. He was in the same position in which I'd left him, his eyes locked on the window, frowning.

"That's a turn-up for the books, huh?" I kept my voice jolly, perching on the edge of his desk.

He looked at me, his eyes glassy. "Huh?"

"Scarlett," I prompted. "Bet you never expected her to turn up here out of the blue."

"No." He stared out the window again.

"It's a lovely day with a pleasant breeze. I think you should get out of here for a bit. We could go out for lunch, maybe. I'm starved."

A muscle beat in his cheek. "No."

"Blay, come on. It isn't healthy to lock yourself away. Or me, for that matter." I flashed a grin to convey I was only joking.

"No one is forcing you to stay here. You're free to leave at any time."

I gasped. "Are you fucking kidding me right now? I'm trying to help you."

"I don't want your help. Go sell that shit somewhere else." He maneuvered his chair, giving me his back.

My mouth gaped open. He'd shown Scarlett kindness

and respect, and I got an attitude. In my opinion, that was the wrong fucking way around.

"Fine." I marched to the door, wrenching it open. I got halfway through when he spoke.

"Don't go, Tilly."

His voice broke. I spun around. His eyes glistened, filled to the brim with tears.

"I'm sorry. You didn't deserve that. You don't deserve any of this." He covered his face with his hands. "I don't know what to do."

I raced to him, dropping to my knees and threading my fingers into his hair as I held him close. He shook in my arms.

"Blay, listen to me. I know you don't want to talk this through with a stranger, but a therapist might be the answer. Someone who isn't emotionally attached who can help you work through all this."

"No therapist." He gritted the words through clenched teeth. "I don't need a therapist."

I wasn't an expert in mental health, but in my opinion, a therapist could work wonders on his state of mind. But if he kept on insisting he didn't need therapy, there wasn't much I could do to persuade him otherwise."

"Then shout and scream at me all you like, but as long as you want me here, then here is where I'll be."

"All of this is my fault."

"No." I reared back, cupping his cheeks and forcing him to meet my gaze. "None of this is your fault. Why would you think that?"

"Because my company hired that technician. Our background checks should have revealed the extent of his gambling but didn't. The badge scanners went down the day before we sailed, which should have alerted me to a weakness in the system, but I was so fucking determined this would be a success that I ignored the warning signs. People died because I didn't do my fucking job."

My heart cracked like a dry riverbed. Blay was a proud man who shouldered everyone's responsibilities, even when they weren't his to bear.

But this... I refused to let him take the blame for a toxic relationship that had turned sourer than anyone would have foreseen.

"Blay, you're reaching and coming to a nonsensical conclusion. You couldn't have known. And even if your checks had uncovered the fact that the man had a gambling addiction, does that mean he shouldn't be hirable? Of course not. Everyone deserves to contribute as long as they can do the job they're being paid for, no matter their personal demons. You're just as much of a victim as the others. You couldn't have anticipated this, nor should you put that expectation on yourself. The fault lies with Jeremy and the fuckwit who fired the gun." And maybe Scarlett a bit, although I didn't say that. "IT breaks, Blay. The issue with the scanners before we set sail and what the technician did were separate events. Stop blaming yourself, or..."

"Or what?" Fear laced his voice.

"Or you might end up falling too far, and it's a hell of a rough road back."

He gave a heavy, thoughtful sigh. "I hear you."

I wasn't sure he did, but that wouldn't stop me from

repeating the same things over and over until he believed them in his heart.

Getting up, I bent over and kissed his forehead. "How about that lunch?"

His lips curved on one side. "On the patio?"

I'd take it. It was an improvement over the last couple of days. "Sounds great to me."

Blay's moods changed from day to day, hour to hour. Each time we came into contact, I braced myself, watching him like a hawk, reading his body language before I spoke. It was like walking blindfolded around a house scattered with eggshells and trying not to stand on any. I was edgy for another reason, too. Yesterday, a week after we'd returned to Miami, I'd plucked up the courage to email my editor and break the news that I wouldn't make my editing deadline, and I completely understood if they wanted to drop me. If I were them, I would. They were running a business, not a charity.

Whatever happened, I'd have to deal. I didn't have the spoons to devote to rewriting that hunk of a mess. All my energy went into bolstering Blay's spirits and supporting him in the best way I could. So far, she hadn't replied. I kept refreshing my inbox, my heart hammering each time a raft of emails came through before my stomach sank when there wasn't one from her.

The not knowing was far worse than the waiting. If I got dropped, then at least I'd be able to plan for the future, albeit a different one than I'd anticipated. I could easily go back to self-publishing. I'd done it successfully for years, and it wasn't as if I'd starve. I had savings to tide me over until I could muster the enthusiasm to write and start putting books out there again.

My phone vibrated in my pocket. I pulled it out, a smile forming.

"Hey, you."

"Jilly." Addison's bright voice widened my smile. "How are you holding up?"

All three of my friends had called or messaged me every day since they'd flown home from the Bahamas on planes chartered by Kingcaid Cruises after the police impounded the ship. Considering I'd been confined to Blay's hospital room and now his house, they were my connection to normalcy. None of them had broached the subject of why I'd given up my life for a man I'd only met a few short weeks ago, because they knew me. They knew I'd fallen so deeply in love that the idea of leaving him was repellent. The thought hadn't ever crossed my mind, and no matter how tough things got, I was in this for the long haul.

"Good days and bad days."

"And what is today?"

"Half and half." I laughed, but it sounded hollow. "I don't actually think in full days anymore. More like moment to moment."

"You're breaking my heart, Jill."

I pressed my knuckles to my chest and rubbed. "I miss you. I miss you all."

"We're here. You say the word and one or all of us will descend on Casa Kingcaid in a heartbeat."

"I know. But you have your jobs and your lives."

"So? You'd do the same for us."

Yeah. I would.

"Don't be a hero, Jill. For one thing, you don't have the boobs for the Wonder Woman outfit."

I laughed properly for the first time in ages. "And for the other thing?"

"Ah, who cares? It's all about the boobs."

I laughed again. "I love you."

"Same, girl. Same. So, tell me. How is he?"

I sighed, my stomach dropping and the moment of levity vanishing. "One minute, he's like the guy I fell in love with. The next, he's snappy, and vicious with it."

"And knowing you, you're absorbing the punches rather than swinging and landing a few of your own."

"What else can I do, Adds? He's grieving, not just for what's happened to him, but for the impact on the company. He's taken the entire blame on his shoulders, no matter how much I try to tell him it isn't his fault."

"Have you tried calling his family? Asking them to have a word."

"No. I think he'd go nuts if I did that."

"Well, keep it on the back burner. You're no one's punching bag, Jill. Not even a man who's as hurt as Blaize. Remember that."

I nodded, even though she couldn't see me. "I will."

"Don't shoot the messenger, but... do you still love him?"

"Of course!"

"Then my advice, for what little it's worth, is to hang in there. Because when he comes out the other side and realizes what a shit he's been, he's going to need you to help build him back up again. And I'm talking emotionally rather than physically."

"It never occurred to me to do anything else."

"He's lucky to have you, babe. Maybe drop that into the conversation next time he's behaving like a pig."

The smile returned to my face. "Don't be a stranger."

"I don't plan to be. As soon as I finish this darned book and meet my preorder deadline, I'm coming for a visit. Tell Kingcaid to prepare to have his ass kicked with a steel-toe boot if he doesn't buck up his ideas."

"I miss you," I whispered. "I miss all of you."

"We're here, babe. We've got your back. Always."

I hung up, drowning in melancholy and lingering in too much self-pity. *Snap out of it, Jill.* I was about to go looking for Blay when an email notification popped up. My heart skittered, missing several beats. My editor had replied to the message I'd sent yesterday.

Oh, God. Nausea swirled in my belly, and my hands were suddenly clammy. I wiped them on my shorts and forced a deep breath into my lungs.

I thought back to what Blay had said to me in Barbados. *"Rip off the Band-Aid."*

I opened it, scanning the text, my mood soaring as I read each paragraph. She was fine. Better than fine. Hugely supportive. Her message said not to worry, that what was important right now was for me to heal from a terrible ordeal and be around to support those I loved. She ended by saying that when I was ready, she'd be waiting.

My vision blurred, and despite furious blinking, tears dripped down my face, one after another. And once I started, I couldn't stop.

As I dried my tears, something incredible happened. Something so out of the blue that I wouldn't have dreamed it in a million years, yet now seemed so obvious.

I know how to fix the damned novel.

Chapter 28

Blaize

Yep. Still using humor to make it through another fucking day.

Before I'd gotten shot, I'd barely gone a week without having sex.

Now, four and a bit weeks later, despite having a live-in girlfriend who probably spent her waking hours searching for an escape route without it looking as if she was abandoning me in my hour of need, I hadn't even gotten a hard-on, let alone engaged in the act.

Just what every new relationship needed to thrive. A helpless cripple with zero sex drive.

It surprised me that she hadn't left already. I treated her like shit most of the time, yet she responded with more kindness and understanding than I deserved.

If today didn't bring a smile to my face, even a small one that lasted less than a second, then nothing would. In an hour, I had an appointment with one of Florida's top prosthetists who planned to fit me with a temporary limb to replace the one the doctors had hacked off.

Yep. Still using humor to get through the day. Whatever it took, right?

I'd have to have several fittings before my permanent leg was ready, but at least with a temporary one, I could dump this damn chair and learn to walk again, albeit with walking sticks and a ball-busting physio I'd hired to put me through my paces.

I'd regain my fucking independence if it was the last goddamn thing I did.

My libido had better damn well follow. I was too young to give up sex.

"Ready?" Jill poked her head into my study, greeting me with that beautiful smile of hers. Today, I found it slightly easier to return it with a grin of my own. The way her eyes lit up when I did made me want to pull out my fingernails with pliers. She'd put up with so much fucking crap these last few weeks.

"Come here." I held out my hand, beckoning to her, then patted my lap. She came to me all too readily. My arms went around her as she hovered over my thighs.

"Legs are fine, Jill. This part of them, anyway. Sit down. I want to feel your weight on me. Make sure you're still real and you haven't cloned yourself and the real you is off living a far better life than this one."

"Blay." She settled herself in my lap, cupping my face

with her warm palms. "I'm going nowhere. As long as you want me here, then here is where I'll be."

I pulled her down for a kiss, sliding my tongue between her lips.

Hot damn.

I'd forgotten what it was like to kiss her, to taste her. My cock stirred, as desperate for intimacy as I was. A groan rumbled through my chest, and I shifted her until her ass was right on top of my dick.

"Grind on me. Let me feel you." I kissed down the column of her neck, returning to her lips once more. She made this sound in the back of her throat, half moan, half sob.

"I've missed you." Her breath hitched on the words, as if she expected a harsh rebuke.

I hated myself.

"I've missed you. And I'm so sorry, Tilly. So fucking sorry. It's just—"

She placed two fingers over my lips. "No apologies. If I were in your position—"

"You'd have behaved with a lot more decorum and a lot less attitude."

She smiled. "None of us know how we're going to behave in a given situation." She kissed me this time, slipping both hands around the back of my neck, playing with my hair that desperately needed a cut.

"We should go." I reluctantly let her get up. "Traffic in Miami is murder this time of day."

"Are you excited?"

I grimaced. "Nervous."

"It'll be fine."

It was a saying, I knew that, but the flippancy of it—a flippancy Jill would not mean—irked me, and I scowled, the words spilling before I could check myself.

"How the fuck would you know?"

Her happiness melted faster than an ice cream in July. She moved behind me, pushing me through the door without saying a word. *You fuckwit.* If I could kick myself in the ass, I would.

"Jill."

"Don't. Let's just get there without taking chunks out of one another, okay?"

I fell into silence, hoisting myself into the car with the help of my nurse and my driver. Jill stood off to one side, staring into the distance. I despised how weak I was, how helpless. Loathed how the selfish part of me clung to a woman that a better man than me would let go.

My thoughts on me and Jill swung from one extreme to the other on an hourly basis. Sometimes, the thought of being without her physically pained me. At other times, I suffocated under her attention, doubting the longevity of our relationship under such trying circumstances.

Maybe once I got this damn leg fitted and rediscovered a sliver of independence, I might settle on one side of the argument. At this point, it was anyone's guess, including mine, which side I'd fall on.

Jill was such a free spirit, a creative wonder whose immense skills would dull tied to a belligerent cripple like me. It was kinder to let her go. I had such a long road ahead of me, not only for my recovery but also for the work involved in trying to save a company my father had built from nothing that I'd single-handedly wounded, if not damaged irreparably. It would take months of PR work to get customers to trust in the brand again. Cruising was a competitive industry with infinite choices for passengers, and a story like this one took a long time to fade from people's memories.

Dad had purposely kept the truth of our employee's involvement out of the media, heaping all the focus on Jeremy and the shooter, both now incarcerated and awaiting trial. I appreciated why he'd done it, and it had certainly helped the narrative of what had occurred not being the fault of Kingcaid Cruises, but *I* knew. And a need so entrenched in every cell in my body urged me to be the one to fix the mess I'd caused.

That, and the physio to recover my mobility, would take all of my attention for the next several months.

Was it fair to expect Jill to put her life on hold for mine?

I wasn't sure yet. But when I found the answer, then I'd know what to do.

Flanked by Jill and Mara, I arrived at the doctor's office five minutes before my appointment time. A nurse took me straight through, and after the niceties were over, the doctor and the prosthetist got to work.

Two hours later, I hobbled out of the doctor's office, on crutches but upright. I could barely keep the smile off my face. Just to look down at Jill instead of craning my neck to look up at her from that goddamn wheelchair gave an enormous boost to my mood. The journey home could not have had a more different atmosphere than the one coming here. Sometimes, my mood changes gave me whiplash, so Christ only knew what they did to Jill. She probably needed months of treatment from an osteopath to fix the problems with her neck.

As I got home, however, my stump throbbed from where they'd messed about with it, fitting, adjusting, removing, and refitting the prosthetic. I swallowed a couple of painkillers and excused myself, retiring to my bedroom on the first floor. I flopped onto the bed, dropping the crutches on the floor with a thud. The prosthetist had warned me of some pain, but this was fucking agony.

My mood dipped so low from such a high that I questioned whether I was bipolar. It would certainly explain a lot. Surely it wasn't normal to flip-flop to this extent?

I sent a message to Dad, updating him and informing him of my decision to return to work tomorrow. I didn't want to wait a second longer to restart my life. The leg was step one. Getting back into the swing of things was step two. I followed that up with a message to my assistant, who replied with a row of thumbs up and a heart emoji, which etched a smile on my face.

A tap came on the door and Jill entered, her steps tentative. "I thought you might want a drink."

"Whiskey?" I gave her a lopsided grin.

She wore her relief on her face, and her entire body relaxed. "Probably not the best idea coming on the back of those painkillers."

"Killjoy." I held out my hand to her. "Listen, I wanted to talk to you about something."

She set a glass of juice on the nightstand and perched on the bed next to me, worrying her lip. "What?"

"I'm going back to work. Tomorrow. I messaged Dad

and told him. And I want you to do the same." I braced for her to tell me it was a bad idea, that I wasn't ready, that my health and well-being should come first.

Instead, she said, "It's funny you should say that, because I have been working these last couple of weeks."

I raised my eyebrows. She hadn't mentioned writing again. "You have? The devil manuscript?"

A laugh spilled out of her. "Yeah. I figured out how to fix it, though, and it's been going really well."

"Care to share?" I tilted my head to the right.

Her cheeks pinked, and she tucked her chin. "Not yet. Maybe never. I'm weird about my stuff until it's ready to publish."

"Fair enough. I'll expect a mention, though."

"You got it." She leaned her head on my shoulder. "And for what my opinion is worth, I think it's a great idea for you to return to work. You need some normalcy and routine back in your life."

"First, your opinion always matters to me. Second, I couldn't agree more." I nudged up my shoulder until she lifted her head and gave me her eyes. "I'm sorry I'm so all over the place. I know it hasn't been easy for you."

"It's been far harder on you. I'm not the one with a life-changing injury."

An uncomfortable pressure settled on my chest, accompanied by a bitter taste in my mouth. My mood nose-dived again.

"At least I'm alive."

She dredged up a heavy sigh. "Blay. I need you to stop with this self-recrimination. I've said it before, and I will say it as often as it needs to be said. This was not your fault. There isn't a single scenario I can think of where you could have foreseen this and put a stop to it. And I make shit up for a living." She flashed a quick smile, which fell as fast as it had arrived. "All you're doing by continuing down this destructive path is making yourself feel worse. No one blames you. Hell, even the press coverage has been, on the whole, supportive. There isn't a single journalist who's out there pointing the finger at you."

Yeah, only because Dad's done a sterling job in guiding the narrative.

I breathed out through my nose, shaking my head. "I know you're right, and sometimes I actually believe that. But then there are other times when I keep going over and over it, looking for the sliver of information I missed that would have put a stop to this entire thing. It'd only take one, and the shooter wouldn't have gotten on board."

"Blay." She covered my forearm with her hand. "That way lies madness."

"And then there's you."

Her brow furrowed. "What about me?"

"All this." I gestured to myself. "Not exactly what you had planned, I'll bet. Giving up your life to care for a cripple."

Anger rippled across her face. She yanked her hand away as if my arm suddenly burned. "I don't like that word, and I want you to stop using it immediately. It's horrible and an affront to the English language. Would you use it about a stranger in the street?"

"No, of course not."

"Precisely. Then stop using it about yourself. You lost a limb. It's a terrible thing to have happened. Two people lost their lives, which is beyond horrific. Another is still recovering from a broken arm and collarbone. But none, I repeat, *none* of this is your fault." Her voice increased in volume, her neck blotching red the angrier she got. "And as for me giving up my life, I've swapped a two-bedroom cottage with a leaky roof in a chilly part of Devon for a beautiful mansion in sunny Miami where I get to see you every day and write in the most amazing of surroundings. So tell me, Blay, what is it exactly I've given up?"

She launched to her feet, pacing and chewing on her thumbnail while flashing me the occasional frustrated glare.

"Okay, okay. I promise I won't use it again." I stuck out my prosthetic limb, stopping her angry stomp in its tracks. "Quit pacing and come sit beside me. And just in case you're thinking of refusing, remember, I can take this leg off and throw it at you." I smiled, the first one that felt truly genuine in weeks.

Jill's lips twitched, and she shook her head. "You're an arse."

"It's true." I reached for her, taking her hand as she closed in and tugging her next to me. "I hear you, Tilly. I can't promise that these thoughts will disappear overnight, but I'll try my very best not to let them consume me or drag me down to that dark place where I'm hitting out at everything and everyone." I cupped her face with both hands. "Especially you."

"At last," she whispered, leaning in to brush her lips over mine.

I deepened the kiss, sliding my tongue between her lips. *Fuck, I need this.* The closeness, the feel and taste of her, the way she took sips of air whenever I broke off to nip along her jawline. I didn't remember lying down, nor pulling her on top of me, nor her unbuttoning my shirt. But when her hands slid over my chest and abdomen, her fingertips exploring the ridges of muscle, I got my first proper erection since that bastard had shot me.

Straddling my thighs, she rocked her hips, rubbing in exactly the right place to get us both off. That day in the pool at my Barbados home seemed like a million years ago, yet my body acted on instinct, my hips lifting to massage her right where she needed me to. Her groan as I made contact told me I'd hit the spot.

Literally.

I unfastened my pants and pushed up her skirt, but as she freed my cock, a knock came at the door.

"Fuck off," I shouted, causing Jill to giggle.

"Charming," Renata said through the solid oak, sarcasm lacing her tone. "Mara is asking if it's okay for her to leave early today or if you need her."

I rolled my eyes, sliding a finger inside Jill's panties. "Fuck," I breathed. "So wet."

"What was that?" Renata asked.

"Is there a reason Mara can't ask me herself?"

"Yes."

"Which is?" I pushed another finger inside her.

"Because she said if you snap at her one more time today, she won't be held responsible for her actions."

Jill giggled. I rolled my eyes. "It's fine, Renata. And unless the president stops by, no interruptions."

I removed my fingers, rolling Jill underneath me as

Renata muttered something, her footsteps fading as she walked away.

"So the president is more important than me, huh?"

Winking, I captured her bottom lip between my teeth. "I mean, he can wait, right?"

Chapter 29

Blaize

**What's one more emasculation
in the scheme of things?**

I MANAGED TWO DAYS AT THE OFFICE BEFORE exhaustion took over, and I had to face facts that resuming my previous punishing schedule wasn't in the cards for a little while longer yet.

And it pissed me the fuck off.

I hated how weak I'd become, how dependent on others for things that I'd usually have relied on them for anyway, such as Carly running down to my favorite deli and picking me up a sandwich for lunch. But when the choice to get my own damn sandwich was taken away, it made me bitter and angry.

My temporary prosthetic wasn't the solution I'd hoped

for. It rubbed like a motherfucker if I wore it for too long, and learning to balance, even with crutches, wasn't nearly as easy as I'd expected. Meanwhile, the promises I'd made to Jill to stop beating myself up over what had happened on Serenity were broken on a daily basis, and my moods still swung like an out-of-whack pendulum.

I was in the middle of deciding which afternoon meetings to shelve when Jill tapped on my study and entered. She looked sexy as hell in an off-the-shoulder red-and-white-spotted dress that gave a hint of cleavage, her skin tanned from sitting outside writing for a few hours each day, yet her beauty wasn't my prevalent thought. That, uncharitably, was the ease with which she moved, whereas I had to plan a trip to take a piss with laser-like precision.

"I'm going to pop down to the grocery store and pick up a few things, and then meet Kelsey for lunch. Can I get you anything?"

I glowered. Something else I couldn't do. I couldn't fucking "pop" anywhere. No quick errands for me. Everything took a fucking age. "Renata can go to the store."

"I know, but I want to do it. I thought I might throw a couple of steaks on the barbecue tonight. Eat under the stars. What do you say?" She smiled. Her efforts to keep my moods high were admirable, but for some reason today, the attempt fell flat.

"Fine." It wasn't fine. Today was the kind of day where nothing would be fine, no matter what Jill or anyone else did to bolster my spirits. Some days were like that. I'd woken up in a shitty mood, and as each minute passed, it was getting shittier.

"I know the barbecue is the man's domain, but I make a mean chargrilled filet."

"What's one more emasculation?" I muttered.

A flash of hurt sped across her face. "Is that what you really think?"

I sighed, closing my eyes for a moment. "No, of course it isn't. Ignore me. I'm tired. That's all."

A wisp of air alerted me to her moving close. When I opened my eyes, she was right in front of me.

"How about you cook the steaks?"

Her soft, tentative suggestion made me feel thoroughly ashamed of myself. I tugged her onto my lap, tucking a thick lock of hair behind her ear. "I'm sorry, Tilly." I grinned. "Seems like I say that a lot right now."

"I forgive you."

"I have no idea why."

She opened her mouth, then shut it, swallowing whatever it was she'd been about to say.

"Any requests?"

"Yeah, no panties tonight."

She giggled. "I meant to bring back from the grocery store."

"Crotchless panties?"

Her head shook at the same time as her shoulders did. "I don't think they stock those."

"Shame. They're missing a revenue stream."

Her eyes glistened as they often did when I tried to be the guy she'd first met. And sometimes I wasn't faking it either. I kissed her, then slapped her ass as she climbed off my lap.

"Drive carefully. Better yet, have my driver take you."

"I can drive. I'm living the SoFlo life, don't you know?"

"There's no such thing as SoFlo, only SoCal."

"Well, there should be." She flashed me a grin and an accompanying wave. "Be good."

The door closed. I grabbed my crutches and hobbled over to the window that overlooked the driveway. A few minutes later, Jill appeared behind the wheel of my convertible Ferrari, a car I'd only driven once before deciding it wasn't for me. I'd considered selling it, but seeing how happy she was as she drove by with a broad grin and the wind blowing her hair, I'd never sell it now.

I returned to my desk and messaged Carly, telling her to cancel all my meetings for the rest of the day. I felt like a complete failure. Every day when I opened my eyes, there was that moment where I forgot what had happened, and I was so goddamn happy. Then reality crashed in, and I had to face up to the fact that I'd spend the rest of my life disabled.

I hadn't come to terms with it yet. Maybe I never would.

Carly confirmed that she'd handle everything, and I sent a quick "Thanks" before shutting down my computer, the screen going black reminiscent of my rapidly lowering mood. I craved the old me, but even flashes of time when I felt like myself were a sort of torture, because they never lasted. I hated spending time with myself, so why anyone, especially Jill, would want to spend time with me was something that played on my mind far too often.

She still hadn't said that she loved me, although her actions showed she did.

Then again, I hadn't told her either.

Did I, though? Or was I so scared of being alone that I was clinging to a future I might not have chosen for myself if I'd never gotten shot?

I didn't have an answer.

"Blaize." Renata knocked on my office door. "You have a visitor."

"Who?" I wasn't expecting anyone. None of my family were in Florida, and even if they were, they wouldn't drop in out of the blue. They'd call or text and let me know they were on their way in case I wasn't around or, far more likely these days, that I didn't want to see them. Both Mom and Dad had offered to rent a house in the area for a few months while I got back on my feet—so to speak—but I'd firmly rebuked that idea, and my brothers had their own lives to lead. "If it's Scarlett Rose again, tell her I'm out."

I didn't blame Scarlett for one second of what had happened, and I'd appreciated her stopping by, as well as her unexpected and unnecessary contrition. That didn't mean I wanted to be besties with her or anything, nor have her think she could turn up whenever she felt like it.

"Upton Barrick," Renata replied.

I frowned. Upton worked for ROGUES, a company with whom my family did an extensive amount of business, but he wasn't someone I'd had much contact with. For one thing, he lived in LA, and for another, his business interests and mine were not aligned.

"Show him in." I propped up my crutches by the side of my desk and faced my chair toward the door. A few seconds later, Renata appeared with Upton in tow. I concealed my surprise. I'd completely forgotten he had a deep scar running down the left-hand side of his face from getting caught up in a terrorist bomb a few years earlier that had killed his younger sister. Like I said, we didn't cross paths very often, so it was easy to forget details like that.

I pushed myself up on my hands and reached for my crutches, but he motioned for me to sit. "Don't get up. I'm sorry to intrude like this without warning."

Hiding how grateful I was to sink back into my chair, I gestured to the guest seat opposite my desk.

"I admit, you've got me curious."

He knitted his fingers together. "I'll get straight to the point. Your dad asked me to come."

My eyebrows flew up my forehead. "Dad? Why?"

"He's worried about you."

Something pinched my stomach. I wasn't sure if it was guilt, confusion, or anger. "I have no idea why. I'm fine."

He cocked his head, studying me with a blank expression, but his eyes gave him away. He didn't believe I was fine.

And he was right to believe that. I wasn't anywhere close to being fine.

"Do you know how I got this?" He pointed to the jagged scar marring an otherwise perfect face.

"Yeah. Bomb, right?"

"Correct. My back is littered with scars, too. I've had more surgeries than I care to remember, each one more painful than the last. But the thing I found the hardest to deal with, other than the crushing grief of losing my sister, was the emotional turmoil. I shut myself away, cutting off everyone who cared about me. I didn't want to engage with anyone. And as for moods..." He flashed a perfect set of white teeth. "How my housekeeper stopped herself from slipping poison into the whiskey decanter, I'll never know."

"Don't go giving Renata any ideas."

His lopsided smile, I realized, was forced into that position by his scar. A moment of shame washed over me. Sometimes I behaved as if I were the only one who'd suffered when there were many, *many* people far worse off than me.

"I'm not here to tell you how to feel, nor how to act, but what I am here to tell you is that I understand. What you're going through, jeez, man, it's fucking tough. It's a roller coaster of emotions, each day bringing a fresh hell to deal with."

I hid my surprise, but it was as if he was inside my head, thinking my thoughts, feeling what I felt.

"How did you get through it?"

"Time." He hitched a shoulder. "There's no shortcutting your recovery. It isn't easy, but it *will* happen. But the worst thing you can do is cut off those who love you the most. Ask me how I know."

"You came all the way to Miami just to tell me that?" I smiled.

"Hell no." He huffed a laugh. "You're not special enough for me to travel from the other side of the country for a fireside chat."

"Gee, thanks." I grinned. He repaid my grin with one of his own.

"I was in town on business, and I promised your dad— or rather, I promised Ryker, whom your dad spoke to, that I'd swing by and see if I could lend an ear." Bracing his elbows on his knees, he leaned forward. "Now, how are you really doing?"

I ran a hand over my face. "I have my good days and my bad days. One outweighs the other by some margin. I'll let you guess which one."

"It's early days. I shut myself away for a year. Don't do that. It fucking sucks."

"A year? Jesus."

"Yeah. It was rough. In the end, my friends staged an intervention, sending what they called companions and I called spies, to try to haul me out of the state I was in. I was so foul to them that no one lasted more than a week. Until Belle." His eyes glazed over, and he looked as if he was keeping a great big secret. "She refused to suffer my moods in silence, giving it back to me tenfold, and then some. Boy, the buttons she pressed." He chuckled. "Then again, she'd had some practice in dealing with grief."

He let the comment hang in the air, possibly to test my interest. I took the bait. "Why?"

"She lost her fiancé in the same bomb that took my sister, and her brother ended up paralyzed from the waist down."

"Jesus."

"Right? Y'know, you should talk to Zak. That's Belle's brother. He's a solid guy. Runs our assistive technology division. He might have some suggestions to make your transition back to work easier. Plus, he's a great listener. A good sounding board for when depression hits." He reached into his pocket and removed his wallet, plucking out a business card. "That's him. Give him a call."

I turned the card over in my hand. "I might just do that."

"You could do worse. My other piece of advice is to find yourself a woman like Belle, someone who won't blow smoke up your ass, who'll push you to put in the work needed to recover, and you'll make it through this rough patch far quicker than you ever thought possible."

Butterflies took flight in my stomach. "I've already found her."

Upton stayed for around thirty minutes before excusing himself to get to his next appointment. I contemplated all that he'd said for a while after, running his experience, and Zak's, alongside my own. They'd had it worse, particularly Zak. He'd lost the use of his legs forever, and Upton had lost his only sister. I still had my family, and Jill, and while my business had taken a crippling blow, it wasn't on life support just yet. As soon as I got my strength back, I'd throw myself into fixing every single issue and putting Kingcaid Cruises back where it belonged.

At the top of the fucking tree.

Sticking my iPad under my arm, I grabbed my crutches and made my way to the patio. I settled into a comfortable chair on the lanai and surfed the net. A dog and cat scrapping in a YouTube video caught my attention. I laughed as the cat romped its way to victory, then plunked on its ass and began licking its paws while the dog slinked off to a corner to sulk. I opened a news app next. As I did, the top story changed, a yellow *Breaking News* ticker running on a loop across the bottom.

Murder and Mayhem on Kingcaid Cruises. Is the CEO at fault?

My stomach dropped to the floor. I scanned the article, reading as fast as my eyes could send the words to my brain. Fuck. Fuck, fuck, fuck. They knew everything. The issue with the badge scanners before Serenity had set sail, the broken door I'd discovered when John had escorted me on a tour of the ship, plus a few other problems that had occurred in the weeks and months leading up to the maiden voyage. The journalist questioned my leadership, my decision-making capability, and my innocence or otherwise with what had happened that resulted in two people losing their lives. The only thing they didn't seem to know about was the part the technician had played in the shooter evading security and boarding the ship.

I reached for my phone to call Dad. My pocket was empty. *Goddamn, it must be inside.* I hauled myself to my feet, hobbling back into my study. By the time I got to my phone, I'd already had several missed calls from Dad, as well as both my brothers, Aspen, and my cousin Asher, who always seemed abreast of everything. I phoned Dad back first.

"I've seen it."

"Don't panic. I've got the lawyers on damage control."

"It's a shit show, Dad. If there's even a whiff of culpability here, it'll ruin us."

"Like I said, don't panic. We're a long way from that. Projects this size have complications. You know this."

"Yeah, but not ones where people die." I sagged onto

the couch and let my crutches fall to the floor. "At least it hasn't come out about the technician yet, although it's only a matter of time."

"Not necessarily. I'm all over it."

"Yeah, but that's the point, isn't it, Dad? *I* should be all over it. This is my business." The line went quiet. I checked to make sure we hadn't been cut off. Nope. Still connected. "Dad?"

"I wish you wouldn't do that."

"Do what?"

"Take the world on your shoulders. You're not super-human, Blaize. A genius, yes, but not superhuman. Give yourself a break."

Funny that. Because Dad never got a break.

"Let me handle this."

"You're handling enough. I've got this, son."

And I thought Jill had emasculated me with the barbe-cued steaks. Turned out Dad's knife was far sharper.

"If you think that's best."

"I'll keep you in the loop. I promise."

"Sure thing." I ended the call. Despondent didn't even begin to cover what I felt after that conversation with Dad. I thought about calling one of my brothers and talking it through, but something told me they'd say the same thing as Dad. *Your job is to get well. Leave this to us. You'll be back in the thick of it soon enough.*

The question was, would there be anything to return to?

I lost track of time, mulling over that fucking story. How had the journalist who'd written this destructive piece dug up confidential company details? There had to be a leak. And if there was, I'd haul that fucker over the coals until their skin melted. They had no idea of the damage they'd caused, and when it came to my business, forgiveness wasn't a concept I got into bed with.

Picking up my iPad, I checked several news apps. Each one carried the same story. There was no escaping it. I navigated to my email to see if Dad had sent anything through. He hadn't, but another email caught my attention. A few weeks ago, I'd set up a Google alert for any mentions of Jill after we'd reunited on the ship. Not for stalking purposes, but more because I'd been curious about what kind of public presence she had. So far, the only alerts I'd gotten were the odd book site or blogger mentioning one or more of her books.

This one was not that.

This one was... was...

Fucking horrendous.

And all my fault.

Trolls had gone after Jill, keyboard warriors whose vicious rhetoric had the power to destroy careers or, at the very least, destroy a person's peace of mind. I navigated to a few of the top book sites. A raft of one-star reviews, all dropped within the last few hours, littered the pages. Warning readers not to buy books or support an author who'd hooked up with the CEO of a company responsible for the deaths of two innocent people. There was even a viral TikTok with over three million views, and the comments were heavily skewed against Jill.

I wiped clammy hands on my shorts and carried on scrolling, like a rubbernecker unable to tear their gaze away from a devastating car wreck. This would destroy Jill.

She'd already had a wobble with her current manuscript, although she seemed to have ironed out the kinks. But still. Confidence was a fragile thing—hard to build, easily destroyed.

My worst fears had come true. Not only had my mistakes single-handedly wrecked my business, but, by association, I'd wrecked Jill's, too.

At least I had the power to fix hers, even if I'd crush myself in the process.

The jury was out on whether my own would survive.

Chapter 30

Jill

**Today's news is tomorrow's
fish and chip paper.
Hopefully.**

Driving a Ferrari was so much fun. I'd never bought into the concept of supercars. To me, a car was simply a convenient way of traveling from A to B. One journey in this pillar-box-red beauty had changed my mind.

Flavia was a dream. Yes, I'd named her. A car this beautiful deserved an equally beautiful name. I might offer Blay sexual favors for years to come if he signed the owner-ship papers over to me. Although, that wouldn't work. I'd already given away the goods for free. Darn it. I'd have to come up with something else to bargain with.

I grinned at my inner thoughts, coasting slowly to a stop outside the restaurant where I'd arranged to meet Kelsey for lunch. It felt so good to be out, even if a twinge of guilt pinched my insides. I pushed the feeling aside. As much as I'd inserted myself as his unofficial carer, he did have a full-time qualified nurse on call twenty-four seven. I deserved a few hours off to catch up with one of my best friends.

The valet came forward, opening my door. I took his hand, climbing out from a car so low-slung that I'd had to perform a deep squat just to stand upright. A few sessions driving Flavia and I'd soon have buns of steel. Better than sweating it out in a gym any day of the week.

My phone pinged. I checked the message. Kelsey was sitting on the patio, and apparently, I was drinking a cosmo. It'd have to be just the one. I could imagine Blay's reaction if I returned to his house in an Uber, having abandoned Flavia after downing several cocktails in the middle of the day. I hadn't even asked him if I could drive her. Then again, he had told me to take my pick of several cars in his garage.

The hostess led me through the restaurant to the patio overlooking a body of water. The sun glistened like diamonds floating on the surface. Kelsey got to her feet as I approached, flinging her arms around me in a hug so tight my lungs protested.

"I've missed you. I'm so glad you called." She peered at me through narrowed eyes. "You're looking a little peaky, which, given that you're in South Florida at the height of summer, is a concern. And you're thinner than when I saw you last, too. Are you looking after yourself? Because you're no use to that billionaire of yours if you don't take good care of yourself."

"I've missed you, too. And I'm fine. I've been writing, not sunbathing." I sat down, as did she.

"You have? Oh, Jill, that's marvelous. You figured out how to fix your manuscript?"

"Yeah. I kind of took the story in a different direction, but since I started listening to my muse instead of what I thought the readers would expect from a follow-up, the words are flowing. Plus, I heard from my editor, and she's not pushing me at all. Said I was to take my time, and they'd fix any scheduling issues in-house."

"As they should, too. They won't want to lose a talent like you, even if you thought they'd dump you because life happened and you had other priorities for a while."

"You can say 'I told you so.' I won't kick you under the table. Well, not that hard, anyway." I sipped my cosmo. "Wow, that's strong. I'd better order some water, too."

We put in our food order. A prawn salad for me and a steak frites for Kelsey. After the server left our table, she gave me one of her motherly looks. "How is it really?"

I heaved a sigh. "Up and down. Some days, he's like the Blay I met on the plane, the Blay who charmed us all on the ship. Other days, it's like he's had a personality transplant, snapping at everyone and everything. On those days, nothing soothes him."

"It can't be easy for him, but equally, it's difficult for you, too."

"I know. Addison called a few days ago and asked me if I loved him. I think she refrained from adding 'enough.' And in case you're wondering, I do."

"Have to say, you're a hero. Not sure I could give up my life to care for a guy I'd known for such a short amount of time."

"That's just it, though. I've always had this sense that I've known him forever. Time isn't always a good measure. He's my soul mate. And as long as he wants me around, then I'll stay."

"He'd be an idiot to let you go."

"Men have been known to behave like idiots on occasion."

Kelsey laughed. "It's funny because it's true."

We caught up over good food and perfect surroundings, but as the time to leave approached, a sense of melancholy descended over me. We hugged, and I promised to call in a few days and arrange another meetup, hopefully with Addison, too, if she'd finished her manuscript in time. Kelsey's eyes bugged out as the valet brought Flavia around to the front of the restaurant.

"Okay, tell me again what attracted you to the billionaire Blaize Kingcaid?"

I laughed, giving her a hefty dig in the ribs. "You'd better be kidding."

"I am, but still." She whistled. "I bet it makes those sour moods a little easier to handle." She kissed me on the cheek and hugged me for a few seconds longer than normal, as if loath to let me go. When she pulled back, all amusement had scattered, leaving behind a serious Kelsey.

"If you need anything, and I mean anything, you just call."

"I will. Love you."

"Love you, too."

I got into the driver's seat and drove away, waving a hand through the open window as I pulled onto the highway. I hadn't driven far when my phone rang. I glanced down at the display. My editor. What did she want? Oh, crap, I hoped she hadn't changed her mind and had decided to hold me to my original delivery date after all. The new book was coming along well, but it wasn't anywhere near ready for her eagle eye yet.

I hadn't hooked my phone up to Blay's car system, so I pulled into the parking lot of a convenience store. By the time I cut the engine, the call had gone to voicemail, but as I picked it up to call her back, it rang again.

"Samantha." I kept my voice light and positive. "How lovely to hear from you. How are you?"

"Not great. And I don't think you will be either. But whatever you do, don't panic."

Whenever anyone said, "Don't panic," the first thing any sane person did was panic. My palms were so sweaty I almost dropped my phone.

"Go on."

"There are a few trolls online who've targeted you, and they're one-star bombing most of your books."

My jaw dropped, and my heart lodged in my ribs. "Why?" I croaked. I couldn't think of a single reason why I'd be the subject of online trolling. I kept my social media feeds professional and didn't use my online presence to get involved in controversial subjects, preferring to steer the conversations toward books and reading. That was what mattered to me.

"It's to do with Blaize Kingcaid."

"What?" I frowned. "I don't understand."

"Neither did I until I did a bit of hunting around. It turns out a journalist has got the inside track on what happened on the cruise, and the rub of the story puts the blame for what happened at the feet of your guy."

Oh God. Poor Blay.

"But... I don't understand. What's that got to do with me?"

"Guilty by association, Jill. Happens too fucking often. You were mentioned in the article, albeit briefly, but you know what social media is like. It only takes a spark, and the next thing you know, you've got a forest fire on your hands."

"Shit." I rubbed my forehead. "So what do we do?"

"I've contacted our publicity department, and they're making damage control their top priority. I think you should make a statement on all your socials, but we'll provide the wording. You can just Jill it up."

I smiled despite the complete disaster facing me and Blay. "Jill it up?"

"I just thought of it. Works, though, right? Look, I meant what I said about not panicking. These things are often a storm in a teacup. Hang in there. It'll pass. I'll be in touch."

She hung up. I dropped my head to the steering wheel. If my publishing house wasn't thinking of dropping me for failing to meet an important deadline, I couldn't blame them if this latest disaster gave them cause for reconsideration. Who wanted a client that brought nothing but trouble to the table?

I went to Google and typed in a few keywords. Less than a second later, the article Samantha had referred to appeared at the top of the search. I scanned it enough to get the gist. There, laid out in black and white, were Blay's worst fears. The article was so heavily skewed toward blaming him, even when none of it was his fault. The written word had so much power to sway people's opinions, especially in this day and age. *Blay must be going out of his mind.*

On purpose, I avoided looking up anything about myself. My confidence was already on a knife-edge. The last thing I needed was to see my life's work trashed by a bunch of noisy and powerful online keyboard warriors. Careers were ended for less. I hoped my publishers could quash this, although I didn't see how. Once something was online, it was there forever. The best I could hope for was, as Samantha had said, to make a single statement, then keep quiet and pray it all went away. It didn't sound like a solid strategy to me, but what else could I do?

Putting my foot down, I raced back to Blay's house. I left the car at the front rather than take the time to drive round to the garages at the rear of the property. I sprinted inside.

"Blay? Blay, where are you?"

I poked my head into his study. Empty. His bedroom was, too, as was the kitchen and the living room. Where the hell was he? I found him sitting out by the pool, his brows pulled into a deep V, his fingers drumming on the arm of his chair.

"There you are." I hurried across, dropping to a crouch. "My editor called me. I'm so sorry. But it'll be okay. Today's news is tomorrow's fish and chip paper."

I didn't believe a word of it, not with a story as big as

this one, but I had to keep his spirits up no matter what I thought.

"Tomorrow's fish and chip paper?" He looked at me as if I'd lost my mind. "Are you fucking kidding me? My business is ruined." He jabbed a finger at me. "And so is yours. Because of me."

"Nothing is forever. People have short memories. They'll move on as soon as another scandal grabs their attention, which, let's face it, in the world we live in, we won't have long to wait."

"You don't get it," he said through clenched teeth. "You don't fucking understand how big business works. I run a multibillion-dollar company that tens of thousands of people rely on to pay their mortgages and feed their families. You make shit up for a living. They're not the same thing at all."

I winced, rising to my feet. "That was unnecessary."

"But true." He stared at me with flat eyes and a stony expression.

"I know you're hurting, but lashing out at me is not cool. I'm not your whipping post."

He grabbed his crutches, hauling himself out of his chair. I went to put my arm out to steady him. He glared at me with abject disdain. I yanked my arm back. "Go, Jill. Leave. I don't want you here anymore."

I gaped at him. "You don't mean that."

"I fucking do mean it," he roared, his face turning red. "I'm no good for you, and you're no good for me."

He took two steps, lost his balance, and fell. I rushed to him, hooking my forearm under his armpit. "Let me help you up."

He wrenched his shoulder up, dislodging me. "I can fucking do it. I don't need your goddamn help. I don't need you. Fuck off back to England and leave me alone."

My heart dried up in my chest. I pressed a hand over it, pushing inward as if I were giving myself CPR. "I don't want to go. I love you."

I should have told him before now, but the timing had never felt right. I'd wanted it to be perfect. *Guess I fucked up on that score.*

His face twisted, but not in pain. In contempt. "Well, I don't love you. I never did. We barely know each other. What I thought might be love was lust. Nothing more. And it's gone. I always knew I wasn't the kind of man to settle down, and being around you twenty-four seven these last few weeks has proved that. So pack up your things and leave. We're done."

He somehow got to his feet with no help from me. Not that I'd have been capable of helping him. I was too busy trying to hold the shattered pieces of myself together. He hobbled into the house and slammed the door. My legs went from underneath me. I grabbed onto a chair just in time and sank into it.

In the space of an hour, my whole life had crumbled. He didn't love me. He never had. All this time, I'd been fooling myself, putting his bad moods down to difficulty in coming to terms with the loss of a limb. Instead, it'd been having me around that had sent his moods spiraling.

They said the truth hurt.

The truth didn't hurt. It annihilated.

Chapter 31

Blaize

**An unwelcome visitor is worse
than losing my leg.**

TWO DAYS AGO, THE WOMAN I LOVED HAD LEFT, AND
my world had gone dark.

I doubted I'd ever see light again.

Despite the constant ache in my chest that far
outweighed the discomfort in my leg, I'd do the same thing
again and again.

And again.

Even if every time I closed my eyes, I kept seeing the
image of Jill's face crumpling when I'd lied and told her I'd
never loved her.

At least I'd been convincing.

If she'd had any idea that I was slowly dying inside, she'd have given up everything to stay with me, and I couldn't allow her to do that. She'd get over me soon enough, move on with her life, and steer her career back on track.

Which she wouldn't be able to do as long as she was associated with me.

Call it an atonement for what had happened on Serenity and my part in it.

I'd done some good, at least. After watching Jill climb into a taxi, taking my heart with her, I'd called the CEOs of every online bookstore and made it clear that if they didn't clean house and remove one hundred percent of those troll reviews, I'd make it my business to be a gigantic thorn in their sides.

All of them had promised to look into it with immediate effect, and this morning, those reviews were all but gone.

The TikTok thing was trickier. I'd hired one of the best hackers in the business to wipe those videos from existence, and any more that sprung up until this shit storm abated. Yes, it was illegal, but if anyone called me on it, I'd chuck a dime at them and tell them to call someone who gave a fuck.

So far, he hadn't managed to take it down, and those videos kept on ticking up and up, the comments so vile they made my stomach turn. The mob mentality was testament to this fucked-up world we lived in. Jill's only "crime" was falling in love with me.

My crimes were far worse.

I'd also had my publicist leak a story about Jill breaking up with me and blast it across as many media outlets as possible. That way, there was a chance this shit would calm down sooner rather than later and Jill could put it all behind her.

Maybe one day, there'd be a way back for us. Not that I'd expect her to take me back after the way I'd behaved, but the dream made it easier to fall asleep at night.

The front gates buzzed. I ignored it. Renata would answer and get rid of whoever it was. I wasn't in the mood to see people.

I wasn't in the mood for anything.

Losing Jill, even if it had been of my doing, had wiped out the progress I'd made. I didn't care about my permanent prosthetic, or learning to walk without crutches or sticks, or seeing the back of that fucking wheelchair once and for all. I couldn't even gather the enthusiasm to return to work, despite my earlier determination. Dad was handling it all anyway. He didn't need me fucking up the progress he was making with the authorities and the public image of my cruising business.

I'd fucked up enough already.

Better to fade into the background and let him assume control. I wasn't in a fit state to be CEO of a rowing-boat business, let alone a multibillion-dollar cruise ship industry.

The door to my office burst open and Aspen marched in, her purple hair whipping around her and her eyes nailing me like two balls of fire.

"Who let you in?" I growled.

"Renata." She planted her hands on her hips and loomed over my desk. "Have you lost your fucking mind?"

Goddamn Renata.

I'd told her I didn't want to see anyone. I should have added *especially Aspen.* It was obvious why she was here. Either she'd called Jill or the other way around. Not that it mattered who called whom.

"Nice to see you, too." I smirked. "That color hair clashes with your beaming red face."

"Jokes? You're making jokes when you've just destroyed one of the nicest, kindest people I've ever met." She snorted, raking me with a gaze that said she'd like to stick a pitchfork into my balls.

Get in line, honey.

"It'd run its course. I didn't see any point in dragging out a relationship that was already dead."

"Ending a relationship is one thing. Doing it with cruelty is quite another. What the fuck has happened to you, huh?"

I dropped my gaze, lifting it slowly. "I lost a fucking leg, and two people died because of me. Keep up, Aspen. I don't have time to spell it out in words of one syllable."

She turned purple. Matched her hair now, at least.

"Out of our entire family, you"—she jabbed a finger at me—"are the last person I'd ever have thought capable of hurting someone to the extent you've hurt Jill."

I kept my poker face on, even if I was cringing inside. Aspen was like a bloodhound. If she got a sniff of what my true feelings were, she'd push and cajole and gift herself the role of Chief Cupid.

But as long as what had happened on Serenity hung over me like a thundercloud, Jill's career would always be at risk of some scandal or other spilling over onto her.

"Are you saying I should stay with someone I didn't have feelings for just to spare hers?"

"No, that's not what I'm saying." She huffed, sitting in the chair opposite my desk without waiting for an invitation. Not that Aspen would wait. She wasn't the kind of girl to wait for anything. She took what she wanted without apology. I envied her.

"I just... I really like her, Blaize."

"You date her, then."

She huffed again, this time through her nose. "Are you being obtuse on purpose?"

"No. Merely truthful." A great fat lie. "Hang on."

I raised a finger as she opened her mouth with what was undoubtedly another comeback and picked up my phone. "I need to take this. Hello, Steve. What have you got?"

Steve was the techie I'd hired to fix the TikTok issue. "Done."

I waited to see if he'd say something else. The line remained silent. I'd discovered that Steve was a man of few words when I'd hired him, but that might be a record.

"Both of them?"

"Yes."

"And what about any new ones that might spring up?"

"They won't."

"How can you be sure?"

A brief laugh was my answer. Okay, then.

"Thanks, Steve."

"Sure."

He hung up. I chuckled. I'd keep Steve's number on my contact list. A man like that could be useful for all kinds of things.

Aspen cleared her throat, reminding me that she hadn't left.

More's the pity.

"What was that about?"

"None of your business. Why are you still here?"

"Because I haven't finished saying what I came to say yet."

"Lucky me. Get on with it, then. I'm busy."

She glowered. "You didn't have to say such horrible things to Jill, Blaize. You could have broached it in a kinder way. She didn't deserve that."

A vise clamped around my chest. The longer Aspen was here pointing out Jill's hurt and my culpability, the harder I found it to maintain the illusion that I gave zero shits.

"I don't appreciate my ex's running off to my family, crying victim."

Aspen made fists with both of her hands and brought them down on my desk with an almighty crack.

"She didn't, you asshole. I called her because I wanted to see how you were doing, and as the decision on whether you pick up your phone blows with the fucking wind direction, it made sense to reach out to Jill. When she told me she was back in England, I almost had an embolism."

"And you got on a plane from New York just to come

tell me I'm an asshole?" I forced a smile. "Wasted journey, cous. I already know."

"Jesus Christ, Blaize."

She shook her head, her shoulders bowing in defeat.

Good.

Maybe she'd leave soon and I could go back to wallowing in self-pity and beating myself up on the regular. Anything was better than thinking about Jill back in England, alone and smarting from how I'd ended things between us.

"I know something's wrong." She pierced me with that fiery gaze once more. "I don't buy this bullshit. Are you somehow trying to play the hero because of those trolls who went after Jill?"

I hadn't a clue how I kept my composure. My heart froze midbeat, then galloped. Beads of sweat gathered on my forehead. It was freezing in my office, the A/C at full blast given the ninety-degree heat outside.

"Because if you are, it's bullshit. Today's headlines are tomorrow's trash."

Jill had said something similar.

I disagreed.

Scandals such as the kind my family and I were caught up in took far longer to dissipate. Jill's career might not last that long. And even if it did, why put the woman I loved through that much trauma?

Now *that* made me an asshole.

"I've already told you why I broke things off. Fuck's sake, Aspen. When did my love life become your business?"

"When you broke my friend's heart, jerkface."

"Oh, so because you've collected another bestie, I can't move on?"

"I already told you that's not what I'm saying. Don't twist my words. You'll fucking lose. The way you told Jill it was over was unnecessary and cruel. I guess this is what happens when a serial one-nighter like you gets embroiled in something that lasts longer than a dog's fart."

"Nice," I drawled.

For the first time since she'd entered my office like a Category 5 hurricane, her lips twitched.

"I can do better, but I won't. You're not worth it."

"Praise the Lord."

"Asshole," she muttered.

"Nosy bitch," I retorted.

I received a proper smile for that one. She rose to her feet.

Oh, good. She's going.

"Thanks for coming. On your way out, grab me some arnica cream for the welts your tongue has left behind."

"I'm not leaving."

My eyebrows flew up my forehead. "Excuse me?"

"No, I won't fucking excuse you. You haven't earned it. I told Uncle Jameson that I'm sticking around for a few days. See if I can't talk some fucking sense into you."

Using my desk to help me to my feet, I stood. "You're not staying here."

"I think you'll find that I am. Renata has already unpacked my things. It's not like you don't have room. Oh, and I've met Mara and told her to take a couple of days off. You're virtually self-sufficient now anyway."

She did a one-eighty, striding over to my office door. I

hadn't recovered my voice when she glanced over her shoulder.

"One last thing. Get changed. We have lunch reservations at one."

With a casual wave, she disappeared, leaving my door wide open.

What the actual fuck?

Chapter 32

Jill

Courage is facing your fears rather than running from them.

A MONTH HAD PASSED SINCE BLAY HAD KICKED ME out of his house, his cutting words ringing in my ears. I'd cried so much on the flight home that the cabin crew must have thought I was dying, or something equally awful.

Each morning I opened my eyes, hoping the heaviness sitting on my chest would have vanished, only to find more weight had been added overnight.

This morning, though, things were different.

Oh, I still ached, but I finally had something to distract me, something to look forward to.

Well, two things, although one of them was so fucking scary I struggled to breathe every time I thought about it.

Scary things were good things, though. A lecturer at university once told me that courage was facing up to fear of the unknown rather than running away from it.

I slotted a few things into a shoulder bag and grabbed a light jacket and an umbrella. My train to London didn't leave for another thirty minutes, and I lived a five-minute walk from the station, yet I always had this habit of arriving for any kind of public transport far earlier than necessary, then cursing my preparedness when I had to hang around for ages.

If Samantha didn't like what I'd done with this book, then too bad. I'd already decided to self-publish it, especially if she wanted me to change large swathes of it. I didn't mind tweaking here and there, but the bulk of it stayed.

All one hundred and ten thousand words of it.

My longest book to date had been a labor of love in some ways and a cathartic exorcism in others.

A way to celebrate the time Blay and I had shared, despite how it'd ended, but also a chance for me to move on, to face up to an uncertain future without the man who'd given me a parting gift I hadn't expected.

My gaze drifted to the pregnancy test I'd taken yesterday morning when I'd thrown up for the third day in a row. It was one of those that baldly stated "pregnant" or "not pregnant," you know, in case women's hormones made it far too difficult for us to process the difference between one line and two.

My eyes rolled of their own accord. I bet a man had designed these tests.

Butterflies swarmed my stomach.

A baby.

I was going to have a baby.

I must have looked at this test a hundred times or more yesterday. I'd taken three others just to be sure, and when they'd all come back with the same result, I'd finally believed it.

It could only have happened on one of two occasions.

Either in Barbados or the one and only time Blay and I had had sex after his accident.

Until I saw the doctor tomorrow and underwent a proper examination, I wouldn't know whether I was in the very early stages or already into my third month of pregnancy.

Unbelievable.

The jury was still out on whether I should tell him. On the one hand, he deserved to know he'd fathered a child. On the other, I worried he'd either think I'd trapped him into it as a way to force him into something he didn't want, or he'd want nothing to do with me or the child.

Being at the end of either scenario wasn't all that appealing.

Besides, I was still newly pregnant. Anything could happen. There wasn't any point in telling him yet when so much could go wrong.

Tears pricked my eyes, and my stomach tilted. I wrapped my arms around my middle.

Already, this bunch of cells ruled my emotions. I couldn't bear to think of an outcome other than a healthy, bouncing baby who'd keep me up all night, give me lifelong bladder problems, and puke on my favorite T-shirt.

Even if I did this on my own, I had several things in my

favor. I was a strong woman—capable, financially independent, and most importantly, able to work flexibly. I didn't have to deal with a demanding boss who'd pretend to be understanding, only to turn into a beast at an approaching deadline.

Within half an hour, I was on the train and headed for London. The knots in my stomach wouldn't loosen until I was sitting opposite Samantha and hearing the words "I love it" spill from her lips.

Despite my vow to self-publish if she passed, I still craved her approval. I might have only released one book with my publisher, but my editor and I had struck up a friendship from the moment we'd been introduced, and her endorsement of a story that included some personal experience meant a lot to me.

Not that I intended to share with the media or my readers that I'd used what had happened to Blay and me when crafting the follow-up to my bestseller. I'd changed enough of the details to ensure that the fictional and real events wouldn't marry up.

Two and a half hours later, I disembarked at Paddington Station and emerged into the clammy heat of inner London just as the lunchtime rush began. Workers, profusely sweating in their suits and high heels, dashed from office buildings to grab a bite to eat before the interminable afternoon meetings got underway.

I dodged several streams of them, wondering, as I often did on the odd occasion I came to London, if I'd missed some sign and was walking in the wrong direction.

I arrived fifteen minutes early for my meeting with

Samantha, so I ordered a coffee and a slice of Madeira cake and grabbed a seat by the window.

Scrolling on my phone, I came across a glowing review a new reader had left on a book I'd published a couple of years ago. I smiled to myself. This shit never got old. I loved it when readers took the time to leave reviews. They owed me nothing other than the price of the book, which made me even more grateful when they took time out of their lives to share their experience when reading one of my stories.

The trolling I'd suffered the day Blay had kicked me out had disappeared as fast as it had emerged. I'd assumed the PR department at my publishers had used their clout, but when I'd dropped Samantha a note to tell her to pass on my thanks, she'd said they'd had no luck with the online retailers, nor did they have any leverage over TikTok, a.k.a. the Wild West of social media apps.

That left only one option: Blay must have somehow cleaned it up.

But why?

A parting gift to assuage his guilt at the heartless way he'd kicked me out, perhaps?

Whatever his reasons, he had my silent gratitude. One day I might tell him that in person.

Maybe.

As if the universe knew I was thinking about Blay, a text arrived from Aspen. She'd taken it upon herself to give me regular updates about Blay's progress, and like an addict craving a fix, I hadn't asked her to stop. When she'd told me how she'd muscled her way into his house, despite his protestations, it'd brought a much-needed smile to my face.

Served him right.

Aspen would give him hell, and he'd hate her invading his home and telling him what to do.

I opened the message, greedily drinking in the information. Blay had had his permanent prosthetic fitted, and according to Aspen, he was doing much better with this one. He was up and walking, taking his rehabilitation as seriously as his job. Mara had left now that he didn't need her to help him with day-to-day things, something his physical therapist had agreed was for the best.

I sent a quick reply and returned my phone to my bag as Samantha dropped into the seat opposite mine. She got in first before I could say a word.

"This, my darling girl, is going to be a smash hit. It's better than the first one. Much better. I could not put it down." As my shoulders sagged, she pointed to her eyes. "See these bags? They're your fault."

I laughed. "God, Samantha, you've no idea how relieved I am. I was all ready to self-publish if you decided you hated it."

Samantha's eyebrows shot up her forehead. "Dear God, girl. Are you insane? On which planet would I not have loved this? I know you struggled with every word, especially as, in that genius writer's mind of yours, you'd already completed Arton and Kenna's story. They'd gotten their happily-ever-after in *Pieces of Me*. Then, in this book, you tear them apart in the most horrifying of circumstances, only to give the reader an ending that's going to break hearts. It's an incredible piece of work, Jill. Incredible."

Every cell in my body cried with relief, and those darned pregnancy hormones went crazy, filling my eyes with tears I couldn't stop from falling in rivers down my cheeks. Samantha looked equal parts alarmed and incredulous. Never a big hugger, she leaned across the table and patted my hand.

"Now, now. No need for waterworks." She grabbed a handful of napkins and thrust them at me. "Dry those tears, girl. We have work to do."

I dabbed my eyes and blew my nose, then squared my shoulders. "I'm okay. It's just—"

"Relief. I know. I get it. I've boosted your ego. Now I'm bringing you back down to earth. I talked to Rosie last night, and we both agree that, with a wing and a prayer and a fuck of a lot of hard work for you, me, and the entire team, we can make the original print run."

Rosie was the head honcho at my publishers, Samantha's boss, and a woman who ran her business with an iron fist. If she'd put her muscle behind making the original print run, I would not let her down.

My insides performed a little jig, excitement warming my belly. "Tell me what I have to do."

Three weeks later, I sat on my sofa with two printed copies of *Echoes of You* resting on the coffee table in front of me.

Severely lacking in sleep, I'd run on adrenaline for pretty much nineteen days straight until I'd received a final copy of my manuscript in my inbox. I'd had my local printer whip up two gold-foiled paperbacks for me, which I'd had to secure Rosie's approval for in case anything leaked. I trusted Pete, though. He'd printed off copies of all my manuscripts without a problem, and I didn't expect any this time.

I hadn't told Rosie I was having two copies printed, though. She would not approve of what I planned to do with the second one.

I picked up a copy, carefully leafing through the pages. Bringing the book to my nose, I sniffed deeply. There was nothing quite like the smell of a new book. Non-bookish people would never understand the pull to stick your nose right in there and get your fill.

Turning to the dedication, my insides collided with each other. I couldn't begin to guess how Blay would take to receiving a copy of this book and reading what I'd put inside the front cover.

In my dreams, I imagined the power of the written word galvanizing him into action. He'd call me and beg my forgiveness—something I was all too ready to give—and say he wanted me back.

If he did, I wouldn't hesitate.

And if he didn't...

I'd have to find a way to live the rest of my life without him, even though I'd always have a part of him in the child we'd created together.

I took the book into my study, sat behind my desk, reached for my favorite pen, and added my signature right underneath the dedication.

It crossed my mind to include a handwritten note, but in the end, I decided against it. I put it inside a box, walked down to the village post office, and handed it over before I lost my nerve.

The ball was in Blay's court now.

Chapter 33

Blaize

**A red-hot poker jammed into your chest
is not a fun experience.**

BETRAYAL WAS ONE OF THOSE THINGS THAT, WHEN IT
happened to you, it took a few days for your brain to recon-
cile the truth of the matter. During that time, the mind
played tricks, whipping you between two contrasting
points. One of hurt and anger, the other of disbelief, that,
somehow, it wasn't true. That you'd misunderstood the
message.

I'd gotten the message. Loud and clear. And I hadn't
misunderstood a damn thing.

How could she do this to me?

Was it revenge because I'd ended our relationship? A

woman scorned and all that? Or did she think she'd used clever prose to hide the fact that she'd taken the horrific events of that day and turned them into a sellable product she could profit from?

Whatever her reasons, the outcome was the same. She'd taken a red-hot poker and driven it into my chest.

While I'd spent the last two months mourning her and working on my recovery in some ridiculously misplaced belief that I'd have to earn her forgiveness, she'd spent her time writing a book. One that laid out in vivid technicolor the destructive bomb that had exploded in the middle of my life and turned it upside down.

It didn't matter to me that only those in the know, such as my family, and Carly, my assistant, would connect the dots, putting two and two together and making four. What mattered was that Jill had shown her true colors with every word she'd bled onto the page.

And she thought I'd be *flattered*?

My gaze drifted to the dedication once more, my hands gripping the book until my knuckles turned white.

To B. The man who made me believe in myself. Thank you.

I'd made her believe in herself so much that she'd turned Judas.

Well, fuck her.

All the pain, the sweat and blood and tears of these last couple of months were worthless to me now.

If my house had a real fire, I'd toss the damn book into the flames and watch it burn. But this was Miami.

Barbecue it was, then.

But first...

I rose to my feet and walked to my study on the one stick I still relied on for balance. I'd worked my nuts off to get back on my feet, and for what? So I could stand tall when Jill nailed me in the balls?

Propping the crutch against my desk, I flopped into my chair and opened my laptop, navigating to the email program. My fingers flew over the keyboard. I didn't address her by name or end with my usual insignia. I wrote two sentences.

You turned the worst time in my life into a money-making opportunity? What kind of person does that?

I hit Send, slamming the lid on the laptop. For the first time since she'd returned to New York four weeks ago, I wished Aspen were here, if only for someone to vent my rage at, knowing she'd absorb it without taking offense.

So many questions ran through my mind. If I hadn't ended things to save her career, would she still have written that novel in the same way? She'd told me she was working on it when she was here, but she'd refused to let me look at it. Was this the reason? Or had she changed tactics after I'd broken things off?

Did I even care?

I spun my chair around to face the window that overlooked the driveway. I didn't even have to close my eyes to conjure the vision of Jill getting into a taxi, clutching her suitcase with white knuckles and casting a glance back at the house in an almost hopeful yet resigned manner. I'd held the shattered pieces of myself together and let her go, certain in my belief that I was doing the right thing. The selfless thing.

And all the while, she'd planned to put her poison pen into action.

The ding from my email program struck me in the gut. It could be a message from hundreds of people, but I already knew it wasn't. My suspicions were confirmed when I opened the laptop again and there it was, right at the top. A reply from Jill. I clicked on it, my eyes darting over the rows of text.

I got to the end and snorted. Sorry, my ass. How the fuck did she think I'd take it? She'd had the balls to write that she thought I'd be flattered. Was the woman insane? And that crap about never meaning to hurt me. What bullshit.

If she never meant to hurt me, I'd happily test the theory.

I typed a reply.

If you feel that bad, pull the publication.

The response was almost instantaneous, as if she'd known to wait for my reply, fingers poised on the keyboard.

I'm afraid I can't do that.

I slammed the lid, wrenched out the power cord, and threw the fucking thing across my office.

Guess I have my answer.

"Your father is here."

My head snapped up from where I'd had my head buried in my computer, sifting through countless emails I couldn't muster the enthusiasm to answer. Nothing soothed me, not even work. I'd assumed it would be the panacea I needed to distract me from the fuckup that was my life, but my focus was off. I couldn't drop in, no matter what I tried. My mind was all over the place, and I'd pretty much cut myself off from everyone. Any day now, I'd adopt a bunch of cats, completing my recluse status.

"What?" I frowned at Renata, asking a question as if I hadn't heard perfectly well what she'd said. "Why?"

An equally idiotic question. How the fuck would Renata know why my father had flown all the way from Seattle to Miami without telling me he'd planned to visit? I knew the answer to the last part. I'd have told him not to bother.

Renata sensibly ignored my query. "Shall I show him in?"

I could hardly refuse now, could I? Inclining my head, I leaned back in my office chair and folded my hands in my lap, the epitome of the calm and in-control son Dad had raised me to be. Inside was a different story. My stomach turned jittery, and prickles raced along the back of my neck, making the hairs stand on end.

Dad was here for one reason and one reason only: intervention. At least he hadn't brought Mom. Against the two of them, I wouldn't stand a chance. They were formidable and relentless when the situation called for it. A little like I used to be before all this had happened.

"Son." Dad patted Renata on the shoulder, his way of dismissing her, and entered my office, closing the door behind him. "It's good to see you."

I swallowed past a lump in my throat, my emotions bubbling to the surface at the worry etched on Dad's face.

"You, too, Dad." I gestured to the seat opposite my desk. "To what do I owe the pleasure?"

He arched an eyebrow. "It's me, son. Your father. Not an associate you once shook hands with at a party you can't remember attending." He sat down and crossed his legs. "Your mother is worried about you. So am I. Your brothers, too. The whole family is concerned. Talk to me. Let me help you."

The steel cage I'd locked around my heart split open as if Dad's softly spoken words had melted it, leaving my heart exposed to emotions I didn't want to face. The lump in my throat grew in size, cutting off air to my lungs.

"I'm fine." I lied, my voice rasping. "Your concern is misplaced."

He cocked his head to the side. "Son. Ever since your mother placed you in my arms thirty-one years ago, I've been the proudest father that ever lived. And I'm *still* that proud father. You and your brothers are my greatest achievements. Your mom and I raised three amazing children. So, please, don't lie to me. Not to me, and not to yourself."

The dam broke with such little effort that it took me by surprise. Tears spilled from my eyes, rolling down my cheeks in a torrent. If the rest of my family were here, Mom would smother me in a tight hug, Kadon would tease me mercilessly, and Nolen would pat me on the back hard enough to crack a bone. But Dad simply sat there, his only action to push a handkerchief across my desk. My dad was one of the few people left in the world who still used cotton handkerchiefs. The familiarity of it brought a faint smile to my lips.

I wiped my eyes and blew my nose. "Guess you don't want this back?"

"Laundered, yes. Snot-filled? No."

A quiet chuckle rumbled through my chest.

"Ready to talk now?" Dad pressed.

"No. But you're not leaving until I do, are you?"

Dad merely jutted his chin and settled back into his seat. I held a breath in my lungs, giving me a few precious seconds to organize my thoughts. I started to talk, and once I did, I couldn't stop. All my pre-sailing concerns came spilling out. The insignificant problems that grew in number, each one eating away at my confidence. The badge scanners going down a couple of days before departure, the security door left open, processes I'd designed that had allowed that technician to get a job on my ship. The guilt I felt for the lives lost, and the damage my failures had caused to the Kingcaid brand. By the time I finished, I could have happily slept for a week.

Dad didn't interrupt me once, and even after I fell silent, he still kept quiet, stroking his chin in deep contemplation.

"How many ships have I overseen from concept to their maiden voyage?"

Where is he going with this? I counted them in my mind. "Nine."

"And how many of those do you think went off without a hitch?"

Ah. That's where he's going. "I'd guess none."

"Correct. So answer me this, son. Why do you think your project was supposed to go smoothly? What do you know that the rest of us don't? Please, share your wisdom so I can share it with the rest of the board." He accompanied his sarcasm with a crooked grin.

For the first time in what felt like months, I cracked up, barking a laugh. "Well, I *am* the genius of the family."

His grin grew, reaching for his twinkling eyes. "It's true. If only we were all such intellectual masters. Look, all jokes aside, things break on ships all the time. You know this. And a build like Serenity was always going to have more than her fair share of problems. But what happened that day was *not* your fault, and I won't stand for you heaping the blame on your shoulders. You are not responsible for every tick and every cross. It's physically impossible to be across the minutiae in a company the size of ours. That's why we have teams."

I opened my mouth to defend my stance. Teams, yes, but since I was the CEO, the buck stopped with me.

Dad got there first. "And don't you dare say that since you're the CEO, the buck stops with you like that means you're supposed to be this perfect being who can somehow stop all mistakes or accidents before they've occurred." He rose to his feet, planting his hands flat on my desk. "You. Were. Not. Responsible. Do you hear me, son? Because you're not too old for a clip around the ear."

"Jill said the same."

My father's lips thinned as he sat back down. "Smart

girl, Jill. A woman like that, son... you're a fool to let her slip through your fingers."

"Dad, you know why I broke things off. I couldn't allow her career to go down the toilet along with mine. But she did something to me that I... I can't forgive."

Dad's eyebrows met in the middle. "What did she do?"

I got up and went over to the bookshelf lining one wall in my office. I couldn't understand why I hadn't burned the damn thing yet. Maybe I'd kept it for an occasion just like this one. I tossed the book onto the desk in front of Dad.

"She wrote a novel, but it's far from fiction. She took the worst time in my life and used it to make money."

He picked up the book, turning it over in his hands, then flicked through the pages. "Is it obvious it's about you?"

"To me, yeah."

"What about to those outside the circle?"

I hitched a shoulder. "Probably not. But that's not the point, Dad."

"Oh? Then what is the point?"

Was he being purposely obtuse? "She shouldn't have fucking written it!" I roared, anger bubbling to the surface. Dad was supposed to be on my side. "Not without asking me first."

"Don't a lot of writers pull on their own experiences to craft interesting stories? Does she make you look bad?"

"No idea. I only skimmed a few chapters. But I got the gist."

Dad rubbed his forehead. "I'm confused. You're annoyed because Jill wrote about her shared experience with you, even though only you and maybe a handful of close confidants would know it was you. And you've made this leap based on a novel you haven't even read?"

I fell silent. He didn't understand.

"What's the general premise of the book?"

A shrug rolled over my shoulders. "Love story, I guess."

"Hmm." Dad opened the book. "Lovely dedication."

"You think?" I couldn't keep the sarcasm out of my voice.

"As a matter of fact, I do." Dad put the book back down. "Son, for a genius, you can be a dumbass at times."

The ridge of my back straightened. "What's that supposed to mean?"

"It means that a woman you'd only known a few days stood by you after you were shot. She stayed by your side in that hospital every day for two weeks. She returned home with you, leaving her own home and country behind her. She nursed you back to health, and even when you were an impossible grouch, she didn't waver in her love for you. To thank her for her loyalty, you dumped her, which, by the way, I didn't agree with. In response, she wrote a love story about her time together with you, dedicated it to you, sent you a beautiful, signed copy, and you're the one who's mad at her?" He shook his head. "She's the one who has every right to be mad, not you."

"She should have asked me," I reiterated, my mouth on the verge of a pout I was far too old to pull off. I thought Dad would be on my side, that he'd agree with my outrage. How wrong could I be?

"And if she had, what would you have said?"

"No."

"Precisely." He got up once more. "Here's what we're

gonna do. We're going to go down to that place by the waterfront I like, have a nice dinner and a bottle of good wine, and enjoy the sunset. And you're going to tell me how you plan to get yourself back to the man you once were so that you're worthy of begging that wonderful girl for forgiveness."

Chapter 34

Jill

Time to face the music.

FOUR MONTHS LATER...

"This was a huge mistake." I wiped clammy hands on a scrap piece of tissue, my heart beating far too fast. This level of panic couldn't be good for the baby, surely? I ran a hand over my extended belly, still incredulous at how big I'd gotten.

"Not as huge as that bump." Addison grinned. "And they say the last few weeks are when you grow the most."

I groaned. "Christ, don't tell me that."

"You know me, babe. I'm the truth fairy."

Kelsey and Raya made their way through the vast hall where my publisher had arranged for me to read an excerpt from *Echoes of You* to a number of the literary world's most influential people and some big-shot film producers. When the idea was suggested to me, it had seemed like a good career move. Now... it might be the worst decision of my entire life.

Well, this and not telling Blay about the baby. But after the angry email he'd sent to me, I'd lost my nerve. I'd hoped sending him the book would open a dialogue channel between us. *Guess I got that spectacularly wrong.* Then, as the weeks had turned into months, the thought of telling him had gotten harder and harder, and now I couldn't see a way through the mess I'd created.

Or rather, we'd *both* created. I refused to take all the blame for this situation.

Surrounded by my girls, I soaked up their positivity and encouragement, and gradually, my heart rate slowed to within normal range. I could do this. All I had to do was sit there and read a couple thousand words to a bunch of strangers who could make or break my future success.

Easy street, right? If only.

"You got this, Jill." Kelsey gave me one of her encouraging looks, accompanied by a shoulder squeeze.

"What if I trip as I walk onstage and fall flat on my face?"

"With that bump?" Addison laughed. "Not likely, babe. You'll bounce right back up."

"You're such a comedienne."

"It's true. I missed my vocation."

Samantha appeared in my sight line, a grin the size of Africa stretching across her face. This was right up her street. I should make her do it. She hadn't stopped beaming since we'd arrived an hour ago.

"They're ready for you."

"Well, I'm not ready for them."

Samantha rolled her eyes. "I get the whole pregnancy hormone thing, but pull on your big-girl knickers, Jill, and get out there."

Have I mentioned that Samantha's empathy doesn't even register on the CliftonStrengths scale?

"You're all heart."

"Swinging brick in there, Jill." She pointed to her chest and laughed. "According to my English Literature professor, that is."

"He was spot-on."

She brushed something imaginary off her shoulders. "Teflon-coated and proud."

Sucking air deep into my lungs, I closed my eyes and imagined a time in the not-so-distant future when this would all be over and I could skulk back to my little cottage by the seaside and bury myself in my next project. I was far more comfortable spending time with my characters than a bunch of strangers, no matter what they could do for my career.

On cheese string legs, I wobbled my way across the stage to thunderous applause. If a genie popped out of a bottle right this second and granted me one wish, it would be for me to send on a clone in my place and have them read the damn excerpt. With all this AI advancement I kept reading about, you would think they'd have nailed cloning.

The chair arranged for me to sit in was a high-backed

affair. Not hugely comfortable, but at least I wouldn't struggle to get up afterward. A couple of weeks ago, I'd made the mistake of choosing a comfy sofa in the coffee shop in my village, and the owner plus two helpful customers—the local butcher and the owner of the village pub—had to help me up again.

Looked as if I was giving up caffeine, meat, and alcohol because hell would freeze over before I'd pluck up the courage to face any of them again.

Hands shaking, I opened the book to the chapter pre-chosen by Samantha and Rosie. *Trust them to pick one of the most emotional scenes in the book.* Told from the point of view of Kenna, my main female character, it was right after Arton's doctor had broken the news that he'd never walk again. Even though it differed from what had happened to Blay, I'd written the entire scene with tears streaming down my face. It was too close to home for comfort, but both Samantha and Rosie had assured me the only dry eyes in the house would be those with empathy lower than Samantha's.

"Thank you for being here," I began, my eyes drifting over the rows of people all gawking at me. I despised being the center of attention. It was one of the reasons why Addison and I were such close friends. She was the opposite of me in every way, and we gelled because of it. "I'd like to read to you the scene where—"

My gaze alighted on a man standing at the back of the room, his hip propped against the wall, arms folded over his broad chest. Dressed in a smart gray suit, crisp white shirt, and cobalt-blue tie, there was no mistaking his identity, even from this distance. Nor was there any mistaking his shocked expression as his gaze fell to my stomach before lifting to my eyes.

I sent a panicked look at Addison standing just out of sight at the side of the stage. She frowned. My eyes flashed back to Blay, then returned to Addison. Her eyes widened, and she gave me one curt nod before disappearing.

What was he doing here?

Oh God. How would I explain my decision to keep the pregnancy from him? Suddenly, my reasoning, once so solid and fixed in my mind, sounded hollow. Weak. Selfish.

Squaring my shoulders, I cleared my throat. "My apologies. The scene I've chosen to read today is one of my favorites in the entire book. It's also one I found the hardest to write. Kenna's excruciating agony when she learns of Arton's prognosis is palpable. I hope you'll agree with me."

I glanced up. Blay was no longer standing at the back of the hall. Sweat dripped between my boobs, several sizes larger, thanks to my impending arrival, and I had this terrible sense of foreboding. Had I imagined his presence? No. He'd been there. And now he wasn't. I shifted my attention to the side of the stage. Addison was still missing. I'd wager that she'd forced him to leave under threat of severe violence.

I couldn't love her more.

My decision to keep my pregnancy from Blay, however well meant, suddenly seemed like the most selfish act. So what if he'd been a bastard to me after I'd sent him a copy of the book I was about to read a passage from? That did not excuse keeping news of the baby from him. I hated the popular secret-baby trope in romance books, yet here I was, living the live-action version.

I feel sick.

Somehow, I read the first line, then the second, and by the time I got to the third paragraph, my nerves scattered, my voice growing stronger with each passing sentence, and I parked the fact that I'd soon have to face righteous anger from a man I still loved. Because I did. The moment our eyes had met across the room, the feelings I'd buried roared to the surface, deafening me in their clamor to run into his arms and beg his forgiveness.

I read the last line, so engrossed in the moment that I forgot about the audience. Only when rapturous applause broke out, accompanied by a standing ovation, did I pull myself back to the present and accept their generous accolades with a bright smile.

Time to face the music.

Rising to my feet, I thanked everyone for coming, then gave the floor to Samantha to close out. I rushed offstage, slap bang into Addison.

"Where is he?"

"Cooling his heels. I told him if he didn't calm the fuck down, I'd make sure he didn't get to see you."

I chewed on my bottom lip, my stomach tying itself in knots. "So he's mad?" Oh, who was I kidding? Of course he was mad, and he had every right to be. My reasoning for keeping my pregnancy a secret sounded thin and without substance.

"More *confused*, I'd say. Shocked, too. And hurt. He said a lot of words, but only a few of them made sense."

Oh God. "Those are worse than mad. Mad, I can cope with. Mad, I can rail against. But hurt..." I shook my head. "This is going to wreck me."

"One of us can come with you, if you'd like." Kelsey rubbed my arm soothingly.

"I should have told him." I shook my head. "I should have told him as soon as my doctor confirmed it, but I was so busy finishing the manuscript and meeting deadlines, and then he was so hateful after I sent him a copy that I... I—"

"Fantastic job, Jill." Samantha beamed and gave me a hug. "Terry Sonnerham has already requested a meeting with Rosie to pitch for the film rights, and it wouldn't surprise me at all if more producers follow suit." She frowned when I gave her a weak grin and managed an even weaker nod. "What's the matter? Aren't you happy?"

"I'm ecstatic. It's great news."

"Ecstatic?" Samantha laughed, looking at each of my friends and then back at me. "Can you let your face know?"

"Blaize is here," Addison said, her tone unusually flat.

I glowered at her. Samantha was my editor, and while I considered her a friend, she was first and foremost a business associate. Her job was to make my words shine and give me a shoulder to cry on when I thought everything I wrote was a pile of shit. Her job was not to get embroiled in my father-of-the-baby fiasco.

"Oh." She grimaced. "I see."

"Where is he?" I asked Addison again.

"I sent him to the coffee shop across the road. I thought the pub on the corner wasn't a good idea."

I dipped my chin. "Right, well, I'd best go and..." I trailed off, the end of the sentence eluding me.

"Do you want company?" Kelsey touched my arm again.

"No. I've got this."

Yeah, right. I didn't have it. Not even close. But I owed him an explanation, and to take whatever outrage came my way.

I waddled over the road to the coffee shop on legs that resembled those of a newborn foal. The place was locally owned, rather than one of the big chains, and the scent of fresh flowers and vanilla candles greeted me as I entered. Blay's gaze burned into me the second I stepped over the threshold, his green eyes swimming with bewilderment and a hefty dose of torment. My hands instinctively went to my bump. His gaze followed, lifting to my face only when I was standing right in front of the table.

"Hi." My voice faltered, almost inaudible over the sound of the espresso machine letting off steam, and the overall business of the place.

Blay rose to his feet, clearing his throat. "Do you want something to drink?"

I rubbed my lips together, staring at his chin because I was a goddamn coward and couldn't meet his eyes.

"Um, water would be good. Thank you." I removed my coat and draped it over the back of the chair. Blay dipped his chin, the confusion and hurt in his eyes replaced with a hardness that unsettled my stomach. I sat down, angling my chair so I could watch him walk away. There wasn't a trace of a limp. He looked as commanding and in control as he ever had. No one would be able to tell he'd lost a limb in such tragic circumstances.

He returned with a water and a plastic tub of mixed

fresh fruit. "Vitamins," he said when I raised my eyebrows. "You look washed out."

Now probably wasn't the time to tell him I only looked washed out because I was terrified of explaining the unexplainable. I murmured my thanks and peeled back the plastic covering, slipping a juicy piece of pineapple between my lips. Flavor exploded on my tongue. Pineapple was one of my favorite fruits. Blay twisted the cap off the water, pushing it toward me, then took a sip of his half-finished coffee.

We sat in silence for a few seconds. He glared at me. I squirmed. Eventually, I plucked up the courage to speak.

"I can explain."

He folded his hands in his lap and knitted his fingers together. Probably to stop himself from throttling me.

"Is it mine?"

My eyes widened. "Yes!" I blurted. "Whose did you think it was?"

"How would I know? I haven't seen you in months."

"And whose fault is that?" I snapped.

He poked his tongue in his cheek and showed me his palms. "I deserve that."

"Yes, you do."

"But I don't deserve this." He indicated my swollen belly. "If I hadn't come here, would you have told me you were pregnant with my child?"

"Yes."

He looked skeptical. Couldn't blame him.

"I had every intention of telling you. In fact, I planned to tell you months ago, not long after I found out."

"Then why didn't you?"

"Because you accused me of using what happened to you to make money. After that, I kind of lost my nerve."

His face twisted, and a hint of shame pulled his features tight. "I shouldn't have said what I did."

"If you thought it, then you had every right to say it. For the record, it wasn't true."

"I realize that now."

I sat upright. I'd expected him to double down on his belief that I'd profited from his pain. "Oh yeah?" My high-pitched tone gave away my level of surprise. "How come?"

"My father made me see things differently than I had." His eyes darkened. "He said it amounted to a love letter. Did it? Was that your intention?"

"In a way, yes. I changed enough of the details that readers won't have a clue I based Arton and Kenna's story on us." I heaved a sigh. "When I met you on that plane, I wasn't in a great place. I'd just had an enormous amount of success thrust at me, and all the expectations that came with it, and instead of giving me confidence, the opposite happened. I'd lost my way, and I didn't know how to fix it. Then you came along and changed everything. I couldn't have written the story I did if you and I hadn't met, and not because I used real-life events to inspire it, but because you made me believe in myself, believe that what-ever I dreamed could come true. It bled onto the page, and the result is something... wonderful. Whatever you think of my reasoning, and however badly you think of me, I wouldn't change a single thing about their love story. This book is an homage to how deeply I fell in love with you."

"What about now? Do you still love me?"

I raised my eyebrows, my hand moving to my stomach as the baby kicked. "Yes."

"Even after what I said, what I did?"

"Yes." I sighed again, picking up my water to lubricate my dry throat. "Feelings aren't negated just because the person we love doesn't feel the same way."

"What if they do feel the same way, but they're a stubborn, stupid fool who took too long to realize their mistake? And even when they acknowledged their idiocy, they didn't want to come to you and beg for forgiveness until they'd worked through the physical and emotional trauma with the best professionals in the business and were whole again."

My heart fluttered, missing a beat. The baby kicked once more. I wondered if he or she was listening to this entire conversation and prodding me to respond favorably.

I gave him my eyes. "And do they feel the same way?"

His face crumpled, and he reached across the table for my hand. I gave it willingly, the feel of his skin after such a long absence making my insides sing.

"They do." He brought my hand to his lips, kissing my palm. "I've missed you so fucking much. You saved my life, and I pushed you away. I broke things off because I worried your career would flush down the toilet after those vile trolls went after you, and then when you approached me, I acted with unnecessary cruelty."

"*That's* why you broke up with me? Because of the online abuse?" I had not seen that coming. Jesus, the guy should be onstage or in the movies, with acting abilities as good as that.

"Yes. I'd destroyed my business. I couldn't sit idly by

and ruin yours, too. But even after I had the one-star reviews removed, and those TikToks silenced, I still couldn't pluck up the courage to call you. I persisted in the belief that until I'd fixed the PR disaster and waited for memories to fade, I couldn't risk associating myself with you. Then the book arrived, and I... overreacted. Dad and my therapist both helped me see things differently."

So he saw a therapist after all. "*You* had the reviews removed? My publisher tried but got nowhere."

He gave me a crooked smile. "It pays to be me sometimes."

"Wow." I blew out a breath. "That's some influence."

"I guess." He shrugged. "The journalist got his hands on a few company emails. That's how he discovered all the problems we'd had before sailing, and he twisted them to his own advantage."

"How?"

"We're still investigating. He won't name his sources. A disgruntled employee, maybe? It'd have to be someone on the executive committee to have access to that kind of information, or an assistant who works for an executive member. But forget that. It's not important."

He sandwiched my hand between his. "Forgive me. I'm sorry for pushing you away. I'm sorry for what I said to you when you sent me a copy of your novel. I'm sorry for so many fucking things. I shouldn't have waited this long to come to you, but I've been mired in my recovery. I needed to come to you when I'd fixed my messed up head and could stand on my own two feet. Call it a man thing, or a pride thing, but I had to make myself worthy of you. If you'll take me back, I promise I'll spend the rest of my life making it up to you. To you, and our baby. Through my own stubbornness, I've missed so much. I don't want to miss another second."

Tears ran down my face. Stupid pregnancy hormones. I cried at anything these days. Only yesterday, I'd cried at a news item about a woman who'd lost her keys at the supermarket checkout, only for a kind Samaritan to track her down and return them. Must've been a slow news day.

He let go of my hand and dried my tears with his thumbs. "Say something. Please."

I stared into his eyes, the burn of love flowing through me like hot lava. "I love you."

"Jill," he breathed, getting to his feet. He came around to my side of the table and helped me stand. Wrapping his arms around my waist, he pulled me as close as my bump allowed. "Tell me, do the British still arrest people for public displays of affection?"

I curved both hands around his face, drawing his lips to mine. "It'll be worth it."

Chapter 35

Blaize

It's now or never.

Ten months later...

Serenity rose from the glistening Atlantic Ocean, majestic in her splendor two hundred and fifty feet above the waterline. It had taken a while to put the past behind me, but that wasn't the only reason I hadn't set foot on a cruise ship since that fateful day eighteen months ago. Life had taken a fascinating turn, and whereas my work had once consumed me to the exclusion of all else, these days, I had a new obsession.

Two of them, actually.

"Lukas, careful." Jill snatched the melting ice cream

357

from our son's sticky fingers but not before several drips dotted my black T-shirt.

I hitched him farther up my hip, grinning at his expression of outrage. "Buddy, you've got more on your face and your hands than you have in your mouth."

He gurgled, then broke into an enormous smile. My heart melted. I'd never known love like this. My world began and ended with my son and my soon-to-be fiancée. Not that she had a clue I planned to propose at dinner tonight in front of my closest family members and her best friends. She didn't even know Addison, Kelsey, and Raya were already on board waiting for us to arrive. Dad had warned me that I was taking a risk in making a public proposal, but, without sounding cocky, I knew she'd say yes.

"How do you feel?" I slid an arm around her waist, grazing my thumb over her hip.

"I'm okay. I was worried all the bad memories would come rushing back, but so far, all I can think of is the fun times we had." She gazed up at me, the sun reflected in her eyes. "I'm kind of hoping we can re-create some of those memories. Especially the ones in Barbados."

My lips stretched into a smile. "Ah, Barbados." I nuzzled Lukas's plump cheek, breathing in his baby smell mingled with vanilla ice cream. We'd created him in Barbados. Maybe this time, we could work on a little brother or sister. "The pool or the bedroom?"

She shivered, and not from being cold. "Maybe both."

"I'm sure I can arrange that."

"Mr. Kingcaid, you can board now, sir."

I nodded at the crew member and took Jill's hand.

Everyone else was already on board, but I'd wanted to wait until last in case some form of PTSD came out of nowhere. The last thing I needed was for passengers to witness the CEO of the company having a meltdown. It had taken many months for my company's reputation to recover, and I had no intention of being the cause of a setback.

From what I'd learned about trauma from my therapist, flashbacks could occur at any time, but as I boarded the ship, holding Lukas in my arms and with Jill by my side, the overwhelming emotion encasing me was one of elation. I might be the boss of the company, but this trip was very much a family occasion. Dad had made it clear that I was not to involve myself in any day-to-day activities, and if anything urgent arose, he would take care of it. That I'd acquiesced without argument told me how far I'd come from the man who'd allowed work to consume him. Losing my leg had taught me that there were far more important things in life, and none more so than my beautiful girl and incredible son.

Six months ago, we'd located the person responsible for the leak. Turned out the girlfriend of the journalist who'd penned the clickbait article had worked for my marketing director. She'd had access to his inbox, read the emails sent to the board about the issues we'd had ahead of the launch, and shared the information with her boyfriend.

Suffice to say, she no longer works at my company.

Passengers fizzed with excitement as they explored, their constant chatter a source of comfort. I loved nothing more than hearing their delight as they discovered what the ship had to offer. This was what I'd always aspired to offer with Kingcaid Cruises. A chance for some much-needed downtime in an environment that aimed to cater to every whim.

None of the passengers sharing the elevator with us seemed to recognize me, which, considering the history of this ship, was a hell of a relief. The last thing I wanted to do was recant what had occurred on its maiden voyage. There had been many sailings since then, but my greatest concern was my proudest work achievement being forever tainted by what had happened.

I made a point of not following the criminal cases against the men responsible, but Scarlett had sent an email last week letting me know the result. The guy who'd shot me had gotten life in prison for murder and attempted murder. Jeremy, Scarlett's ex, had received fifteen years for conspiracy to murder. I'd sent a polite reply thanking her for informing me, and I hadn't heard anything since, not that I'd expected to. The aftereffects of that day appeared to have affected her as much as they had me. Last I'd heard, she'd all but withdrawn from public life, preferring a quieter existence on a ranch in Wyoming.

I opened the door to the owner's suite. A bottle of champagne stuffed in an ice bucket sat on the coffee table along with a note. Jill picked it up, smiling as she read it.

"It's from your dad. He said to settle in, relax, and he'd see us for dinner at eight."

Lukas squirmed in my arms. I set him on the floor, holding his hands as he tried out his legs. He hadn't walked yet, but each time he got closer. It wouldn't be long now before he was bombing around the place and keeping us on our toes as we chased after him.

Right on cue, he landed on his padded butt with a

thump. He let out a wail, part tiredness, part frustration. I scooped him up, peppering his face with kisses.

"Someone is tired. I'll put him down for a nap, then what do you say you and I take this bottle of champagne to bed?" I waggled my eyebrows. "That is, if you're not too tired."

"What time is it?"

I checked my watch. "Five o'clock."

"Hmm, three hours. Not sure that's enough time for what I want you to do to me."

"Good thing I brought a selection of toys, then, isn't it?" I winked, running my free hand over Jill's ass on the way to the second bedroom. The staff had set up the crib as I'd requested. I settled Lukas down, tucking him in tightly. He was asleep before I closed the door.

"Right, then, sexy. It's just you, me, a bottle of lu—" A loud knock on the door interrupted my dirty talk. I frowned. "Whoever that is, fuck off."

"Blay!" Jill went to answer the door. "It might be your dad."

I shrugged. "Same response applies. Besides, he said he'd see us at eight, so it isn't him."

She opened the door, and the next thing I knew, a bunch of women surrounded her, squeals of excitement piercing my eardrums. I groaned. Fucking Aspen. My cousin shot me an unapologetic grin while Addison, Kelsey, and Raya all spoke at once with Jill standing in the middle, dumbfounded.

"Did you know about this?"

I grinned. "Might have."

She extricated herself from the group hug and came

over to me. Standing on tiptoes, she pressed her lips to mine. "Thank you."

"I'll do anything to make you happy."

"Anything?"

"Yes."

She motioned to her friends still hovering by the door and chattering at warp speed as she unfastened the top two buttons on her shirt.

"You just volunteered to tell them we're busy and we'll see them later. Good luck."

And with that, she sauntered into the master suite, dropping her shirt to the floor as she disappeared from view.

God-fucking-damn.

K

"You look well fucked." I draped Jill's hair over one shoulder, kissing her neck.

"Great. Just what a girl needs to hear right before she's due to have dinner with her kid's paternal grandparents and his aunts and uncles."

I chuckled, wrapping my arms around her from behind to cup her breasts. "They won't care."

"*I* care." She leaned into me, sighing as I brushed my thumbs over her nipples.

"One of these days, I'll knock that British reticence out of you."

"I'm only reticent in public."

"Oh, that I know. Just as well, too. Otherwise, I'd have

to let you go." She elbowed me in the ribs. I grunted and stepped back. "Vicious."

"I barely grazed you."

"My cracked rib begs to differ." I went to answer the door, letting in the babysitter I'd hired especially for this trip. Childminding wasn't a required service on an adults-only cruise. I called it owner privilege. I'd raised the subject of a permanent nanny with Jill more than once. Each time, she'd met my suggestion with a glower and a firm "No." Maybe when we had more kids, she'd change her mind, but for now, she worked her writing around the baby's schedule and seemed pretty happy with that structure.

"Come on in, Diandra. We're about ready to go."

"You have our phone numbers, right? And any of the crew can find us at a moment's notice, I'm sure," Jill asked, worry drawing her eyebrows inward.

"Relax." Diandra smiled at us both. "Go, have a wonderful time."

"If he wakes up, there's a bottle made up in the fridge, which should settle him right back down. "

"Jill. She's a professional. And we're literally a few decks down."

"I know, I know." She grimaced. "It's a mother's right to worry."

"Of course it is," Diandra said in solidarity. "I promise, he'll be fine."

Hustling Jill out the door before she decided she couldn't leave Lukas, I surreptitiously patted my jacket, making sure I had the engagement ring. Nerves knotted my stomach as we rode the elevator down to deck seven. I

hoped this wasn't one of those situations where pride—or rather, overconfidence—came before a fall. The idea that I'd drop down onto one knee and ask Jill to marry me in front of family, friends, and an entire room filled with passengers, only to have her say no... the thought made me want to puke.

Our group took up an enormous table in the center of the restaurant. Everyone got to their feet as we arrived. Multiple hugs and many minutes later, Jill and I took our seats—and at that point, I lost her. Everyone monopolized her attention, asking about her latest novel, the baby, whether I was driving her crazy, and if she wanted tips on burying bodies. The last one, courtesy of Aspen, was rewarded with a sharp kick under the table.

Food was brought, consumed, and empty plates removed. As the waitstaff cleared away the last of the dessert dishes, my stomach tilted. Dad met my gaze, giving me an encouraging nod. Mom clasped a hand to her chest, basically giving the game away if Jill happened to glance in her direction. I'd told them both what I'd planned, but kept it from the rest of my family. The fewer who knew what I was about to do, the better.

It was now or never.

I tapped a spoon against my wineglass until the chatter subsided. Standing up, I put a hand on Jill's shoulder.

"Firstly, we'd both like to thank you all for coming. Neither Jill nor I knew how we'd feel about coming back here after what happened, but knowing we wouldn't be alone in facing our demons made it all that much easier. In the end, it's been a joy rather than a tribulation, but that doesn't alter the appreciation we feel at having you all around us."

I looked down at her and she gazed up at me, the love in her eyes shining so brightly that I got a lump in my throat. Clearing it, I took a deep breath and lowered to my prosthetic leg. I'd been practicing this move for weeks, occasionally losing my balance. Even now, there were moves that felt strange, although most days, I hardly noticed the weight of the prosthetic. I'd wanted my proposal to be normal. Jill deserved nothing less.

Her eyes widened as I reached into my inside pocket and pulled out the ring box. Opening it to show the nine-carat diamond, I held it toward her.

"I love you, Tilly. I loved you before I knew that I did, and I'll love you until my dying day. I'm forever grateful that I met you when I did, and the gift of our son is something I shall never forget. Marry me. Be mine for the rest of our lives."

There was a split second where the room fell silent and fear took hold. The next thing I knew, she was on her knees, too, kissing me, her salty tears wetting my lips.

"Is that a yes?" I asked when we broke apart.

"It's a yes," she whispered.

I slid the ring onto her finger as our friends and family gathered around, and the entire restaurant broke into loud applause.

If I lost every cent in my bank account tomorrow, I'd still be the richest guy alive.

Epilogue

Jill

The best Christmas gift ever.

TWO WEEKS LATER...

Sunlight warmed my face, the weight of Blay's left leg over mine comforting. He removed his prosthetic each night to allow his stump to breathe, but other than that, he wore it pretty much all the time. Nowadays, those without knowledge of his amputation would never know. He walked without a limp, although it had taken a lot of work and painful physiotherapy for him to get this far. His strength astounded me. I couldn't say, in all honesty, that I'd have coped nearly as well as he had.

I listened to his steady breathing, his hand on my

breast twitching as he slept. Snaking my left hand through the covers, I examined the huge diamond on my finger. I'd lost count of the number of times I'd stared at it in a stupor over the last couple of weeks.

I hadn't seen it coming.

Fourteen days since I'd gotten engaged, and I still couldn't quite wrap my head around it. Not an inkling of suspicion had crossed my mind that Blay had planned to propose. He hadn't shown an ounce of nerves. If the roles had been reversed, I'd have been a blubbering wreck. Thank goodness the tradition of men predominantly proposing had survived the feminist age.

The baby monitor resting on the bedside table remained mercifully quiet. Two nights ago, Lukas had fussed all night, and nothing had soothed him. Last night... he'd slept like the dead. That was babies, I guessed.

Speaking of babies...

My stomach tilted. I really should—

"Merry Christmas, soon-to-be wife." Blay kissed my shoulder, rolling me onto my back and settling between my legs. "You look beautiful."

He'd made the *soon-to-be wife* statement every morning since he'd proposed to me. "Are you still drunk from last night? I bet my hair looks like a bird's nest, mascara gloop is in the corners of my eyes, and as I didn't remove my foundation last night, I've probably stained the pillowcases."

He nodded sagely. "Hmm, now that you mention it, *beautiful* might be a stretch."

I put on my best resting bitch face. "I decline your marriage proposal."

"Too late. You're tied to me for life." He kissed me before I could protest, sliding his tongue over mine. I lost myself in his kiss, wrapping my arms around his neck and pulling him closer.

"Lukas..." Blay nuzzled my neck.

"Still asleep. For how long is anyone's guess."

"Better take advantage, then."

He grazed his teeth over my nipple. I arched into him, moaning, pleasure gathering low in my stomach. Tilting my pelvis, I reached for him. Mother's instinct told me we didn't have long, and as much as I adored my perfect bundle of joy, a girl had needs.

Guiding him inside me, I sighed in bliss. He filled me so perfectly, as if we'd been made for each other. He rolled onto his back, taking me with him.

"Ride me, fiancée. And if you're good, I'll give you your gift."

I laughed, circling my hips and clenching my muscles around his cock. His eyes closed, and he groaned.

"Feels so amazing."

A faint stirring noise came from the baby monitor. I upped my pace, sweat gathering across my forehead despite the efficient air-conditioning. Blay held on to my hips, supporting me as I bounced on his dick with a sense of urgency, my palms on his chest. My climax crashed into me with the speed of an asteroid hitting the planet. Blay followed me shortly afterward as the aftershocks went on and on. I collapsed onto his chest, panting.

"Sorry," I muttered, my lips traveling along the column of his neck.

"What for?"

"Too fast."

"No such thing, especially with the world's best cock-blocker in the next room."

On cue, Lukas let out an indignant wail. I groaned. Blay's softening cock slipped out of me, and I flopped onto my back, still trying to catch my breath.

"I can go. Won't take a second to fit my leg."

I shook my head. "I got it." Tossing the covers to the side, I climbed out of bed and slipped into a robe hanging on the back of the door. Lukas stopped crying the minute he spotted me, his chubby arms reaching up. I leaned into the crib and gathered him in my arms, peppering his face with kisses.

"Your timing is still off, buddy. We need to have a chat about that."

He grinned at me. Already his fourth tooth had come through. He was growing up so fast that I was scared to blink in case I missed an important milestone.

"Let's go see Daddy."

I carried him to our room. His eyes lit up as he saw Blay, and he squirmed in my arms. Such a daddy's boy. I handed him over. Blay tucked him into his side, sprinkling kisses on the top of his head.

"Can you say Dada? Dada. Da-da."

I chuckled. "Might be a little early."

"Pah. He's a genius, just like me."

"Hmm, I wonder if he'll also have your amazing modesty?"

"Nothing wrong with confidence."

"Good thing, too, considering you're brimming with it."

I left father and son to it and went to the bathroom. As I shut the door, my heart flailed in my chest, and my fingers trembled as I opened the bathroom cabinet. I'd suspected for a couple of days that I might be pregnant, so I'd bought a test when we'd stopped in Nassau yesterday. Blay had made it clear he wanted another child as close to Lukas as possible, so we hadn't used protection for a few months now, but so far, nothing. Every time I got my period, I saw the disappointment sweep over his face before he hid it behind one of his brilliant smiles and, with a wink, told me we'd have to try even harder.

I dove into the brown paper bag and retrieved the kit. I read the instructions even though I knew what to do. Pee on the stick. Wait. Pray. *Hopefully, celebrate.*

After setting a timer on my watch, I prowled around the small bathroom. Why did time go so slowly on these types of occasions? It was the eternal unsolvable mystery.

The timer went off. I jumped, releasing a shaky breath. I grabbed the stick and muttered a silent prayer before looking at it.

Pregnant.

A gasp spilled from my lips, and I clutched a handful of my robe. *I did it. We did it.* My chest was full as I opened the door into the bedroom. Blay was tickling Lukas, my baby's peals of laughter making my heart burst.

With a grin that wouldn't quit, I tossed the stick onto the bed, where it landed in Blay's lap.

"Merry Christmas, soon-to-be husband."

He glanced down at it and then up at me. He picked it up, his eyes widening.

"Is this...? Is this...?"

I nodded. "It is."

"Oh, baby." He held out his arms to me, and I sank into his embrace, hugging him and Lukas.

"You hear that, baby boy." I kissed his hair, breathing in his unique smell. "You're going to be a big brother."

"Another baby." Blay looked shell-shocked. He placed his hand on my stomach. "And this time, I get to be a part of it from the very beginning."

Guilt tasted sour, sucking all the joy from the moment. I hung my head, shame licking through my veins. It was my fault Blay had missed out on most of my pregnancy. I'd never forgive myself for not sharing the news earlier. That he'd found out the way he had would be a source of regret for the rest of my life.

"Hey." He tilted up my chin with his forefinger. "I know where that gorgeous mind of yours has gone, and I'm ordering you to quit."

I lifted one eyebrow. "Ordering me?"

"Yes. I mean it, Tilly."

The familiar nickname raised a smile, and the feeling of remorse lessened.

"I kind of like it when you boss me around."

"Is that so?" He lowered his gaze to the gap in my robe. Reaching inside, he skated a finger over the swell of my breast. "You know, you never did tell me what the *T* stands for."

"I guess you'll have to wait for the wedding." I giggled.

"Speaking of." He picked up my hand, tracing the ring with his thumb. "How do you feel about bringing it forward? Before you start to show."

"You're only saying that because you can't wait to find out my middle name."

"It's true. I'm transparent." He ran his fingers over my cheekbone. "What say you, pretty lady?"

"I say that I'll marry you anywhere, anytime, anyplace."

"Today? Here?"

My forehead wrinkled. "What, in bed?"

"I mean, it's an idea, but I was thinking more of on the ship, before we disembark. Enough of my family are here, and your closest friends are here, too. The captain can perform the ceremony."

"But won't your entire family expect an invite?"

He brandished his hand dismissively. "We'll throw a party in a few weeks. That'll satisfy them. They won't be upset. I promise. Although, if you'd always dreamed of having a big event with a designer dress and a seven-tiered wedding cake, that's perfect, too. Whatever you want."

"I just want you. You and Lukas and our newest addition. Nothing else matters."

He kissed me, then Lukas, and reached for the phone beside the bed.

"John," he said. "Merry Christmas. There's one more duty I need you to perform before you disembark."

Considering it was Christmas Day, my friends and Blay's family performed wonders, and at fifteen minutes to twelve, I walked down the makeshift aisle, holding a posy of pink and white flowers in a flowing white dress heli-coptered in by... someone. I hadn't a clue where it had come from or who'd designed it, only that I felt like a princess about to marry her prince. I locked gazes with Blay standing beside his brother Kadon, whom he'd chosen as his best man. The three brothers had a pact so they all got to perform the role once and no one felt left out or pushed to the side.

As I walked by, Raya looked on the verge of tears, Kelsey clutched her throat, and Addison gave me a goofy grin and stuck both thumbs in the air. Unlike Blay, I hadn't been able to choose between my three best friends. In the end, we'd decided I wouldn't have a maid of honor, and to have three at such a small gathering seemed like overkill. My friends didn't care. All they wanted was for me to be happy.

And boy, was I happy. Deliriously so.

Blay's mom bounced Lukas on her lap, and he played with the flower pinned to her floral dress, oblivious to the momentous occasion. I shot her a smile as I passed, then joined Blay in front of the captain.

John leaned forward, whispering to us both, "Ready?"

Blay took my hand and kissed it. "I was born ready."

The ceremony was over in five minutes. Blay walked me back down the aisle to a smattering of applause from the compact group, his arm around my waist and a smirk on his face. I braced myself. There was no way he'd let this go without making some kind of comment. I looked up at him. The corners of his mouth were twitching.

"Get it over with." I sighed.

"And you told me your parents wouldn't be cruel enough to call you Jilly Tilly Rowe."

"Which they didn't."

"No. They went one better."

I could hear the contained amusement in his voice. "There is nothing wrong with Jillian Tabitha Rowe."

"Instead of Jilly Tilly Rowe, it's Jilly Tabby Rowe." He couldn't hold back a second longer, bursting into fits of laughter.

"I can get a divorce just as quick, you know. Or an annulment."

"Can't get an annulment if the marriage has been consummated."

"Which it hasn't been."

"Not yet." He scooped me into his arms, marching out of the room and into the nearest elevator. As soon as the doors closed, he pressed the emergency stop button. "I fucking love you, Tilly-Tabby. Every goddamn inch of you."

I groaned. "I'm going to have to live with that double-barreled nickname forever, aren't I?"

He broke into another shit-eating grin. "It's endearing."

"It's bloody annoying."

"You love it."

I'd never admit it to him, but I did. It was ours, special, just like him.

"I love you, although I don't know why."

"Yes, you do." He ground his hips into me. "It's for my huge... intellect."

I rolled my eyes. "It sure isn't for your huge... humility."

He laughed. Bracing his palms on the wall behind me, he took my lips in a searing kiss.

"What say you, Mrs. Kingcaid? Consummate this marriage here, or on a nice, comfortable bed?"

Smirking, I traced a fingertip down his shirt. "Both sound good to me."

A Thank You from Blaize

Thank you for reading! I truly never thought I'd be the kind of man to settle down with one woman, but I guess we meet our soul mates in strangest of places - including transatlantic flights! I fully anticipate Nolen and Kadon to rib me about it at every single family dinner from now on. God knows, I ribbed them enough when they fell for their better halves.

If you're not ready to say goodbye to me and Jill just yet then I have a surprise for you. Remember Barbados? Well, if you want to know what happened when I introduced Jill to my kinky side, *sign up to Tracie's newsletter* and receive a **bonus scene** to *Devoured By You*.

Don't worry if you're already subscribed. You

won't be added to the list twice. Just go to...
https://authortraciedelaney.com/dby-bonus/ to grab your copy.

Have you read the ROGUES series yet? If not, pick up your copy of the first book, ***Entranced*** today.

Or, if you'd like a free prequel to the ROGUES series, all you have to do is go to her website at www.authortraciedelaney.com and click on "Claim My Free Book" on the home page.

Books by Tracie Delaney

BILLIONAIRE ROMANCE

The ROGUES Series

The Irresistibly Mine Series

The Kingcaid Billionaire Series

PROTECTOR/MILITARY ROMANCE

The Intrepid Bodyguard Series

SPORTS ROMANCE

The Winning Ace Series

The Full Velocity Series

CONTEMPORARY ROMANCE

The Brook Brothers Series

BOXSETS

Winning Ace

Brook Brothers

Full Velocity

ROGUES Books 1-3

SPINOFFS/STANDALONES

Mismatch (A Winning Ace Spin Off Novel)

Break Point (A Winning Ace Novella)

Control (A Driven World/Full Velocity Novel)

My Gift To You

Acknowledgments

I sometimes wonder if, after releasing thirty-five books, I should stop writing acknowledgements. It feels as if I say the same thing each time, but that's because I have the most amazing team, a lot of whom have been with me right from the beginning when I released Winning Ace. I'll never be able to fully express how grateful I am for each and every one of them, and how much richer my life is by having them be a major part of it.

With that said... here we go.

To my incredible husband who has been a complete rock during one of the most challenging periods in my life. I never forget how fortunate I am to have met you thirty-nine years ago. Never.

To my wonderful PA, Loulou. There isn't much more I can say other than thank you for being there. You're right at the center of the small group of people I know I can trust. It's a select group, but goodness me, we're mighty. Love you to bits.

Lasairiona and Clare, my amazing wifeys. If a day every

goes by when we don't speak (rare I know but it happens), I feel as if something major is missing from my life. I'm so glad I met you both. Here's to all three of us achieving our dreams.

Bethany - thank you so much for your brilliant editing as always.

Katie - My heartfelt gratitude for reading my words, continuing to unearth my Britishisms, for your friendship, and the wonderful daily uplifting Instagram messages. They, and you, mean everything to me.

Jacqueline - Okay, what is going on? Two typos. TWO! Have I excelled myself with this book? I think I may have. Thank you, as always, for your diligence and endless support. Can't wait to see you again soon.

To my ARC readers. You guys are amazing! You're my final eyes and ears before my baby is released into the world and I appreciate each and every one of you for giving up your time to read.

And last but most certainly not least, as ever, my gratitude goes to you, the readers. Thank you for being on this journey with me. I'm so incredibly lucky to do this for a job, but without you, I wouldn't be able to. I have lots of exciting things in store in the next 18 months, and I can't wait to share them with you. Stay tuned!

If you have any time to spare, I'd be ever so grateful if you'd leave a short review on Amazon, Goodreads, or Bookbub. Reviews not only help readers discover new books, but they also help authors reach new readers. You'd be doing a massive favor for this wonderful bookish community we're all a part of.

About the Author

Tracie Delaney is a Kindle Unlimited All Star author of more than twenty-five contemporary romance novels which she writes from her office in the freezing cold North West of England. The office used to be a garage, but she needed somewhere quiet to write and so she stole it from her poor, long-suffering husband who is still in mourning that he's been driven out to the shed!

An avid reader for as long as she can remember, Tracie was also a bit of a tomboy back in the day and used to climb trees with her trusty Enid Blyton's and read for hours, returning home when it was almost dark with a numb bottom and more than a few splinters!

Tracie's books have a common theme of women who show that true strength comes in all forms, and alpha males who put up a great fight (which they ultimately lose!)

At night she likes to curl up on the sofa with her two Westies, Murphy & Cooper, and binge-watch shows on Netflix. There may be wine involved.

Visit her website for contact information and more www. authortraciedelaney.com

Printed in Great Britain
by Amazon